Fridays in April
-
The mysterious Box

Mike Herman

It's my pleasure to acknowledge my family and friends for the encouragement I received from them to finish writing this book.

The strongest and unwavering encouragement came from my best friend, wife, and companion: Paula

Fridays in April- The Mysterious Box

Episode 1-Greg's Friday

CHAPTER 0NE

"What've you got in the bag, Greg?"

"It's a nice little box, about the size of a shoe box. It might be a small jewelry box. It looks like it's hand made, and it has some fantastic carving all over it. Whoever made it had a lot of artistic ability. I figure it's got to be worth ten bucks at least."

"Let's see it."

"Here. Take it out and tell me what you think its worth."

Stu opened the bag, just stared at it and said, "Greg, I knew if you didn't get off that cheap wine this was going to happen to you someday."

"I don't know what you mean. I'm only asking ten dollars for it."

"This is just a piece of wood. It's nice and square, and smooth but, it's a long way from a piece of art. And, it's definitely not worth ten bucks. As a matter of fact it looks like a piece of plain white pine."

"What? What are you talking about? I found that box this morning and put it in this bag. Open it up and you'll find 5 soft and neatly folded cloths inside. I swear to you."

Stu pulled it out of the bag, handed it to him and said, "Greg, look at it. Does that look like a box to you?"

He couldn't believe his eyes.

"No! But, I don't know what happened. I don't understand it. I'm sure I didn't set it down anywhere, and it hasn't been out of my sight since I put it in the bag."

"You've never asked for any handouts, and you've always paid your own way in the five years that I've known you, so if you need some money I'll loan you $20 or so. I know you're good for it."

"I don't want a loan. I had something to sell you. I'm not drunk. I haven't had anything to drink in 2 days. If someone's trying to pull something I'm going to find out who it is and kick their ass. I'll get that box back and show you. Give me the bag, I'll be back later.

With that, Greg put the block of wood in the bag and, angrily headed for the door.

Stu yelled after him as he ran out, "Hey Greg, don't forget I'll see you Monday morning around 9:00 so we can start fixing the floors."

***

Stu is in his early 40's and owns the neighborhood pawn shop. He took it over when his dad retired and moved to Arizona ten years ago. Greg, who's homeless, wandered in one day with a wrist watch to pawn. As they began talking they found a lot of common ground between them and a formed an immediate friendship.

***

As he walked back toward his lean-to he thought about how this morning started.

This is weird. An hour ago I woke up with this beautifully carved box beside my head, and now it's a block of wood. Who's trying to mess with my mind? I don't even know where it came from or how it got here. Did my dream have something to do with it? Was it really a dream?

He began to calm down while he sat on his bedroll staring at the bag with the block of wood in it.

It really doesn't make sense to get that upset over ten dollars. The bag with the box in it has never been out of my sight, so it couldn't have been tampered with or stolen. Is Stu right? Is the wine getting to me? No! I know it was a box. What happened?

He picked up the bag and cautiously reached inside and pulled out the…box!

"What the? This is unreal."

He opened the box and the cloths were there, undisturbed, so everything was the way it started out to be.

"This time I'm not taking my eyes off the box, and I'm going to slip it into the bag, and tightly wrap the bag around it. I'm keeping it under my arm till I get back in front of Stu. Then, he can see I wasn't just imagining everything."

He tucked the bag under his arm and headed toward Stu's. As he stepped out onto the sidewalk, he looked up and froze on the spot.

Oh hell. Here comes Mitch and his gang. The village idiots. Those four clowns are absolutely useless, and a menace where ever they go.

No one knows where the gang came from. They just showed up one day and started bullying the homeless and extorting what little money and valuables they have. Although they are mental midgets, they have the cunning and coordination of a pack of wolves. It didn't take the locals long to realize, any resistance to them brought on a methodical beating that took you within an inch of your life.

Mitch, the leader and mouth of the four is a real piece of garbage with long unruly reddish blond hair and scraggly beard, and a look in his eyes that makes you think he hates the world and every one of his actions back it up. His flunkies, Petey, Slug and Flop not only look like garbage, they smell like it.

"Hey Wino. Watch'ya got under your arm?"

No use trying to lie. I guess I won't have to prove anything to Stu after all, because if I don't give it to them I'll end up beaten to a bloody pulp and they'll take it anyway.

Greg quietly replied, "It's nothing special. I was going to ask you if you wanted it."

"Sure you were. We ain't dumb. Gimmee that bag, or we're gonna kick your ass."

"Here take it."

Mitch grabbed the bag, reached inside and pulled out…a block of wood.

"Hey Wino. What the hell you tryin to pull on us? It's a damned old piece of wood. Slug, you an Petey learn him real good so he don't ever do that again."

Petey hit Greg in the mouth half a dozen times. Slug jammed the block of wood into his mid section, and when he doubled over he hit him on top of the head with it then threw it in his face as he fell to the ground. Just for giggles Flop kicked him in the ribs a couple of times while he was laying there.

After they left, Greg lay there for what seemed like an eternity. Finally, he looked up at the bank clock.

"Holy cow! It's almost 9 o'clock, and this is Friday. I've got to get over to Charley and Barb's

Charley and Barb own the neighborhood tavern, and every Friday they pay Greg $20 to clean the restrooms, then they let him lock the men's room door, so he can shave and wash up out of the sink. It's not as good as a full hot shower, but he can get clean top to bottom. There is a catch though. He has to do it all in two hours, because they open the tavern at 11:00 o'clock for lunches.

Reluctantly, Greg pulled himself up and stuffed the block of wood back into the bag. He was totally bewildered. He wasn't stupid by any means, but he couldn't figure this one out.

Where did the block of wood come from, and where did the box go? Stu was right. I really have lost it. It has to be the fog I'm in because of the cheap wine. I'll have to straighten it out later though, because I've got to get to Charley's.

Dragging himself to the tavern he couldn't stop thinking about what has happened since he woke up this morning. As he passed by a trash can, he started to throw the bag away and noticed through a rip in the bag that the block of wood was once again a box. He pulled it out of the bag, opened it, and saw that the cloths were there, just like before. Now he knew there was no doubt at all. He had completely lost his mind.

What the hell is going on and why? I wish this box had never shown up. I thought I was lucky, but all the luck I've had

since I woke up has been bad. Well, I don't have time now, but when I get done I've got to do something about this thing.

He didn't think it was possible to hurt this badly and still be alive. Up to this point he had been able to avoid the gang's wrath. Now he knew first hand why the rest of the street people cowered when they were around.

***

"Greg, what happened to you?"

"I made the mistake of getting within sight of the four stooges, Charley."

"Man, you look like you've been stomped by a 2,000 pound bull."

"It was three guys with the strength of bulls, and the IQ of a marble. I hurt from head to toe."

"I can't figure out why the cops won't do anything about them."

"They can't do anything if people won't file charges, and they won't file charges because they're afraid."

"Yeah, I know, but it still isn't right."

"See you later Charley. If I don't get my work done, the boss is going to fire me."

"Yeah, right."

Greg went in and looked at himself in the mirror.

Oh man, this is really rough. I don't know how I'm going to get cleaned up and shaved. My face is all puffy and cut up. Well, I'm going to have to try when I get finished.

Greg limped his way through the normal routine of getting the restrooms cleaned, and then locked up so he could get himself clean. He washed very gingerly, carefully avoiding the cuts on his face. He decided to pass up shaving this week, because his face was way too sore. When he started to dry himself off with the paper towels like he usually did, he knew that wasn't going to work. His body was so sore and tender that even trying to dab with the paper was out of the question. The paper was far too rough.

Then, he remembered, the cloths in the box were very soft. Providing it was still a box and not a block of wood. He reached into the bag and pulled out the box. Opening it he saw the cloths were there. He took a cloth and gently put it to his face.

Wow! This cloth really feels good on my face and body. It's so soft and soothing, like it has some kind of lotion on it. I'm glad I didn't throw the box away yet.

After he finished drying off completely, he watched astonished, as the cloth started to shred and disintegrate, right there in the palm of his hand, suddenly there wasn't anything left of it. It just disappeared. He knew he was running late, so he had to run around and gather all the cleaning stuff up and put it away. It dawned on him that he was feeling better. As a matter of fact, he was feeling very good. He figured doing the cleaning must have worked out the kinks and sore spots. In a hurry, he went out to see Charley and get paid.

"Man, you clean up real well Greg."

"What do you mean Charley?"

"Well, somehow you cleaned up all those cuts and bruises till they disappeared."

"Yeah, sure. I feel better, but I don't think it works that quickly."

"OK, if you say so. What do you have in the bag?"

"I'll let you look and see what you think."

"It's a block of wood. What are you carrying that around for?"

Greg let out a long sigh and said, "I'm not really sure. I found it this morning and thought it looked interesting. I guess I've finally lost it."

"Well, the bags ripped. Do you want another one?"

"Sure, I might as well carry it in a good one."

"Here you are. Greg, I'm serious, you need to look in the mirror."

"I will later. Right now I've got some thinking to do. See you next week."

"OK. Take care of yourself."

In the past, he never allowed himself to use the $20 he got from Charley on anything but food. Today he decided to make an exception to his rule and picked up a bottle of cheap wine and a pack of cigarettes, and then he headed for an old familiar refuge.

***

"The Anthill." It's a place where, in the past he could hide from the rest of the world, gather his thoughts, and pull himself back together, so he could face things with a renewed vigor. While there, he doesn't have to worry if anyone will intrude, because no one knows about the place.

The only thing Greg held onto from the past was an elaborate bomb shelter he had inherited from his grandfather. Greg was an only child and his father died when he was a young boy. He was also the only grandson on his mother's side, so he and his grandpa were very close. They did a lot of things together while Greg was growing up. Greg called him Pop.

Pop was exactly 6ft. tall, about 165 pounds, bald, and loved his shot of whiskey followed by a cool, but not cold beer.

As he slowly walked, long ago conversations with Pop came to mind.

"Why do you like your beer that way, Pop?"

"I started drinking beer when I was in Europe in the 1950's and that was the only way they served it. I got used to it that way. I feel it's got a lot more flavor when it's not ice cold."

"Are you building this place for you and Grandma to live in?"

"No. we'll live in our house till we die."

"Why are you building it then?"

"Those rotten commies are going to drop the a-bomb on us someday, so I'm making this shelter. That way my family will have a safe place to stay when it happens.

"How are you going to make it into a shelter?"

"I got the idea when I was stationed at 'Wright Patterson Air Force Base' in Dayton, Ohio. They had built this reinforced concrete laboratory underground, and piled a huge mound of dirt on it to make it bomb proof. They called it 'Mound Laboratories'."

"Why are you building it here?"

"Well, I couldn't get enough dirt to make my own big mound, so I bought this old hill with nothing but woods and wild pasture land around it. It's far enough out of town so I don't have to get building permits. That way I don't have people out here asking what's going on.

In the 1940's and 1950's there were oil wells around here. So, I also acquired the mineral rights to this property when I bought it, because there's still an old natural gas well here. Now, the well doesn't provide enough gas to make it commercially profitable, but it'll supply the power needs of the average family indefinitely."

"Are you going to put the shelter underground like the laboratory?"

"No, not exactly. I'll go up about thirty feet, then, dig into the side of the hill. That way I don't have to worry about flooding. And, at thirty feet I can still pipe the gas to the generator and furnace. I'll keep all the dirt from the digging, so when I'm done building I can cover the shelter and hide the entrance to it."

"Why do you want to hide it?"

"After they bomb us I don't want them to know where we are."

"How are you going to build it?"

"Well, since I have my own construction business and I operate heavy equipment I can do almost all of it by myself."

***

After all these years the entrance had so much heavy brush growing around it that it took him a while to get to the door. Even if wasn't overgrown, you couldn't find it if you didn't know where it was. You can't even stumble upon it. If you do happen to wander through the massive overgrown maze, when you get to the end of it, it isn't recognizable as a doorway to anything.

The South side of the hill is used by off road motorcyclists for hill climbing competition. The bottom 2/3 of the East side is covered with thick thorny bushes, and that's where the maze begins. That side also has medium sized boulders stretching from about twenty feet below where the bushes stop to the top of the hill.

When he finally got there, and went inside, he sat back, got comfortable, and tried to sort out the pieces of his life.

Man, I haven't been here in years. I wonder why it's been so long. Whenever I come here I can relax and contemplate all sorts of things about myself. I guess I've answered my own question. I've avoided coming here because I couldn't bear to face what I needed to know about myself.

Today, for the first time since it all went sour he really started to question why he let his life get so screwed up. For five years now he had been in some kind of denial about everything. Of course being in a drunken stupor most of the time made that easy. Even being considered a big man at 6' 2" and 220 lbs. he probably couldn't have prevented getting beaten today, but he might have gotten in a few good licks and done some damage to them as well if he hadn't been in an alcohol induced fog.

Deep inside I've always known that if I stayed drunk, and didn't think about all this, I wouldn't have to accept any of the responsibility for it. That way I could blame everything on Larry and Delores. The reality is, it's not their fault I'm on the streets.

He recalled the conversation with Larry that started, or perhaps ended it all.

Larry said Greg was just jealous when he tried to have a talk concerning some things that bothered him about Delores.

"What about Delores, Greg?"

"I'm not sure I can put my finger on it, but something just doesn't feel right."

"And, you don't like Thelma either, do you?"

"I think Thelma's wonderful. She's been the best thing to come along for us. Why do you say that?"

At that point Thelma had been their secretary and office manager for about nine months. Delores is her daughter.

Delores was very beautiful and well built, so I guess I can understand Larry's interest in her.

"Delores told me not to tell you about us, because she said you'd be upset and try to fire her mom. She said when you tried to get her to go out with you, and she turned you down, you threatened to fire Thelma. I think you're just jealous of her and her mom."

"I did what? I didn't ask her to go out with me. She asked me to go out with her. Why would you believe something like that?"

"Because, she told me you'd say she asked you to take her out. She said she told you she loved me, and you went into a jealous rage. When you said she had no business going with us to the tooling convention I knew she was telling the truth, and I'm not going to stand here quiet while you attack her."

"I never said I didn't like Delores, and I'm not attacking her. I just said I had some concerns and wanted to talk to you about them."

"There's nothing to talk about. I love her, and I'm not going to stand here and let you say things against her. So, get the hell away from me before I slug you."

"Larry, we've been friends a long time, and we could always talk things out. What's going on?"

"I said get away from me, Greg. I'm tired of you and you and your superiority."

***

That was the last conversation between them.

Yeah, Larry accepted a little over a million dollars from some want to be investors, and put their company on the hook for it, then, proceeded to take the money and run with Delores by his side. After he left that meant Greg was alone to face all the people who had advanced the money for the new projects.

Larry and Greg met in high school and became fast friends. After their own individual stints in the military, they opened a product and service business. By the eighth year they were very successful and had drawn the attention of some big investors.

Larry is one of the smartest people I've ever known. Even though he's 2 years younger than me, we were in the same grade because he skipped 2 grades in elementary school,

so I can't understand why he was willing to chuck it all
and run away with Delores. With several investors interested
in us, they could have waited another year and taken a world
cruise if they had wanted to. And, we wouldn't have lost our
business.

All the investors said they would work with Greg to
repay the money, but this deal with Larry, along with the fact
they had been swindled out of a large sum the year before, just
drained all the fight out of him.

Even though he figured he had grounds to prosecute
Larry, he just couldn't do it to him. So, instead he went into a
deep depression, and thus began his pity party. He took what
money he had in his pockets, went to the nearest bar and
started his new life. It surprised him how easily he climbed
into the bottle without ever looking back.

Until now.

Why am I thinking about all this now? In the past five
years I've always been able to drink myself into the land of
forgetfulness. Something's different now.

He sat for a long time staring at the bottle in his hand.
He set the bottle down. Suddenly he no longer wanted it. He
then pulled the unopened cigarette pack out of his pocket, and
set it down next to the bottle.

I don't know why I started smoking. I never did like it.

He went into the bathroom and looked at his reflection
in the mirror.

"Wow! Charley was right. The cuts, bruises, and
puffiness are all gone. And, I'm not sore anywhere either. As
a matter of fact I haven't felt this good in years. Whew. This
is scary. I feel like I'm coming out of a deep, deep fog. It's
almost as if the last five years have been a dream and I'm
finally starting to wake up."

He decided to sit around for a while to try to determine
what was going on, and where to go from here.

All of the sudden my mind's on the future. How can
that be? I'm so deep in debt. Logically I can't see anything
positive. I turned and walked away from everything, so I know
I let a lot of people down, and they've got to be really pissed at

*me. And yet, for the first time in quite awhile, I feel there
has to be something good ahead. All this started this morning
since I found this box. Is there some kind of connection? If so,
how does it fit in? Where did it come from? Why am I the only
one who sees it as a box? I'd say, it's black magic, but I don't
believe in it. The ever changing box does worry me, because I
know there is no free lunch, so sometime in the future there's
going to have to be a reckoning.*

*My life was so simple, and now I have a strong feeling
that's about to end. And to think when I went to sleep last
night I was convinced that my 37th birthday would be one
more in a long line of boring days. Oh well, so much for being
convinced.*

That year Greg's birthday was the first Friday in April.

*For the last 5 years I've not only accepted the fact that
I'd spend the rest of my life on the streets. I've looked forward
to it. I figured I'd die there with no worries, no problems and
no hassles. It would just be over, and the world would be
better off with one less useless person to deal with.*

*Now, I don't know why, but I can't get my mind off the
dream I had last night. It was really weird. I dreamed I was
walking on a sidewalk under some trees and heard a noise
above me. The next thing I knew I was on the ground with a
terrible headache and I couldn't move my left arm. Something
strange woke me up before I could figure out what happened.*

He was beginning to sense things were about to change.
As a matter of fact, he didn't know it, but his whole life was
getting ready to turn him inside out.

After spending the afternoon in reflection, Greg started
to get hungry. This was a new sensation for him, because
usually by this time on Friday he was starting to get into his
first bottle of wine. Well, he reasoned, he could easily sell the
wine and cigarettes on the street for half what they cost, and
get something at Mindy's coffee shop.

***

Mindy is a really neat person. She bought Fred's
bakery 2 years ago, about 6 months after he'd died.

Fred and Jean owned and operated the bakery for 35 years, and they lived in the apartment over the shop all that time. After Fred passed, Jean said she just couldn't bear the thought of going back to their home alone. So, she turned the building with all the furnishings and equipment over to a real estate agent to sell, and moved to Atlanta to be near her sister.

One day there was a big sign in the window, announcing that Fred's bakery would soon become Mindy's Coffee Shop. The whole neighborhood awaited the arrival of Mindy. They certainly weren't disappointed.

Mindy is a very sexy, tall, classy natural blonde with brown eyes. On top of all that she's highly intelligent. She has never mentioned her age, but she looks to be in her late thirties to early forties. She has a slow easy way of speaking that makes you want to listen to everything she says. She is always friendly, but no one knows anything about her or where she came from. If anyone does ask personal questions she doesn't answer and just changes the subject.

Like Stu, she is another one of many who has taken a liking to Greg, and can't understand what he's doing on the streets. He won't take any handouts, so she's had him do some odd jobs and handy-man work around the shop, and she's watched fascinated, as he breezed through the work.

Greg always enjoys conversations with her. Their philosophies and outlooks are quite similar. Many times he's looked at her and wished they had met before everything in his life had turned sour. But, then he sees all the good looking guys talking to her and realizes he wouldn't have had a chance even then. Still, he's very satisfied with the relationship they have. One of the reasons they are so comfortable together is because neither one tries to get into the other's personal life.

***

"Hi Greg, strange seeing you here today. I don't think you've ever come in on Friday. You usually show up on Tuesday or Wednesday."

"Well, I've had an interesting day, and I thought I'd come and talk to you about it, if you've got the time to let me bend your ear. By the way, how are you Mindy?"

"I'm doing great. And, I always have time to listen to a friend. I hear you had some problems this morning with the four jerks."

"Boy, news really travels at super sonic speed around here."

"I didn't mean to offend you."

"Oh, I'm not upset. I just didn't realize I was such a topic of conversation."

"You make quite an impact on the people in this neighborhood. Everyone who knows you likes you."

"I don't understand why. I'm nobody special. I'm broke, homeless, and I can't do anything."

"People are drawn to you because they feel comfortable around you.

You listen to them and make them feel like you care about them."

"I do like people, but unfortunately I don't trust most of them."

"I'm sure you have your reasons, and certainly can't say I blame you. By the way, you look pretty good for someone who got worked over this morning."

"That's what I wanted to talk to you about. After I got beat up I was so sore I didn't think I'd be able to make it to Charley's let alone do my work after I got there. I had a hard time getting through it, and I would've bet anything I had a couple of broken ribs. But, after I got finished and washed up, I started feeling pretty good. As a matter of fact, I couldn't believe how great I felt."

"Why don't we have a cup of coffee while we talk?"

"OK. Let's go over and sit in front of the bay window. I love sitting on these new padded bar stools, and we can watch the outside world go by. It's very cozy and relaxing to me."

"OK. What do you want to talk about?"

"It's been a real weird day right from the moment it began, and as the day moved on it got weirder by the minute."

"How so?"

"For starters, I was in the middle of a strange dream when something jolted me awake."

"You mean like a noise?"

"I don't remember hearing anything. Have you ever waked up feeling like someone was watching while you slept?"

"Yes I have. Why?"

"That's what woke me up this morning. I laid there a while pretending to be asleep, but I didn't hear anything. So, I slowly opened my eyes and didn't see anyone there, but I was startled by something setting right next to my head."

"What was it?"

"At first I thought it was just a piece of wood someone had done great carving on, but when I examined it more closely it dawned on me it was a box, about the size of a shoe box."

"Do you know where it came from?"

"I have no idea. Like I said, I had the feeling that someone was there, but I didn't see anyone."

"Where is it now?"

"I've got it here in this bag."

"I'll try to show it to you, but so far that's what makes things get weirder."

Greg picked up the bag and was reaching into it to show her the object of his day's activities when they heard tires screeching and a distinctive thump of someone or something being hit by a vehicle. They looked outside and saw a mid sized blue car sitting stopped in the middle of the street. The driver had gotten out and was standing in front of the car, looking down. Suddenly he turned, got back into the car, and drove around the object in the street, and sped off.

They ran out to see who was hurt. As they approached the figure lying on the pavement, they realized it was a dog.

"Greg, he looks like he's hurt real bad. There's a lot of blood."

"I know. Why don't you call the Humane Society and then bring back some rags?"

"OK."

As Greg got closer he recognized the dog. It was the neighborhood stray who always growled and snapped at him, which scared the hell out of him.

The dog is a very dark gray color similar to a wolf, and large, about seventy pounds. He looks like he might be a mixture of Lab and German Sepherd.

When he knelt down next to him, the dog looked over at him and tried to snap at him, but was too weak. Greg could see a long, very bloody gash on the dogs' right side, and his rear leg on that side had a large knot on it, and was misshapen enough to be broken.

Realizing he was carrying the bag with the box in it, he reached inside, took the box out and opened it, then pulled out a cloth and started dabbing the wound, hoping to stem some of the blood gushing out of it until Mindy could get there with some rags. He watched in amazement, as not only did the blood stop flowing, but the gash started closing.

This can't be happening. What I'm seeing isn't possible. The wound has stopped bleeding and completely closed up,

Almost trancelike he began rubbing the cloth on the dog's injured leg.

I don't believe this. The knot's shrinking and his leg's going back into place.

After everything had healed, he sat there and watched as the cloth started shredding and finally disintegrated right in his hand.

That's the same thing that happened to the cloth in Charley's restroom today.

He was snapped out of his deep thought by Mindy's voice, "Greg. I couldn't get through to the Humane Society. The line was busy. But, I did bring some rags and gauze."

"Thanks Mindy, but I don't think we'll need them."

"Wait a minute! When I left to go back to the shop, the dog's side had a big gash in it that was bleeding profusely. Where's all the blood? Where's the gash? How'd you get him cleaned up so fast?"

"That's what I came to talk to you about. There's something really weird going on, Mindy."

"Is this part of what you were talking about?"

"The thing in this bag is at the center of the dog being healed."

"That doesn't make sense. Nobody heals that fast. So, what's in the bag?"

Greg put his hand into the bag and pulled out the item and said, "This."

"A block of wood? What's a block of wood got to do with it?"

"Greg was astonished. "It's happening again. This is freaking me out."

"What is happening? What are you talking about?"

"I don't know, Mindy. Nothing has made sense today. Somehow I'm involved in this and I still don't have clue what's going on."

"Involved in what?"

"I don't know, but I can't talk about it now. I've got to go."

"Please don't go, Greg. I'm not doubting what you say. I just don't understand."

"I don't understand either. That's why I can't talk. I'll see you later, Mindy."

***

Greg walked off totally confused, and so deep in thought he didn't realize the dog had jumped up and was walking beside him.

Why is this stuff happening to me? When I was in business I felt my life was set. Then, that fell apart and I was sure I'd have an uncomplicated life on the streets. Now, this happens and so much for the simple life. This is turning everything inside out. I've got to get rid of this thing. I want my life back to the way it was. Besides, there's something going on that isn't right. What if it's something evil and I have to give up my soul. Damn, I need to listen to myself. That's ridiculous science fiction stuff. It doesn't matter, because I'm throwing this box/block of wood in the first trashcan.

As he passed a trashcan he threw the bag into it and walked off. He still wasn't aware of the dog walking beside him. When he got to his lean-to, and sat in shelter of it, he finally saw the dog.

He screamed at the dog, "What the hell are you doing here? Go away. Get out. I thought you hated me. The last thing I need is another mouth to feed. I don't want any more complications in my life."

The dog just sat there and looked at him, not moving. So, he lit his propane stove, heated some canned soup and made coffee. Thinking about today's events, Greg realized he had lost his appetite. After having half of a cup of soup he gave the rest of it to the dog, and sat sipping his coffee, deep in thought.

I'm glad I got rid of that box. Just for starters it got my butt whipped, and every time I tried to show it to someone, it wasn't a box. It was a block of wood. And those cloths. How did they heal the dog's wounds? Obviously they also healed me today as well. Until now I never believed in black magic or sorcery, but this isn't natural. The whole thing is scary. There definitely is no such thing as a free lunch, so there has to be a payback. I keep wondering what it's going to cost in return. I just want my life back to the way it was yesterday. I've got to get a good night's sleep, and everything will be alright in the morning.

***

It was chilly the next morning when Greg woke up, and he was wishing he had stayed the night in the local homeless shelter, so he could've taken a nice hot shower. For some unknown reason he really felt the need for one.

He saw movement out of the corner of his eye, and looked over to see the dog was still there, waking as soon as Greg stirred. When he saw Greg, his tail started wagging and he came over to lie beside him.

"What am I going to do with you? This time yesterday you hated me and wanted to eat me alive. Now you act like we've been lifelong friends.

I know one thing. If you're going to be with me, you are getting a bath. You stink.

After we eat something I'm taking you up to 'The Anthill' and we're both taking a shower.

I must be nuts. I'm talking to you like you understand me, and you're standing there looking at me like you know what I'm saying."

When they finished eating they started toward the bomb shelter. As they walked along Greg heard a voice behind him say, "Where you goin Wino?"

He turned around to see two of the four idiots standing there.

Mitch said, "You look pretty good for someone who just had his ass beat yesterday. Maybe you need another whippin. This time we'll do a better job, so you won't look so good tomorrow."

They started toward Greg, but they hadn't seen the dog, so they didn't realize he had come around behind them. As they tried to grab him, the dog sank his teeth into Mitch's right calf. He screamed and went down. When Flop saw that, he made a move to hit the dog with a club. Greg doubled up his fist and hit Flop square on the jaw, knocking him out cold. Mitch was on the ground in a ball trying to protect himself as the dog kept nipping at him.

Greg called the dog off, and as they walked away, he heard Mitch yelling, "You're gonna pay for this Wino. We'll get you and put your ass in the hospital for a long time. Maybe we'll take our time and kill you, real slow."

All the way to "The Anthill", he kept talking to the dog about what happened.

"Boy, we've gotten ourselves into a nasty mess now. When they get a hold of us we're dead, because those jerks don't have enough brains among the four of them to know when to quit.

Hmm . . . I guess I can still hold my own in a fight, because Flop, dropped like a rock when I hit him. I didn't know I still had such a strong punch. It all happened so fast I just reacted without thinking and decked him. I hope he isn't hurt too badly.

Well, here I am talking to you again like you should understand me. I am losing it. Oh well, I guess while I'm thinking you know what I'm saying, I might as well give you a name. Let's see… Since you've got such a strong bite I'll call you Snapper."

At that the dog looked at him, and started wagging his tail.

When they finally reached "The Anthill", Greg got the generator going and put on a pot of coffee. They didn't have to wait for the shower water to get hot, because Pop installed an on demand water heating system. He also built something unique into the master bathroom. The shower stall is 7 ft. by 7 ft. with benches built into the corners. It has eight shower heads, all coming from different locations, and heights, including one 12 in. in diameter coming straight down from the ceiling to simulate rain. Each one can be turned on and off individually. So, you can have them all on at the same time, or choose only the ones you want.

While waiting for the coffee to brew, he got undressed and coaxed Snapper into the shower with him.

He definitely has some Lab in him, because he really loves the water.

It became obvious that he had found a new friend, because Snapper wouldn't leave his side.

They spent the rest of the weekend at "The Anthill". Greg hadn't relaxed that much in years, and the dog seemed quite content with lazing around and unwinding as well.

For the first time since he walked away from everything Greg actually slept in a bed. Just before he drifted off, he sighed. *Boy, I really miss this.*

By Sunday night he knew he was getting back in to enjoying some of the creature comforts of a life he had rejected five years ago.

He laid there reflecting on the events of Friday, and about how everything in his life seemed to change that day. It was hard to believe it was only two days before that. Although the cloths in the box helped him and Snapper, he was glad he threw them in the trash. It all scared him. How could a box turn into a block of wood, and then back into a box several times? Even worse, where did it come from? Who left it there? Why him? Well, it doesn't matter any more, because it's all gone.

He went to sleep Sunday night remembering that last week he had offered to go to Stu's shop about 9:00 AM Monday to help him repair the flooring that had started to rot under the display cases. It was going to be at least a 2 or 3 day job, because the cases had to be emptied and moved just a few at a time.

CHAPTER TWO

Monday morning Greg woke up refreshed and feeling pretty good. He didn't want to have to clean up a mess at "The Anthill", so on the way to Stu's, he stopped at his lean-to for breakfast. All the way there he hoped they wouldn't run into Mitch and his gang.

When they got there and Greg started Breakfast, he happened to glance over in the direction of his bedroll, and saw a familiar sight.

"The box is back. How? What's going on? There isn't anything slightly funny about this. Frankly, it's getting scarier and scarier.

I don't have time to do anything about it now, so I might as well take it with me. If I don't, it'll probably be waiting for me when I get there.

Well, at least this time when it turns back into a block of wood. Mindy can back me up about what happened to Snapper on Friday."

**

After breakfast Greg put the box in another bag and they both headed for Stu's. When they got to the pawn shop, something was wrong. The door was unlocked, but Stu was nowhere in sight, so Greg cautiously went in and started looking around. He saw that one of the display cases was knocked over, and broken glass seemed to be all over the place, and still no sign of Stu. Not knowing if someone had broken in and might be hiding inside, Greg looked around for Snapper, and he was gone as well, so he slowly and very quietly made his way toward the door to Stu's office. As he got near the door he could hear what sounded like a person groaning. He carefully pushed the door open and saw Stu lying on the floor in front of the couch. Looking around the rest of the room, he didn't see anyone else present, so he stepped in and went over to Stu.

"Stu, what happened? Did someone break in and beat and rob you?"

In between groans he tried to respond, but all he could do was say, "Who is it? Who's there?"

He seemed to be almost incoherent.

"It's Greg."

"What are you doing here Greg?"

"I told you I'd come over and help you move the cases out of the way and repair the floor. So, what happened? Who beat you up?"

"I don't know. I just woke up hurting like hell. My leg's killing me, my side feels like a mule has kicked it in, and I just want to sleep. I'm so sleepy."

"I'm going to call 911."

No. No. No. Absolutely not. I'll be Ok if I can just get some sleep."

I don't know what to do. I've got to call 911. He's seriously hurt.

I know! It'll only take a minute to try one of these cloths on his leg. If it doesn't work I'll make the call. If it does, I'll use it on his side, and that'll prove to Stu that it's not just a block of wood.

Greg took the box out of the bag and removed one of the cloths. He didn't have to ask him which leg was hurting, because he had shorts on, and about 6 inches below the knee, his left leg was very swollen and bent where it should have been straight.

Greg began to gently wipe the cloth over the injured part of Stu's leg. He watched enthralled as the swelling started going down, and his leg slowly went back into normal alignment. Then he wiped the cloth over his lower left rib cage, and as he did, he listened while Stu's breathing gradually became more relaxed and deeper. He waited a moment. Then pressed his rib gage, and when he didn't wince he knew the area was all healed. But, something was wrong. The cloth didn't shred and disintegrate like it did before, when he and the dog were healed. Greg was baffled, and yet this could be a good thing, because if Stu woke up and saw the cloth, he'd know that Greg was telling the truth and wasn't nuts.

Hold on. What if Stu has another injury? But, where? Oh! He said he was sleepy, so maybe he has a head injury. He didn't say his head hurt, but it looks like there's some glass in his hair.

Greg looked at his head, but couldn't see any damage, because his hair is so thick. Stu was definitely out of it, because he didn't even ask Greg what he was doing when he was feeling around his head. Bingo. It was a large knot, just above and slightly behind his left ear. When Greg touched it Stu groaned. As he rubbed the cloth over the knot he could feel it slowly receding. When he couldn't feel the knot any longer, the cloth began to shred, and disintegrate. Greg watched as, just like before, it completely disappeared without any trace of it ever having existed. After that, Stu seemed to be sleeping comfortably, so Greg placed a small pillow under his head, and went out front to get a pot of coffee going, and clean up the mess.

***

After he got the pot going, he went to look more closely at the case that had been knocked over. When he did he saw that there was a hole in the floor in the area that was under one of the corners where the case had been setting. So, what must have happened was, when Stu tried to move the case, the corner dropped into the hole, and with him using his weight against the case, he lost his balance and fell on top of it.

Soon Stu came out of his office, looking quizzically at Greg.

"What's going on here Greg?"

"I don't know. I wasn't here. You need to tell me what happened."

"Well, this all seems like a strange dream, but while I was waiting for you to get here I emptied the case that's on the floor. Then, when I tried to move it, it tipped over, and I remember falling. I must have been knocked out, because the next thing I knew, I became aware that I hurt almost everywhere. I couldn't stand up, so I with all the effort I could muster, I forced myself up on my hands and knees and managed to make it to my office. I must have passed out again, because I woke up just now on the floor with my head on a pillow. I don't know how long I was lying there, but I don't hurt anywhere. Actually, I really haven't felt this good in years. I've lost all track of time though. What day is it Greg?"

"It's Monday. Don't you remember me coming into your office a little while ago?"

"No. Like I said, everything is all fuzzy. I'm not sure it's real, because nobody gets over hurting that badly in just a few minutes. Wait a second. This whole thing can't be real. It has to be a dream, because I keep thinking I'm seeing you kneeling down beside me, and touching and wiping the places where I hurt."

"Is there anything else?"

"That's all, until I woke up feeling great and smelled the coffee. Then I came out and saw you standing there. But, then it couldn't all be a dream, because if it were, the display case wouldn't be laying on the floor with glass all over the place. Something's really strange. I don't understand what's going on."

As Greg stood there sipping his coffee, he came to a sobering conclusion. *It won't do any good to talk to Stu about the box and the cloths, because he didn't see it happen and there's no evidence left after the cloth disintegrates. Plus, when I show the box to anyone it becomes a block of wood. Whether I like it or not, Snapper and I are the only ones who know what's happening. This seems weird, but I think the only reason he knows is because he can't talk. So, he must be part of all this. I guess until this has played out and I see where it's going, I might as well keep my mouth shut, or risk looking like I've lost all my marbles.*

"I don't know what's going on Stu, but I'll try to put it together the best way I can. And, as soon as I do I'll let you know."

"Somehow you're involved aren't you, Greg."

"I'm just as much in the dark about this as you are."

"OK Greg, I'll leave it alone for now. While you're here and I'm feeling good we might as well get to work."

Stu closed the store in order to get the job done as quickly as possible, and they both worked two 10 hour days and repaired all the flooring in the shop and rearranged the cases and displays.

Greg knew what to do without being told to, and worked very quickly. Something Greg found interesting was the fact that anytime he looked outside while they were working, Snapper was nowhere in sight. But, as soon as he came out at the end of the day, Snapper was sitting at the bottom of the steps waiting for him.

Stu gave Greg $150.00 a day, because he felt like he worked as hard and as well as any other handyman would have.

Greg was ecstatic. He hadn't seen that much money in five years. He had a feeling he should put as much of it away as he could. But where? "I know, I'll ask Mindy if she'll hold it for me."

***

"Of course I'll hold it for you. All you have to do is tell me when you need it, or just some of it."

"I'm usually here at least once a week, so I'll just get enough to live on each week."

***

For several weeks Greg went about his regular routine and everything seemed to slip back into a state of normalcy. He continued to work at Charley and Barb's on Fridays. On Tuesday afternoons when Mindy's business was slow, he'd go to her shop to get enough money to run on and see if she needed any work done. Then if she had the time they'd sit and drink coffee while philosophizing and solving all the world's problems.

In between those times Greg spent a lot of time with Stu, and their friendship seemed to grow stronger each time they got together.

One day just after he stopped by the pawn shop, the sky opened up and a deluge hit the area. Stu and Greg were standing and talking. Suddenly, he could see anger flash across Stu's face. Although he was built like a pro wrestler, Stu always maintained an easy going, happy, live and let live attitude. Greg had never seen him angry in the 5 years they had been friends. Following Stu's gaze he saw Mitch and his gang gathered under the awning out front. Stu stopped talking and went behind the counter. When he came out he had a double barreled shotgun in his hands, with a 45 pistol in his belt, and he headed straight for the door. He opened the door and hollered, "You scumbags get out of here. Get off my property or I'll blow you all away."

Mitch yelled back, "Don't get your shorts tight bud. We ain't hurtin nothin. We're just tryin to stay dry."

Stu pulled the hammers back on the shogun and said. "I don't care what your problem is. I said get off my property or I'll shoot."

"You ain't shootin nobody, cause you'll go to prison."

"No I won't. See those holes in the wall beside me? Well, those holes were put there by the 45 in my belt. All I have to do is blow you creeps away, throw the 45 out there and tell the cops you fired first. I was just defending myself. Knowing your reputation I bet they'll believe me."

That was good enough. They took off running in the downpour, and Stu came back inside.

"I've never seen you like that Stu."

"I can't stand those blood suckers. They go around the neighborhood preying on people who are down and out, and can't protect themselves. They wouldn't dare go up against anybody who can fight back."

"Would you have really shot them?"

"No. Even if I did, it would only sting them. The shells have rock salt in them."

"What about the gun in your belt?"

"It doesn't work. But, they obviously don't know that. Besides it doesn't mean I don't hate them."

CHAPTER THREE

Greg purchased a small zippered gym type bag with handles, and put the box in it, along with some other personal items. He finally accepted the fact that he was involved in what was going on with the box, so even though things were calm and peaceful, he figured he'd keep it with him wherever he went and see how it all played out. Besides, he found out it didn't do any good to try to throw it away.

Although Snapper was a constant companion for Greg, whenever he went inside for any length of time Snapper disappeared, only to show up when he came back out.

***

One day while Stu and Greg were talking, Stu made him an offer, "Greg, there's something I'd like to talk to you about."

"OK. What's on your mind?"

"I've got a huge Victorian style house a couple of miles north of here that used to belong to my grandparents. Do you know anything about that area?"

"I've only been to the north side of town a couple of times, so I'm not real familiar with it."

"Do you know where 'High Road is?"

"Yeah, I think I remember seeing it somewhere."

"The house is on High Hill."

"I can't say it rings a bell. What about it?"

"Well, my mom died when I was 3 years old, so my dad and I moved in there right after that and lived there with my grandparents until 15 years ago. Then I bought a house in the suburbs below Santos Hill, so dad and I moved to my new house."

"How did you end up with it?"

"After dad retired, he moved to Arizona, so my grandparents put the house in my name, with the provision that they could live there till they died, or wouldn't be able to stay alone."

"Is anyone living in it now?"

"No."

"What happened?"

"Well Grandpa died 2 years ago, and Grandma couldn't live there alone after that, so she went into assisted living. She died last year. Now, I don't need a house that big, which means I'm not about to move back there. So, it just sits there, empty."

"What do you have in mind?"

"It's a solid house, but it desperately needs some TLC. You've got an excellent eye for decorating and home repair. I don't know if that's what you did before you became homeless, and I'm not asking, but if you ever decided to make your living at remodeling you could make a lot of money at it. Well, here's what I'm thinking about. I'd like for you to restore that house to as near original as you can."

"I've never done home repair before, other than a place I owned years ago. I don't know if I could do it well enough for someone else."

"I know you can. You just tell me what supplies you need in order to do it, and we'll get them. I'm not a bottomless pit in the money department, but I can pay you just for your time and have you go out there every day. Or, what I'd prefer to do is pay you the same amount of money, and have you live in the house while you do the work."

"But Stu, I can't afford the utilities."

"You won't have to. I have to turn the power on while you do the work anyway, so it won't cost that much more for you to live there."

"Is the house totally empty now?"

"When Grandma left, I went in and shut everything down; gas, water, and electric. I took all of her personal things to my house, then covered all the furniture and closed the house up. So, everything you'll need is there, including dishes and linens. You will have to do some house cleaning before you move in. What do you think?"

"I really appreciate the offer, but I don't' know, Stu. What if I can't do everything you need done? Besides, I don't know if I want to go back into living in . . . er, get into a job routine. Can I have some time to think about it?"

"Sure, but I don't want to wait too long, because the place isn't getting any better. Let me know when I see you next week. OK?"

"OK"

Greg was in a real quandary now. Needing to talk to someone about this, he headed straight for Mindy's.

***

"Hi Greg, how're you doing?"

"Hey Mindy, I'm OK, how about you?"

"I'm good. But, you look like a man with a troubled mind."

"Yeah, I need to bounce some things off of you, if you have the time."

"I don't know if I'm qualified to give advice, but go ahead, and I'll try to help if I can."

Greg proceeded to tell Mindy about Stu's offer, and how he wasn't sure if he'd be able to do as good a job as Stu would expect.

"I don't know why Stu has so much faith in me. I'm a homeless nobody who has no background or qualifications for that kind of work."

Mindy listened while he tried to explain his doubts. When he finished she said, "I hear what you're saying, but you aren't telling me what's really going on inside."

"What do you mean? I've told you everything."

"I've got one question. What're you afraid of?"

"I'm not afraid. I just don't think I have the ability to do it."

Mindy sat silent for a long time, just staring out the window. Finally she said, "Look, we've never talked about our lives and what brought us to where we are today, but I'm going to tell you some things I swore I'd never tell anyone."

"Whoa! Hold it. You don't have to say anything about your past."

"I know I don't, but I trust you. Deep down inside, I know you won't ever make me sorry for telling you about it."

"No. Of course not."

"Well, here goes. Quite a few years ago, I was deeply involved with a guy. I'm sure you wouldn't know him, but I won't use his real name. I'll just call him 'Sam'.

'Sam was a class A Con Artist, who could manipulate people in ways that are unbelievable. He could swindle you out of everything you had and make you feel like it was your idea.

I didn't realize this until much later, but In order for 'Sam' to get me to do his bidding, and take all the heat for his cons he had to beat me down emotionally.

He did this by showing me how much smarter he was than me. He took everything I did and picked it apart until I was convinced that I had no value, or self worth without him to guide me, and direct my every move in life. It was like being brainwashed.

He did a very good job on me, because I was so infatuated and awestruck by him that I got to the place where I felt I couldn't go to the bathroom without his approval."

"That's hard to believe, Mindy. You come across as a very confident individual."

"I am now, but I let him rob me of all my confidence and self respect. Basically I lost my own identity to him, but I have no one to blame for that but myself."

"So what happened to him? Why aren't you with him now?"

"One day he sent me into a store to get him some cigarettes, while he sat out front in the car. It was something he had done many times before. This time he waited till I came out of the door, he looked at me and smiled, then drove off before I got to the car. I was so blinded by his charm that I didn't even see that one coming, so I waited there for three hours, expecting him to return for me. Well, the more time went by, the more and more afraid I became. I cried and cried till there weren't any tears left.

I walked to the motel where we were staying and he was gone. I couldn't even get my clothes, because the desk clerk said 'Sam' left there owing money, so he wouldn't let me into the room. I was now penniless and homeless with only the clothes on my back. I couldn't go back home, because my parents had passed away and there was no home to go to. But, that's a story for another time.

There were also some people looking for me, because the con jobs 'Sam' pulled on them were made to look like I did them. I have never been so, afraid of anything in my whole life as I was then. That fear was so strong that I even considered suicide. If I live to be a 100 years old, I'll never forget how it felt. I was begging for food and went to an organization that gave me some clothes. This went on for several months.

Finally, I woke up one morning under a bridge, looked around, and realized although I was scared to death, I was getting pissed. I made up my mind to overcome any and all obstacles that were in my way. 'Sam' could go to hell, and I was going to help him get there by proving he was the one pulling those cons, not me."

'Were you able to prove your innocence?"

"It took along time, but I finally cleared myself."

"What happened to 'Sam'?"

"He was convicted of fraud and grand theft, and sentenced to 15 years in prison. I didn't find out if he would be eligible for parole, so I don't know if he's out and if he is, I don't know where he is. And, I don't want to know. I just knew I had to get past my fear and restore my own life."

"So, what does that have to do with me?"

"There's no doubt that you have the ability to do what Stu wants you to do. If you look inside of yourself you'll know it as well as everyone else does. So, what are you afraid of?"

"I'm not afraid. I couldn't spend 5 years on the streets and be afraid."

"Oh yes you can. I think you're afraid if you do it, it'll be like having a job and you'll be back into everyday life. You know, it's what we call the rat race. You have a fantastic ability to do things with your hands, but there's something you're trying to avoid, and only you know what that is.

I just knew that if I didn't create the opportunity to get off the streets I wouldn't survive. And, if I didn't survive, then

'Sam' would have won and beaten me down to nothing. There wasn't any way I was going to let that happen."

"How did you do it?"

"Before I could regain my confidence I had to be sure of my determination.

Greg, you can let your 'Sam' defeat you. Or, you can take charge of your life and become what you are capable of. It's totally up to you."

"I don't think I agree with you Mindy, but I did ask, and you've given me a lot of food for thought. Now, I need to go somewhere and think things over. Thanks for listening. I'll see you next week."

"See you then, Greg."

As Greg left, Snapper walked up beside him. Mindy watched out the window as they went side by side down the street. Standing there looking at them, she had no idea that their little neighborhood was about to change in a big way.

She was wondering though, what it was that had Greg so tied up in knots. *Greg is such a nice person. It seems like there isn't anything he can't do. He's very intelligent, just as sharp as a tack. On top of it all he's quite handsome. I can't help but wonder what happened to him. Why is he on the streets?*

Greg and Snapper went back to the lean-to, and after having some lunch he laid down on his bedroll to take a nap. In a little while he sat straight up, looked at Snapper and said, "You know what? She's right. I am afraid. I'm afraid I'll fail *again*. And the reason I failed the last time is because I've never set any goals. When you have solid, determined goals, failure is not an option.

Our business was successful, but it wasn't because of any goals I had. We did work hard, and everything seemed to fall into place. I guess when you work that hard you're bound to have some degree of success. But, without good solid goals you set yourself up for failure. And, fail we did.

If I had been determined and set some goals, I would've worked through all the crap that Larry left me with. Without them, I just walked away with my tail between my legs.

I've got to talk to Stu."

***

"Hey, Stu, were you serious with the offer of remodeling your house?"

"Hi, Greg, sure, but I'm surprised you're asking. When I first brought it up you didn't seem too interested."

"Well, I've thought it over and I'd like to try it. I hope you can be patient with me, because I'm not a pro at that kind of work."

"Look, I know you've gotten used to being independent since you've been on the streets, and you'll need some crash time occasionally, but as long as you're making progress I'll be happy."

"Do you still want me to live there?"

"I'd prefer it, yes. I know I can trust you, so just turn in the time you work each week, up to 40 hours, and I'll pay you $15.00 an hour. I can't pay you any more than that,"

"That's the same rate you paid me to work in your shop. Shouldn't you charge me for living there?"

"The only thing you'll be using is a little electricity, and it'll be a great benefit to me to have someone in the house till I can decide what I want to do with it. I know at this time I can't bring myself to even consider selling it."

"OK, you've got a deal. When can we look at it?"

"If you aren't doing anything this Sunday, you can meet me here or at the house. Then we can go through the place and decide where to start."

"I'll meet you at the house around noon, if that time's OK with you."

"That works for me. Here are the directions to the house. Oh, yeah, I've got all the tools you'll need, so I'll bring them over with me. Monday you can take my pick-up to the lumber yard and buy the necessary materials to get you going. I'll also bring my generator, because it may be a few days before we can get the electricity turned on."

***

Greg was getting nervous. *What am I doing? I don't know why I agreed to this. Oh well. I did, so I hope I can do a good job for him.*

"Come on Snapper let's head for the 'The Anthill'. We can spend some time taking it easy before I go to work."

CHAPTER FOUR

Greg decided to get to the house a little early, so he could walk around the grounds and look things over. It was a three story house, and it sat about 100 feet back from the road, on a slow easy rise in the middle of about 2 acres. It definitely had a Victorian style and appeared to have been built somewhere in the early to mid 1900's

The bricks were dull and looked like they could use a good cleaning, but they seemed to be solid and in pretty good shape. Some of the gutters and downspouts were coming apart, so they were going to have to be replaced.

There was a lot of gingerbread trim and most of it looked to be in decent shape, but it needed to be painted.

The steps going up to the front entry way were quite wide, and had a handrail on each side, leading up to a screened porch. The porch extended across the front, and halfway down both sides of the house. The entry way door was beautifully carved, with a half round, etched glass window near the top, and two etched glass side lights.

As he stood on the front lawn, watching the sunlight filter down through the large oak trees, he felt himself being blanketed with a warm calmness. He took in a deep breath and could feel and smell the coming fall crispness in the air. As he exhaled, all kinds of jumbled thoughts and pictures flashed through his mind. The thoughts didn't bother him. He was just surprised by them.

"You know, Snapper. I've never been here before, but somehow I feel I know this place. Standing here studying it all, it feels like a long forgotten memory. I have an idea what the back area looks like. Come on. Let's go see if I'm right."

It was just as he saw it in his mind. There were two out buildings. One was a two story garage big enough to be a barn, and the other was a tool shed large enough to handle plenty of lawn and garden equipment. The garage was in pretty good shape, but the tool shed was leaning badly to the right, and looked like a good stiff wind would blow it over.

How did I know that? I must have seen a picture of it at Stu's shop.

He was so deep in his own thoughts he didn't hear Stu walk up behind him.

"Have you been here long?"

"No. Not very long."

"What's wrong Greg? You've got a strange look on your face."

"Do you have any pictures of this place in your shop?"

"No. My grandmother was a Native American Indian, and wouldn't let anyone take pictures here. She believed that pictures could expose your home and soul to evil spirits. Why do you ask?"

"Well, when I started walking around I had the feeling I had been here before. And yet, I knew I hadn't, so I thought maybe I'd seen a picture of it."

"My grandparents had this house built in the 1940's, right after World War II. They lived here all the time since, so it's not likely you ever saw a picture of it."

"This is a beautiful place Stu. I can see why you want to keep it in good repair."

"Yeah, it is nice. I'll never get rid of it, but I'm not sure what to do with it, because like I said, it's too big for me to live here."

"When do you want me to start on it?"

"With fall being around the corner, the days will be getting cooler and shorter, so I'd like for you to start as quickly as you can. There are definitely some things needing to be fixed before the winter weather makes them worse."

"Man, you weren't exaggerating about the size of this place. It's gigantic."

"It sure is. It's got three floors, with a full basement, and a big attic that could become a fourth floor."

"How many bedrooms?"

"Seven, each with a large closet."

"How many bathrooms?"

40

"Four and ½. Two full baths on the second floor.
One of which is accessible only from the master bedroom, and
two on the third floor. There is a half bath on the first floor."

"Why such a big house? Did they have a lot of
children?"

"No. They just had two. My father and his sister, who
was five years younger than him. I think she died when she
was around eighteen. I don't know what she died from, because
Dad never talked about it much.

I don't know if they entertained a lot, but when I was a
kid there were always people staying in the spare bedrooms.
When I became an adult there weren't as many staying there."

"Do you have a time table for finishing the job?"

"I'm pretty flexible with when it's finished."

"I don't know if I can do any large outside jobs, like
cleaning the bricks, and painting the trim. I'm not thrilled with
working off a scaffold."

"I'm not concerned with the outside right now. I had
the roof replaced last spring, because it had started leaking
badly and ruined some of the ceilings and floors, so everything
I want you to do at this point is inside. We can make a
decision on the outside stuff after winter."

"OK, let's go inside and look it over."

As they started up the steps Greg expected Snapper to
wander off, but he stayed right by his side.

When Stu put the key in the lock Greg stopped him and
asked, "Is there a foyer just inside the door?"

"Yeah. Why?"

"Is the living room to the right of the foyer?"

"Yes. But, how'd you know, and why are you asking
about it?"

"I'm not sure. I just know that as soon as we stepped
on the porch, I had the definite feeling I'd been here before."

"This is getting interesting. What else are you thinking
about?"

"Is the stairway going up to the second floor on the left
side of the foyer? And, is there a door under the stairway that
leads to the half bath?"

"Yes and yes"

"I don't have a picture in my mind of the upstairs, but let's see if I have the whole first floor right. The door to the left of the foyer leads into an office, and the office has a door on the back wall that goes into the dining room. The dining room of course goes to the kitchen.

Walking down the right side of the hallway past the stairs leads you right into the kitchen. A door on the right, just before the kitchen door, leads you into the parlor, or as some say, the sitting room. A door on the back wall of the parlor also leads into the kitchen.

There are two doors on the back wall of the kitchen. The left one goes to a utility room, and the right one goes to a screened in porch on the back of the house. A door in the utility room leads to the basement."

"You walked around and looked in the windows, didn't you?"

"Come on, I'm tall, but not that tall. Look how high the foundation is."

"Yeah you're right. You couldn't see in those rooms without a ladder. My grandparents had this house built from their own plans, so even though the style is Victorian, this house is one of a kind. So, how is it you know the layout?"

"I don't have the faintest idea. I really don't know."

"I'll tell you. You definitely are an interesting character."

As they walked around looking at the things Stu wanted repaired, Greg couldn't shake the feeling he had been in the house before, a long, long time ago. It was almost as though he was seeing things through a child's eyes.

Surprisingly, Snapper was content to walk all through the house with them, sticking right by Greg's side, until they got back to the foyer, then he went to the door and wanted out.

"Now that you've seen all of it, are you still willing to do it?"

"Sure. If you want me to, I can start tomorrow."

"Here're the keys to the house, the other buildings, and the truck. If you'll take me back to the shop so I can get my car, you can keep the truck while you work on the house. The tools are in the bed of the truck, so you should have enough to do the work. You can get your stuff and move in when you're ready. OK?"

"Yep."

"I forgot to ask. Do you still have a driver's license?"

"Yes, they don't have to be renewed till my next birthday in April."

"Oh, one more thing. I don't feel the same as my grandmother, so if I leave a camera here, would you mind taking some pictures of the different stages of improvement? Sort of, before and after pictures."

"I'd love to."

The next day Greg went to Charley and Barb's, and then Mindy's to tell about his job for Stu. Tuesday he started tearing out damaged, floors, ceilings, and walls.

Snapper was by his side a lot of the time, but once in a while he still wandered off. Sometimes Greg didn't even notice he was gone until a couple of hours had gone by. Greg had no idea where he went, but figured he must have a girlfriend. He came back to the house every night and stayed inside with Greg.

Occasionally Stu stopped by, and they would take a break together to sit and talk. For the first two months Greg was so busy on the house that he didn't take time to see Mindy. Finally, he decided to take a Tuesday afternoon off and go talk some things over with his friend.

***

"Wow, hi Greg. I was beginning to think you'd walked off the face of the Earth. It's been a long time since I've seen you."

"Hi Mindy, how're you doing?"

"I'm doing well. How are things at Stu's mansion?"

"The work's going great, and I'm obviously busy. But, I needed to take an afternoon off and just relax."

"Have you had lunch?"

"Yes."

"OK. Let's grab a cup of coffee and sit by the window."

"Boy, it's good to finally stop for a little while. I've been working seven days a week."

"I thought Stu was only paying you for 40 hours."

"That's all I charge him, but once I begin a phase of a project I don't want to stop till I finish that part of it. Besides, I just pace myself and before I know it the day has flown by. Stu has been a good friend and I don't mind."

"I'm sure Stu knows he has a good friend too."

"You know, while I'm here I've got something I'd like to talk to you about."

"Sure. What's on your mind?"

"Well, I keep having this recurring dream, and I don't know what to make of it."

"What's it about?"

"In my dream I'm a young boy. I think I'm about seven or eight years old, and I'm lying on this big bed.

I'm very uncomfortable at first and in a lot of pain. My head really hurts, and I try to reach up and touch it, but I have so much pain in my left arm that I can't move it. I don't know what's going on, but I see this woman sitting on the edge of the bed. While she's sitting there she pats and rubs my head and arm very gently. Soon she softly strokes my cheek.

She has such a warm and gentle expression on her face that I feel comforted just looking into her eyes. I don't know how old she is, but when I look at her I would guess her to be my grandmother's age.

All the time she's patting, and rubbing me she is talking to me. But, she's speaking so softly I can't hear what she's saying. So, I ask her what she's saying, and I always wake up before she has a chance to reply.

At first I didn't think too much of it, but it keeps happening at least once a night. And, it never varies. Do you know anything about dreams?"

"There must be something significant about it. But, boy, when you talk dream interpretation, you're way out of my league. I wouldn't know where to begin. I don't even know who you could talk to about it."

"I don't either. I just know it's been happening since I moved into Stu's house."

"That's fascinating. I wonder why. Do you think it's connected to the house?"

"It certainly seems like it, because this never occurred before I moved there."

"Speaking of the house, what all are you doing in there?"

"Well, I've torn out ceilings, walls, and floors; some that were damaged by water when the roof was leaking, and some were just old and needed to be replaced. I'm almost done with the walls and ceilings now. Very few of the floor and ceiling joists were damaged, so I won't have to replace too many of them. Next, I'll start replacing the sub-flooring, so I won't have to worry about where I walk. Right now I have to watch my step, because I've only got plywood sheets lying over the floor joists."

She reached over, putting her hand on his arm, and said, "You know. I sure miss the long discussions we used to have on those lazy afternoons."

"He looked into her eyes for a long time and replied, "I miss them too. I definitely get a lot more pleasure out of talking to you than talking to myself or Snapper."

"Thanks."

"Hey, I've got an idea. Have you ever seen Stu's place?"

"No. I don't even know where it is."

"If you aren't busy Sunday afternoon why don't I pick you up around 2:00 o'clock, and take you up there for a grand tour of the place?"

"OK. I'll bring a large thermos of coffee and some sandwiches, so we can have a late lunch."

"That sounds good to me. I'll see you then."

Driving back to the house, it dawned on Greg that he was smiling, and humming along with the music on the radio. He thought. *I'm really looking forward to spending Sunday afternoon with Mindy. I don't remember the last time I was this happy to be with someone.*

All the rest of the week he was in a good positive mood. That and staying busy made the time fly right on by.

***

"Are you ready to go Mindy?"

"You bet. Can you help me with some of this stuff?"

"Sure, but what is all this? If you're planning to move into the house, you can't. It's not ready yet."

"This bag is our lunch, with desserts, and these other things are my drawing supplies, and camera."

"Drawing supplies?"

"Oh yes. I love to draw with colored pencils and charcoal."

"Those pictures in your shop, did you do those?"

"Yes. It's been a hobby of mine since I was in elementary school."

"They're beautiful. Are they scenes of places you've been to?"

"Yes."

Even though it was mid fall, the sun was shining brightly and the temperature was in the 70's, so they ate lunch on the screened in front porch. After lunch they strolled around the grounds.

As they began walking she reached for his hand and they continued on holding hands.

Greg was surprised at how natural it felt to walk along holding her hand.

"You know, Greg. It's very relaxing and comfortable here. The people, who made this a home, must have had rich rewarding lives, because this place has good vibes."

"That's interesting, because I feel the same way."

"Before we go inside I'd like to walk around again to make some sketches and take pictures."

"You don't just sit down at your easel and draw?"

"No. I don't have time to sit and draw a scene all at once, or to keep coming back. So, I make rough sketches and take pictures. Then at home when I have the time, I match the color pictures to the sketches. That way I'll know the shading for charcoal, or if I want, I can draw it with colored pencils."

"If you don't mind, I'm going inside. Come on in when you're ready. Be very careful where you walk though, I've got a lot of loose plywood down to cover the floor joists."

"I'll be in shortly."

Greg couldn't believe how good it felt to be out here with her. He had dated several women, and nothing ever developed. Now, here he was with a woman he'd never dated, and considered a friend, but his thoughts were quite confusing.

"This place is even more beautiful inside. The woodwork is amazing. Let's look around."

"Sure, but be careful, and walk where I do."

As they walked through the house, he explained who originally owned the property and how Stu ended up with it. She couldn't get over how magnificent, and yet homey the atmosphere was every where she went.

"You know, Greg. It's obvious the material that went into building this home is top quality. Money was no object, yet the warmth and comfort I feel while I'm in here is mind boggling. You can tell everything about this place has their personal touch on it. They must have been some fantastic people."

"It's nice to know I'm not the only one to feel that way."

"This is my first time here, and I know I could live here easily."

"I know. Now you see why I get lost in time while working all day here."

"Yeah, I sure do."

Looking at her watch, she said, "As much as I hate to leave, I'm afraid I have to. It's almost 6:30, and I've got a lot to do to get ready for tomorrow."

"I wish you could stay, but I understand. Let's get your stuff together, and I'll take you home."

As they stood in the foyer facing each other, Greg said, "I don't want you to get the wrong idea Mindy, but I really enjoy being with you, and I hope we can spend some time off together again."

She took both of his hands in hers, saying, "I won't get the wrong idea. I've enjoyed this afternoon too, and I'm looking forward to the next time we can get together."

He stood for a long moment, gently squeezing her hands. Looking deeply into her eyes, he said, "Mindy, when we're touching like this, you feel the same thing I do, don't you?"

"Right down to my toes."

"I certainly didn't see this coming. I don't know where my life's going, so I can't make any promises."

"I have no expectations. I just know I look forward to spending time with you, and I greatly treasure our friendship. All we can do is take things as they come, Greg."

After dropping her off at home, Greg had some new feelings and thoughts to try to sort out in his mind.

CHAPTER FIVE

The following Wednesday night after Greg quit working for the day, things got very interesting.

After he had showered and the lights had been turned off for a while, he was lying in bed thinking how glad he was that he'd finished the wall and ceiling repairs in the rooms. Now all he had to finish was the ceilings and floors in the walkways outside the rooms. Suddenly Snapper's head and ears perked up, and he let out a low growl.

"What is it boy? What do you hear?"

Snapper got up and quietly went out of the room.

He's never done that before. I wonder what that's all about. Hmm, it sounds like I'm hearing voices. I'd better see what's going on.

"Is someone there?"

Mitch's voice came out loud and clear, "Hey, you stupid Wino. We found you. You can't hide no more. We're comin for your ass. We're gonna give you time to pray, then we're gonna kill you, so you better get on your knees."

Greg's eyes were adjusted to the darkness and he could see movement in front of the bedroom on the other side of the stairway. He yelled out, "Don't come over this way, or you're going to get hurt."

"How you gonna hurt us Wino? You gonna hit us with a wine bottle?"

"I'm telling you if you come over here you'll get hurt."

"Sure Wino, here we come, let's see how you're gonna hurt us."

After Mitch took three steps, a plywood sheet tipped up on one end and slid down between two floor joists. When it landed on the second floor it hit another plywood sheet, and both went between two joists on that floor.

Mitch followed the two sheets of plywood to the first floor, screaming all the way down. When he landed with a sickening thump, he became silent. You could've heard a pin drop until Flop yelled in pain as Snapper growled and sank his teeth into the back of his thigh, just above his right knee.

Unable to see in the dim light, Petey said, "This place is booby trapped. Let's get out of here."

He and Slug ran down two flights of stairs and out the front door, with Flop screaming in pain and limping behind them.

To everyone's relief they were never seen or heard from again.

Greg, standing there watching it all, started to break out in laughter, and then he realized Mitch was probably very seriously hurt. He may even be dead.

Oh my god! I don't even have a telephone. I can't call 911. What the hell am I going to do? Wait a minute. The box with the cloths. I'll get the box, if I can remember where it is. If he isn't dead I might be able to keep him stable till I can get him to a medical facility.

Greg found the gym bag with the box in it and took it downstairs. When he got there, he turned on the light and Mitch was gone. But, there was trail of blood leading into the kitchen.

The blood trail was smeared, so it looked like Mitch was crawling or dragging himself across the floor. When he walked through the doorway, he saw Mitch lying in the middle of the room.

He went over and knelt down beside him. As he did, Mitch slowly opened his eyes and said, "You win Wino. I'm busted up pretty bad, so if..."

Then he slipped into unconsciousness. As Greg was reaching into the box, Mitch came to and said, "If you're gonna finish me, do it quick."

Then he drifted out again.

The front of Mitch's head was bleeding profusely from a large gash just above his hairline. Greg began wiping the cloth on the wound, and once again watched wide eyed as the gash stopped bleeding and closed up. The cloth was still intact, so he knew there were other injuries. As he was taking Mitch's jacket, shirt, and pants off, he came to again, this time saying,

"Get off me you damned pervert. Ain't it good enough that you killed me?" Then he passed out once more.

Greg listened to his breathing, and it was very rapid and shallow. He was fading quickly, so Greg knew he couldn't waste any time. He could see a large bluish looking knot about the size of a grapefruit on his chest just below his right nipple, so he wiped the cloth over it until the knot disappeared.

The cloth was still there, and his breathing hadn't changed, so he still had another injury. His left ankle looked broken, so Greg worked on it with the cloth, and when the swelling went down, he knew something more serious was going on, because Mitch's breathing was still labored, and the cloth hadn't disintegrated.

He turned Mitch onto his left side, and saw it. There was a large indentation on the lower, rear section of his right rib cage. It looked as though someone had slammed a 2x4 across the right side of his back. Some ribs had to be broken, and maybe his lung or kidney was punctured. The skin all around it was scraped and raw looking.

Man, this looks bad. He must have hit one those floor joists directly on his side. I hope the cloth can handle this.

He wiped the cloth over the area, and once again, he sat there staring as it healed.

I don't care how old I get I'll continue to be amazed at what I've seen these cloths do.

The cloth began to shred and disintegrate, so he new Mitch would be alright. As he sat there watching, he heard Mitch's breathing become deep and relaxed. He picked him up and carried him to the couch in the parlor, and then covered him with a blanket.

He sat in the lounge chair the next morning and glanced over at Mitch as he slept. Sipping his coffee, he wondered what Mitch's reaction would be when he woke up.

Pretty soon he opened his eyes. As he looked around it was evident he was totally confused. When he saw Greg, it startled him, and he stared at him for a long time before asking, "Am I dead?"

"No."

"Where are we?"

"In the parlor, in Stu's house."

"Why are you sitting there watching me? What's going on here? How in the world did we end up here together?"

"If you like coffee I'll get you a cup, and then try to answer all your questions."

"Yeah, I do. I'll take it black."

When Greg came back with coffee Mitch was sitting up, gingerly touching his chest and right side. He still had a befuddled look on his face.

"Thanks. OK, now tell me what's going on."

"You tell me what you think, and I'll see if I can fill in some of the blanks."

"There are so many things in my head I don't know where to start."

"Take your time. I've got all day."

"That's a good place to start. What day is it?

"Thursday."

"Then it was just last night we came here, right?"

"Yes."

"When we came here, I said we were going to kill you. Why aren't you mad at me?"

"What makes you so sure I'm not?"

"Well, you haven't killed me."

"Killing you wouldn't benefit me in any way."

"Where are the other guys?"

"They ran off when you fell."

Mitch had a look of surprise on his face and said, "Then, my falling wasn't a dream?"

"No."

"When I landed, I remember hurting like hell. My head, my chest, and right side were killing me. I know my ankle had to be broken, because I couldn't walk, so I crawled as far as I could, and that's the last thing I remember."

"You don't remember anything more?"

"Can I have another coffee?"

"Sure."

"Thanks. That's good coffee. I'm sitting here in my underwear and tee shirt. Where are my clothes?"

"In a pile at the end of the couch. They're in pretty bad shape."

There was a look of shock on Mitch's face when he saw them.

"Is that my blood?"

"Yes."

"I don't get it. I'm not cut or bruised, and I'm not sore anywhere."

"Do you remember anything else after you fell?"

"No. I passed out and the next thing I knew . . . Hold it! It was kind of like dream, and you were in it. Why are you being so nice to me?"

"Because, it doesn't make sense to fight with you. So, go ahead, as you were saying?"

"In my dream you were on your knees beside me. You weren't saying anything, but you were wiping my head with a towel or something, and my head felt better. Next thing I knew, you were taking my clothes off, and I was getting pissed. That's the last thing I remember till I woke up just now."

"Is that all?"

"Why were you sitting there watching me? Are you Gay?"

Greg couldn't help but chuckle at that one. "No, I'm not"

Mitch stood up and walked around the room. When he saw the ladders and construction equipment, he said, "I remember laying on the floor thinking you had set traps for us. But, you're just restoring the place for Stu, aren't you?"

"Yep."

"He doesn't live here now, so is he going to move in after you finish?"

"No. It's way too big for him, but he won't sell it, because it used to belong to his grandparents."

"What's he going to do with it?"

"The last time we talked about it, he didn't know."

Pointing upward Mitch said, "We both know that I fell through those floor joists right up there. True?"

"Yes."

"I'm lucky to be alive, because we were on the third floor, and yet I'm not even sore."

"So, what are you trying to say?"

"Well, everything between when I fell and when I woke up on this couch, seems like a hazy kind of dream. Only it wasn't a dream was it? Yet, I couldn't haven't fallen that far and not been seriously hurt. Right?"

"It would seem that way. Now, I've got a question for you."

"Yeah?"

"Mitch, since I've known you, you've had terrible grammar. Frankly your diction was rotten. You talked like you had absolutely no education. Well, it's quite obvious that you are well versed in grammar. What's that all about?"

"I'm educated. I have bachelor's degree in math. I felt I had to talk that way, so I could make the other guys think I was like them."

"OK."

"You still haven't answered all my questions."

"I don't have all the answers. The only thing I can tell you is, in the last several months some things have taken place that have allowed me to help people who've been hurt. I don't know why I'm the one to do this, but it's definitely changed my whole life. I was content to spend my life on the streets, and now look at me."

"By the way, what's your name?"

"My name is Greg."

"Greg, how do you help people when they get hurt?"

"I'd try to tell you, but I can't prove it, so you'll have to take my word for it."

"If what happened to me wasn't a dream, then that means you helped me. But, you can't show me, or explain how you did it?"

"That's right. I can show you something you've already seen, but I don't think it'll clear anything up for you."

"What do you mean?"

Reaching into the gym bag, Greg pulled out the block of wood.

Mitch stared in disbelief, and said, "Is that the same block of wood you were carrying that day when we . . . ?"

"Yes."

"What in world can that thing do?"

"You wouldn't believe me if I told you. So, we'll have to let it rest there."

"Man, this is the craziest thing I ever heard of."

"You think I don't know that? So, what are you going to do now?"

"Right now, I'm going to put my clothes on and get out of here. My life just did a 180 degree turn around, so I've got to figure out what's next."

"Are we finished fighting with each other?"

"You saved my life, and when I think about some of the things I've done to you and others, I don't know if it was worth saving. But, now that you have, I certainly couldn't fight with you. I just know I've got a lot of soul searching to do though. I don't know if I'll ever see you again, but I think I'd better leave now."

After getting dressed, Mitch shook hands with Greg and walked out.

CHAPTER SIX

Things were pretty quiet through the holidays. On Thanksgiving, Christmas, and New Years Day, Charley and Barb closed the tavern and fed as many of the homeless in the neighborhood as they could.

Barb and Charley aren't from this area. She's from a small town in the Midwest, and she felt stifled there, so finally one day she got on a bus for anywhere to try something new. He's from a wealthy family in a large city up North, and didn't want the trappings and pressure of all that money, so he hopped on a bus to strike out on his own and that just happened to be the same bus she was on. That's how they met. To see them side by side you wouldn't take them as a couple. He's about 5' 10", thin and wiry. She's about 5' 2", and heavy set. You can see though, when they tease back and forth that they really like each other.

Somehow Mindy and Greg got roped into helping serve the food and drinks at all those dinners.

At one of the dinners Mindy said, "Greg, I've been worried about you being out at that huge house and not having any way to contact the outside world."

"I don't have problems with it."

"If you had an accident and couldn't get out, how would anyone get to you in time? The nearest neighbor is a quarter mile away. If you were hurt you could die before anyone knew about it."

Thinking about what happened to Mitch, he responded, "What do you have in mind?"

"With my cell phone plan I can get a second phone for only twenty five dollars more a month. Why don't I get it for you?"

"I guess it's a good idea, but I don't want anything fancy, just enough to make calls. I'll pay you for the phone"

"OK. Come by the shop Wednesday, and we'll get you one."

***

After the holidays Greg was able to spend more time on the house, so the repair work was going along pretty well. It looked as though he'd get all the subflooring finished before March.

It was a quiet mid winter afternoon. Greg was installing new subflooring in the third floor hallway when he heard, "Hey Wino. Where are you? I'm comin after your ass."

Greg said aloud, "I thought this crap was over, now the boneheads are back and no Snapper when I need him."

He listened carefully and could hear footsteps on the lower floors. Then suddenly the footsteps were on the stairs, heading in his direction. He went in the large bathroom and over to the other side of the cabinets where he couldn't be seen, and waited. He knew the walk area was narrow enough that if they came in, they'd have to be single file and he could at least take out the first two.

As he waited, he could hear Mitch yelling, "Come on out Wino. You can't hide. I know you're in here."

The door opened slowly and Greg could hear at least one of them coming into the bathroom. He doubled up his fist, and drew back to punch. But, he was standing there staring into the eyes of a nice looking, neatly dressed, clean cut reddish blond haired man in his mid thirties, and said, "What the? Who are you?"

"Don't swing Greg. It's me, Mitch."

"Mitch! That's unbelievable. I never would have known you. Man, you clean up real well."

"Geez, I'm glad you didn't hit me. I remember what you did to Flop that time. Did you know you broke his jaw?"

"Really? I didn't know that."

"They had to wire his jaw together. He was eating through a straw for two months."

"No kidding!"

"His jaw was broken in three places."

What are you doing here? I didn't think I'd ever see you again. As usual I've got coffee going in the kitchen. Want some?"

"Sure. By the way, where's the dog? I can tell you first hand, he can do some damage too."

"Here you go. Oh, Snapper, he's out roaming around somewhere. I think he's got a girl friend. Let's go sit at the table. You know, you really had me fooled. I thought, hear we go again."

"I figured I'd jerk your chain just one more time. I was looking around here. You've moved along on this place."

"I've stayed busy since you were here last. What have you been doing?"

"I told you I had to do a lot of soul searching. Well, I have, and I still have a lot more to do. At this point, it's forced me to come to grips with the things I've done to people and why I've done them."

"Have you come to any conclusions?"

"I sure have. When I look at some of the things that took place in my life, it makes it easier for me to understand why I was so angry. Don't get me wrong. I'm not saying that just because I had bad things happen to me, that it was OK for me to hurt others. There's no way I can justify the things I've done to hurt people. I just feel I can't solve my problems if I don't know what caused them."

"If you don't mind my asking, did these things happen to you as you were growing up?"

"I don't mind. I won't bore you with all my problems, but maybe I can give you enough to fill you in. Just for starters, the man who was my biological father was the most brutal, ruthless person I've ever seen."

"What did he do?"

"When I was six years old he came home one night and told us he'd quit his job. He said the idea of being homeless was far more attractive than having a wife and two kids hanging on to him and dragging him down. Then, he turned around and walked out, taking nothing with him but the clothes on his back."

"Never to be seen or heard from again?"

"It would have been a blessing if that had been true."

"Where did he go?"

"Oh, he never left the city. He just went downtown to the homeless area."

"You said two kids."

"I had a sister, four years older than me."

"Had a sister? What do you mean had?"

"She couldn't live with the things he did to her. She committed suicide. She and I were very close. When she died I felt like all of the good things that were in me died as well."

"What about your mother?"

"She was driving drunk and hit a tree at a hundred miles an hour. I think in her own way she committed suicide too."

"What a terrible shame it is when a person feels there's nothing to live for. Do you know why?"

"Periodically my father would come back to the house for sex and money. My mother couldn't say no to him. After he'd leave she'd lay in bed for days in a drunken stupor. I tried to get her to change the locks, but she wouldn't do it. She told me, some day he'll come to his senses and come back to stay. I didn't want him to come back.

I was really getting to hate him, so one day when he showed up, I tried to stop him. He picked me up and threw me against the wall breaking my leg and my collar bone. I laid there in pain and unable to move, and he was in such a rage that he beat my mother till she was unconscious. Then, he went into my sister's room, and I listened to her scream as he raped her several times."

"Is he still alive?"

"After that day I swore I'd kill him when I got big enough. Don't you know, the rotten bastard even cheated me out of that?"

"How did he do that?"

"The day I buried my sister, I went down to the ghetto to kill him. Five minutes before I got there he stepped out of a doorway into an alley in front of a garbage truck. Witnesses said he didn't know what hit him and he died instantly. All that did was intensify my hatred for him.

"How did you get an education?"

"My grandparents were very wealthy and they never did like my father. So, they decided that the way they could protect the three of us would be to create a sizable trust and put it in Mom's name. Mom could take out just enough money to support us each month, and only if my father wasn't around.

It's a good thing they did that for us, because two weeks after my father left, my grandfather died. Mom didn't know about the trust till after my grandfather died. When his funeral was over, my grandmother left and we never saw her again.

When Mom died, the trust rolled over to us. As soon as we were old enough, we could draw money out for the college of our choice. I went to school, and my sister didn't want to, since she had plenty of money to support herself, so she did volunteer work for the Red Cross."

"Why did she commit suicide?"

"After Mom died we didn't see our father for a couple of years, and we figured he was dead too. Thanks to some advanced courses in high school by the time I was sixteen I was ready for college.

College was pretty uneventful. I'd come home for the holidays to see my sister. We never talked about our father, and I never saw him, so I just assumed he was dead.

When I graduated, my sister came for the ceremony and then flew home the next day. After some celebrating, I drove home the following week-end.

When I got home I found my sister lying across her bed, and a letter to me under an empty pill bottle on the nightstand. In the letter she said, our father had been coming back about once a month or so, raping her and taking what money she had on hand. She said she didn't tell me, because she knew it would mess up my school work. But now that I was out of school, and she knew I'd be alright, she said she just couldn't bear to live with the shame any longer."

"Man, that had to be nearly impossible to take."

"When she died I wanted to die too, but I was so filled with hate when I discovered my father was dead, that I knew I had to stay alive, if for no other reason than to exact my revenge. To my way of thinking he was a terrible beast that chose to be a homeless bum, so every homeless person must be as bad as he was, and I was going to see to it, they got everything they deserved."

"How do you feel now?"

"I realize that was stupid thinking. I think deep down inside, I always knew it, but that was the only way I could vent my frustration and anger.

Now, I have to learn how to take each person as they come to me, not prejudge anyone. The weird thing is I've never had any prejudices against minorities, races, politics, or religions. I just hated all homeless people."

"I noticed you used hate in the past tense. What changed your mind?"

"You."

"Why me?"

"I can't get my mind off the events of that Wednesday night a few months back. The more I think of it the more I'm sure I wasn't dreaming about all those injuries, and you being there. I remember lying there touching my right side and feeling the bottom half all caved in. Plus, my chest was hurting so bad I could hardly breathe. Those injuries alone were life threatening, and left alone, I probably would've been dead by morning.

Greg, you knew I was coming here to kill you, and you could have left me there to die. You could've said you didn't know I was there and no one would've known any difference."

"I would have."

"I still can't figure out how you did it, but I know, that the how doesn't matter. What does, matter is the why, and the fact that I'm alive and healthy. All because of you. You've seen to it, I've been given a chance to try to make up for some of the rotten things I've done to people who didn't deserve it."

"How do you plan on doing that?"

"Well, you said Stu didn't know what he was going to do with this place. I have an idea, but I'm going to need you to help me convince Stu of it. My reputation obviously precedes me, so he isn't going to listen to just me."

"So what's your idea?"

"When you get finished restoring the house, we could turn it into a place where people down on their luck could come to, as a safe haven, until they are able to lead a productive life again."

"That wouldn't be cheap. Just the cost of food, clothes, and bed linens alone would be pretty high. I can't speak for Stu, so I don't know if he'd be willing to do it."

"No. I'll carry the daily expenses. The only thing I'd ask him to do is keep the property in good repair. I'll take on all costs including food, bed clothes, towels, medicine, the utilities, water, sewer, and trash."

"Since we're being open and above board about everything, I've got to bring something up here."

"Go ahead."

"You and your guys were stealing from the homeless and destitute people in the neighborhood. How are you going come up with the money to finance an undertaking like this?"

"I told you we had a sizable trust left to us. While I was going to college my sister quite wisely invested our money in some high dividend stock. After she passed I sold the stock at a wonderful profit, so I'm very comfortable, to say the least."

"If you are financially well off, why steal from others?"

"Stealing from the homeless had nothing to do with money for me. It was all about power and anger. I let the other guys keep the money and valuables."

"Hmm . . . that's interesting. It sounds like a fantastic idea. I don't know if Stu will go along with it though. He grew up in this area, and feels that your gang poisoned the whole neighborhood. He really hates you guys."

"I know, and he has every right to, so will you go with me to talk to him? He might believe me if you're there. Look!

I'll even help you get this place finished, and maybe together we can have it ready in a month or two."

"What makes you think he'll listen to me?"

"He knows you're an honest man. If he trusts anyone it'll be you."

"I'm not sure I have the same faith in me you do."

"If you can just keep him calmed down until I explain my plan to him, that's all I can ask for."

"Alright I'll do it, but I'm going to see if he'll meet us here."

"Thanks Greg. When do you want to meet with him?"

"After your accident I got a cell phone, but I keep forgetting to plug it into the charger, and it's dead now, so come back tomorrow about the same time. I'll call Stu before you get here and set up a time for us to meet with him."

"Alright, I'll see you then."

CHAPTER SEVEN

"Hey Stu, its Greg how're you doing?"

"I'm OK, how about you?"

"I'm good. I called, because there was someone here today that wants to give you some ideas about what you can do with this house."

"I'm not selling it under any circumstances."

"He knows that. As a matter of fact he hopes you never do."

"What's this all about? I don't have any money to put into changes."

"It's nothing like that. Look, I won't say anything right now, because I don't know all the details and I don't want to tell you wrong. He said he'd like to meet with you and explain everything."

"When does he want to meet?"

"He said he'd be back tomorrow afternoon around two o'clock, if that's all right with you."

"OK, I can be there by then."

***

"Hi Greg, I thought I'd get here a little early and try to get a heads up."

"I figured you might. I don't have all the info, but I'll tell you what I do know. When he gets here he'll lay it all out for you. OK?"

"Alright. Tell me what you can."

"He'd like to set this house up as a refuge for people down on their luck. It would be a retreat, where they could stay long enough to recharge their batteries and get back on their feet."

"That's spooky."

"What do you mean?"

"After I talked to you last night, my dad called. We were talking about this house, and I told him you'd probably be done by summer. He asked what I planned to do with it then. I said I had no idea. Then he said, 'Why don't you do what your grandparents did'?"

"What was that?"

"Here's what's spooky. He told me that all those people who stayed in the house when I was a kid were down on their luck, and my grandparents took them in to give them the chance to get back on their feet."

"Wow! That is eerie."

"I told Dad I didn't have the time or the money, so there was no way."

"The guy who proposed this said he'll supply all the money for it, if you'll keep the house in good repair."

"Who is this guy? Where did he come from?"

"That's the part you're going to find difficult to deal with."

"What do you mean?"

"Just hear me out before you go off half cocked."

"Come on Greg, who is it?"

"You're not going to believe this. It's Mitch."

Stu's normally resounding voice rose about ten decibels as he responded with, "Mitch! Mitch! You mean the gang leader, Mitch?"

"That's the one."

"All this time they've done nothing but abuse the homeless, and steal from them, including you. Now we're supposed to believe they've made this miraculous turn around and want to help all of you? Greg, are you back on that cheap wine?"

"No. Of course not. I definitely won't try to influence you in any way. For one thing, on a personal level I won't be involved. Once I'm done fixing this house I'm going to go about my own business."

"You know how I feel about bloodsucking leeches that prey on helpless people. You were there when I threatened to kill them."

"I remember it all too well."

"I don't want that gang of cutthroats anywhere near my house. Let alone in it."

"One thing I can guarantee. There is no more gang."

"How do you know that?"

"The last time I saw Mitch's gang they were running away screaming. That was several months ago. To the best of my knowledge no one around here has seen them since, including Mitch."

"What happened?"

"That's a whole different story. Sometime when we get together I'll tell you all about it. Actually it's quite funny."

"I'm still trying to figure out how this ever got to the place where the two of you could sit and talk together. He had vowed to kill you."

"Now, that is a very long story. Perhaps he'll fill you in. If he doesn't, I will later. A lot of things have taken place recently. The real Mitch is nothing like the person we've known and seen in the past. I think you'll be surprised when you see him.

He is coming onto the porch now, so will you please be civil, and listen to what he has to say?"

"Sure Greg. I trust you like a brother. I'll hear him out. Besides, I'm not that hard to get along with. You know that. But, when this is over, no matter how it turns out, I deserve to know the whole story."

"OK. I'll tell you everything I know. I promise you."

Greg let Mitch in the door, then stood back and watched with amusement at Stu's reaction to him.

Mitch put both hands up in front of him with his palms out, and said, "Before we start, I want to tell you that if I have done anything in the past to harm you, or cause you any problems, I'm very sorry. I swear to you. I will never hurt you or anyone else ever again."

Stu stood for a long time with his jaw hanging open, and finally said, "You're Mitch? You don't look like the Mitch I know."

"I knew I had to change my image when my life took on a new direction, or nobody would believe me."

"You don't even talk like the Mitch I know."

"I'm guessing Greg told you at least a little bit about what I'm proposing that we do with your house. So, why don't you ask me some questions? I'll answer all that I can."

"Alright, for one thing, it's going to take a lot to convince me that you are for real, and whether I go along with you or, throw your ass out, depends on your answers to all my questions."

"Believe me. I know that I can't ever begin to make up for what I've done to people, but I have start somewhere,"

"Mitch, Stu, you guys don't need me here, and I've got some things to do, so I'll leave the two of you alone to iron this out."

"OK Greg, we'll catch you later."

As Greg walked toward the steps he looked back to see them sitting down in the easy chairs across from each other in the parlor.

***

"Alright Mitch, what caused this miracle turn around in your attitude?"

Mitch pointed in the direction Greg went and said, "Him."

"What do you mean him?"

"Greg saved my, up to that point very unworthy life. And, when he did, I realized I was being given a second chance to do something I had tried to throw away the first time around."

"How did he save your life?"

"Well, I fell through the joists on the third and second floors. By the time I landed on the floor, right here between us, I was seriously hurt. I probably would have died."

"So what did Greg do?"

"I don't expect you to believe this, but somehow he healed my injuries. I don't know how he did it, because it's all like a hazy dream. I feel like I woke up one time, and he was touching the injured areas and soothing me. I do know for a fact, I woke up the next morning feeling great. I wasn't sore or hurting anywhere."

Stu sat there, thinking about his own injuries, and how Greg was involved in that. He finally said, "So far, that's the first thing you've said that I *don't* have any doubts about."

Now, it was Mitch's turn to be surprised. Looking quizzically at Stu, he replied, "There's only one reason you wouldn't doubt what I just told you. You've had the same thing happen to you, haven't you?"

"Yeah, but that's something for another time maybe. You've got my attention now, so give me a broad overview of what you want to do in this house."

"I want to use it as a refuge and shelter for people who are down on their luck, and are trying to get back into the mainstream of society. Plus, I want to put programs and projects in place to enable them to do that. When I say people, I mean both genders, and all races."

"After the way you've treated the down trodden, I still don't understand the turn around."

"I need to do this in memory of my sister. I feel if I don't, she will have died in vain."

"I didn't know you had a sister. What does she have to do with the homeless?"

Mitch went through the whole story about his father, mother, and sister. He also told him about the money and college. The biggest point of all this was why he reacted to the homeless with such rage and hatred after his sister died.

Stu asked him, "Why my house?"

"To start with, Greg said you weren't planning to live here, and you didn't have any idea what you were going to do with it. Plus, I almost died here that night. It's very important for me to have my new beginning here. And, I'd like to call it 'Annie Neville's Second Chance', in honor of my sister."

Stu sat there in stunned silence for the longest time.

"Finally Mitch said, "What's wrong? Are you alright?"

"Annie Neville was your sister? You are Billy Neville?"

"Yes. How do you know her?"

"For four years she and I did volunteer work at the Red Cross. She was the most wonderful person I ever knew. God, she loved you. She talked about you all the time. She was so proud of you."

"I can tell you right now I don't deserve it."

"You are the only one who can change that."

'That's why I'm here talking to you. Do you still volunteer there?"

"No. After she died I kind of lost my drive and spirit for being there."

"Were you in love with her?"

"No . . . Yes . . . I don't know. I really don't know how to describe it. I don't think I ever expected anything to come of it. I just know how good I felt being around her, and being her friend."

"Now maybe you understand why I can't disappoint her any longer."

"Yes. Since you came into the house I've been trying to figure out why you look so familiar, and now I remember. I saw you at the Red Cross one time when you were home on Christmas break from school."

"Yeah, I did that a lot."

"Is Mitch your middle name?"

"No. That was the name of a tough macho guy I saw in a movie years ago, and I always thought it was cool."

Stu thought Billy's idea was great and he wanted Billy to run it. After a lot of conversation to get to know each other, they both agreed there was enough time to work out the details while the house was being finished.

They both went upstairs to find Greg and fill him in.

***

"I think it's a wonderful project guys, because it'd be a shame to see this beautiful home just sit here and not be used for what the original owners intended.

I have to admit though. I had my doubts about the two of you being able to agree on this."

"As it turns out, Stu knew my sister very well. After I told him what we grew up with he understood why I wanted to do it."

"Mitch, I know you had my endorsement, but it's not my house, so I couldn't give you the OK."

"Something else you need to know, Greg. My name's not Mitch. It's Billy Neville, and you can call me Billy or Bill, I don't care which."

'Man, you guys are full of surprises today. So, what brought the two of you together?"

They both said in unison, "You."

"Me? What did I do?"

Billy said, "It had something to do with a block of wood that you carry around with you."

"Look you two. All I know is, I don't have any mystical or magical powers, so don't set me up as some kind of healer, because I'm not."

Stu said. "One thing I do know is, the day I was injured so badly I passed out from the pain, you came by. When I woke up with no injuries and no pain, you were still there with me."

Billy says, when he fell through the floor joists in this house, and was in terrible pain you were there, and when he woke up pain and injury free, you were there with him. And, we all know, nobody heals that fast, on their own."

'If you don't want to tell us how it happened we can't make you, but we both know that if it weren't for you, we wouldn't be here today. It's that simple."

"It's not that I don't want to tell you. It's just something I don't know how to explain."

"Why don't you try?"

"Look. If I tell you that this block of wood is really a box that has magical cloths in it, and when I take one of these cloths out and wipe it over someone's injuries it heals them, would you believe me?"

"No, we'd doubt your sanity", said Billy.

"OK, then. I didn't say it, did I? Right now I'm not able to explain how this happened. Maybe someday I'll be able to, but I have my doubts."

CHAPTER EIGHT

The next day Bill showed up at the house bright and early to start working with Greg. The two of them got a lot of things done in a short time. On the days that weren't so cold, Bill started some of the outside work. He rented scaffolding, and as weather permitted; cleaned the bricks, repaired the trim, and replaced the gutters and downspouts. The outside painting would have to wait until the temperature was constantly in the seventies.

As much as they worked together it still took Greg a long time before he finally got into the habit of calling him Bill and not Mitch.

Bill only worked Monday through Friday, and Greg would spend the occasional weekends that he didn't work with Mindy.

As time went along Stu, Bill, and Greg formed a strong bond between the three of them.

Also, to Greg's relief the question of how they were healed was never brought up again.

***

It seemed as though Snapper could read Greg's mind because every time he wondered where Snapper was, he would suddenly show up.

***

One of the times Greg went to Mindy's shop and business was slow he told her the story of Mitch/Bill's life while growing up. She was a little reserved at first, so Greg offered to bring him over the following week, so she could draw her own conclusions.

After meeting and talking with him as Bill, she began to feel better, so when they could, they'd take an hour or two and go to Mindy's for lunch.

Mindy and Greg discovered, Bill shared many of their own outlooks and philosophies, and it allowed the three of them to have some very lively discussions.

One of those Tuesdays when they arrived, Mindy had a surprise. She showed them two, eleven by fourteen size drawings of the property.

They were both done in charcoal. One was a view from the road out front, looking at the right front corner of the house, with a man and woman sitting on the steps in front. The second was closer to the house, and looking at the left side, so you got a partial view of the out buildings in the rear, with a young boy and his dog in the side yard.

The guys were extremely impressed. After they showered her with all kinds of accolades, Greg asked, "Is there anything you can't do?"

"There are a lot of things I can't do, but I don't tell anybody what they are.

I want you guys to come here next Tuesday at three o'clock. It's very important that you bring Stu with you too."

"OK."

For the week, Bill worked on the tool shed, getting it squared and plumb, then bracing and reinforcing it so it would stay that way.

Greg in the meantime, finished up all the flooring in the house.

The only projects left to do were mostly small things like replacing faucet washers, toilet hardware and cleaning up the hardware on the doors and windows. Stu wanted any broken fixtures replaced with original equipment whenever possible, so Greg and Bill were going to spend a lot of time in salvage yards, antique stores, and flea markets looking for things.

***

"Now that you all have your coffee and donuts, I want to tell you, I'm glad you could all come by. I've got something I want to give you Stu."

Mindy walked over to the corner of the room and pulled the cover off a large drawing that looked to be twenty four by thirty six.

The scene was Stu's house in the spring. It was looking straight at the front of the house from around thirty feet away. In the foreground, to the right, standing in the grass, was a grandmotherly looking woman. She had a gentle smile on her face and was dressed in the style of clothing a woman her age would've worn in the 1960's. Mindy had drawn it with colored pencils, which made all the spring colors jump right off the paper at you.

They were all awestruck and just sat there staring. Finally Stu said, "Mindy, that's the most beautiful thing I've ever seen. Did you do this?"

"Yes I did, and it's yours. My only request is you hang it in your house."

"I will, I have the perfect spot in mind in the living room. I'm forever in your debt. I don't know how to ever thank you enough."

Greg asked, "Who is the woman Mindy?"

"She's no one in particular. If you look around at my other drawings, you'll see a person, and/or animal in each one.

I always draw the scene first, without people. Even if there are people present when I make my rough sketch, I don't draw them in.

When I'm finished with the drawing, I close my eyes and picture in my mind what the person or animal looks like, and where they belong in the scene. Then I draw them into it. To the best of my knowledge it's never anyone I know, or have ever seen."

Bill stood transfixed, staring at the picture and finally said, "She looks familiar, but then I suppose everybody would say that."

They all sat around for a while with their coffee and donuts laughing and teasing with each other. Finally Stu said, "I don't know about you guys, but I'm going to the house and hang this picture when I finish my coffee."

After coffee the three of them went to "Annie's House". That's the name that Bill had affectionately given to Stu's house. When they got there, Bill said he had some things to do, and he left.

***

After they'd hung the picture, Stu and Greg stepped back about ten feet and stood there admiring it.

"You have a strange look on your face Stu. What's wrong?"

"Oh, nothing's wrong. I didn't notice it when Bill brought it up, but now that I think of it, he's right. She does look familiar. She looks like a woman who stayed here for a while when I was a kid. I remember my grandparents saying she did things for people, but I never saw what she did, so I didn't know what they meant by it."

"Stu, I think I'll go make a list of things Bill and I need to pick up tomorrow."

"Yeah, I've got to get back to the store and wrap everything up for the day. See you later."

"OK."

Greg walked around trying to make a list, but he couldn't keep his mind on it.

I can't stop thinking about the picture. Every time I look around here I keep seeing it in my mind. I've got a feeling the weird stuff is going to show up again.

***

The following week Greg went alone for coffee at Mindy's

"Mindy, do you remember the dream I told you about?"

"Of course I do."

"Well, it has changed a little."

"How so?"

"Now, when I ask her what she said, she bends down close to me and says, 'Someday this opportunity to help will come to you. You must then help those who need it'."

"That's interesting. What do you think it means?"

"I wouldn't begin to have any idea. I just know it has been the same thing every night since we were here last week."

"Since it's the same night after night, you would think it has to have some significance."

"There's one more thing."

"What is it?"

"The woman in the picture you drew for Stu is the one in my dream. She's even wearing the same clothes."

"Oh my god Greg, that's unbelievable. It's giving me goose bumps. Look at the hair on my arms."

"Yeah I know. I couldn't believe it when I saw it. I haven't been able to get my mind off of it all week."

"Where is this coming from? What can all this mean?"

"I wish I knew. Because, there are other things going on, and I have a feeling it's all tied in."

"What do you mean by other things? What other things?"

"Well, do you remember when Snapper was hit by that car, and was suddenly healed?"

"Sure, and I also know you had something to do with him being healed."

"Since that day many things have been so mixed up and confusing. Things I don't have any answers for. You don't know how much I appreciate the fact that you've not asked me about it."

"Greg, there've been a lot of strange things going on around here in the last year. That was only one of them. Besides, you were so upset when you showed me that block of wood that I was determined not to discuss it unless you brought it up."

"What do you mean, when you say strange things are going on?"

"For one thing, the relationships between you, Stu, and Mitch, er, I mean Bill."

"Why is that strange?"

"I can understand you and Stu, but when you throw Bill into the mix, that's where it gets odd. Don't get me wrong. I think he has wonderful ideas for Stu's house. It's just that it's so totally opposite of when he was Mitch. What made him do a complete turnaround like that?"

"The block of wood is at the center of it."

"Are you saying it has some sort of magical or mystical quality to it?"

"No, not exactly, but I am trying to let you know that I'm not responsible for those healings and changes in people. I don't have any special power or ability."

"What do you mean *those* healings? There was more than one?"

"Do you remember telling me I looked pretty good for a guy who got worked over that morning?"

"Yes."

"I was badly hurt. My face was bruised and cut, and I'm sure I had a couple of broken ribs. My injuries were healed that day."

"How did a block of wood do that?"

"That's the part I don't know how to explain. Hopefully some day I'll be able to, but right now I'm as confused as you are. Can you accept that, until I'm able to work it out?"

Of course. I have no problem with it. Whenever you want to talk, I'm here, and I won't sit in judgment in any way."

"I know that, and if I ever get things figured out, you'll be the first one I'll talk to about it."

"What did Stu and Bill say when you told them about the woman in the picture?"

"I didn't mention it, because I hadn't told them of my dream."

"I'm surprised you haven't talked to them about it."

"Why do you say that?"

"The three of you have become pretty tight. I assumed you'd tell them anything."

'Men will talk to other men about a lot of things, but most of us won't tell another man what we dream about."

"And yet, you'll tell me."

"I think the relationship between a man and a woman is different. Have you told me things you wouldn't tell another woman?"

"Yeah, I guess I have. Speaking of that woman in the picture, it makes me wonder if someone, somewhere else, has had dreams about the people in my other drawings."

"Wow! That's a deep and heavy thought. I think I'd better leave on that one. Seriously, I do have to get back to the house. I'll see you next week Mindy."

***

Greg looked around totally fascinated at how everything came together, and said to Bill, "You obviously don't have enough room to house all the homeless people, so how are you going to decide who can stay and who can't?"

"To begin with, each person will have duties of some kind while they live here. This home will be a hand up, not a hand out. By doing their share they will, in effect be paying their own way."

"How will you know who can do what?"

"I'm working up a list now on everything from; cooking, laundry, and cleaning, all the way to setting the table for meals, and to taking out the trash.

As part of the interview for each individual I'll go down the list to determine who can or will do what job. If they aren't willing to something, they won't qualify to live here. Also, if they don't do what they're assigned to do after they're here, they won't be here long."

"Do you have all your appliances hooked up yet?"

"Fred's going to finish them up tomorrow."

"When are you going to be open for boarders?"

"I hope to have everything ready sometime in April."

"Will that give you enough time?"

"I think so."

"I don't have a lot of work left Bill, so if I can help you, let me know."

"OK. If I need it I'll holler. What are your plans after the house is all finished?"

"I've given it a lot of thought, but I still don't know yet. I don't have a particular place to go, so I'll probably go back on the streets."

Stu and I have talked this over and we both agree if you want to be the maintenance man here, you can renovate the attic and turn it into nice living quarters for yourself."

"That's something to consider, because it definitely gives me another option."

CHAPTER NINE

On the last Sunday in February, Charley and Barb decided that it was too long between holidays so, they closed the tavern and put on a free dinner for the needy in the neighborhood.

They're in the southern part of the country, and yet, they and many others in the neighborhood are from the northern part, consequently they served the traditional New Years meals of both areas. For the North of course, they had pork roast with sauerkraut and mashed potatoes. For the South, black eyed peas, with ham, fried okra, and southern style cornbread.

They got so much pleasure out of it that they decided to do it again at Easter and at least one more time in the summer. That would be six times that year, and they agreed to do it a minimum of six times every year from that time on.

Even though Mindy and Greg's relationship had not gone beyond being good friends, they were spending a lot of time together. So, no one was surprised to see them side by side, setting up and serving the food at the tavern.

After the meal, as they sat drinking coffee and watching the cleanup, Greg said, "Let me know when you're ready to go Mindy, and I'll take you home."

"I'm ready now, so we can go anytime. Would you mind stopping on the way and taking a walk along the river?"

"It sounds good to me. I need to walk off some of this wonderful meal anyway."

All the way there Mindy was very quiet, almost to the point of being withdrawn. By the time Greg pulled the truck into the parking place the sun had already gone down and it would soon be dark. There was a damp winter chill in the air as they silently walked hand in hand along the river bank. She finally stopped and said, "I saw something today that really unnerved me."

"What was it?"

"Right after I opened the shop this morning, a car drove by very slowly. It was going slow enough for me to see the driver. Even though I haven't seen him in years, I'm certain it was 'Sam'."

"How could he find you?"

"I don't know. I thought I'd put all of my past behind me, and discarded it, but I guess I was wrong."

"Is there anything you can legally do if it is him?"

"I don't know what the terms of his release are. I didn't even know he was out. I did hear that he threatened to get back at the ones responsible for putting him in prison, so it's kind of scary, because I have to be at the top of that list."

"If I'm not being too, nosey; how did you get involved with him?"

"I don't mind telling you. A friend of mine met him at a business conference, and liked him. She said when she met him she thought of me right away. She also said if she hadn't been happily married she would've tried to go out with him. Naturally, at that time I wasn't looking for any companionship, so that's probably why I got sucked in and blindsided by him."

"He was that smooth, huh?"

"Well, that was part of it; but the biggest thing for me was his real obsession with campaigning for and contributing to 2 different charitable organizations. It got my attention, because right up front he asked me if I would have any problems helping him raise money for those 2 charities.

"Did he use that as part of a con?"

"No. That's the weird part. Every month he gave 20% of the money he conned people out of to those charities; and he was adamant about keeping all that separate, which he could do by being an anonymous donor. He never let those aspects of his life mix."

"What were the charities?"

"They were both children's hospitals that treated children from all over the world at no charge. I guess that's the main reason I stayed with him even after I found out he was a com man."

"What do you mean?"

"I think I felt that anybody who cared that much for injured and sick children had to have some redeeming qualities."

"Did he ever say why that was so important to him?"

"No. As a matter of fact he'd get pissed if I asked anything about his personal life before I knew him."

"It would be interesting to find out what that's all about. Look why don't you stay at the house for a while? I'm sure Stu or Bill wouldn't mind. They're not going to be open for boarders till April, so there's plenty of room and it would get you out of his line of sight."

"I couldn't drag you into this. If you help me you'll be a target too."

"I'm your friend. But, I wouldn't be much of a friend if I just stood back and let you take abuse from someone. Besides, there's strength in numbers. Not only would I have your back, so would a lot of others in the neighborhood."

"Greg, please don't tell anyone about him."

"I'd never do that. I'm just telling you, if anyone in the neighborhood found out you were being threatened they'd definitely come to your aid."

"That's nice to know, but as long as we can, I'd like to keep them out of it."

She reached out and hugged him very tightly. It felt wonderful to hold her in his arms, she was so soft and warm, and her body seemed to fit perfectly with his, so he had to keep reminding himself. *We're just friends. We're just friends.*

As they walked hand in hand back to the truck, he asked her, "Are you going to stay at the house with me?"

"No, not at this time, but it's good to know I have it as a refuge if I need it. Try to keep your cell phone charged, that way if I have to run out, I can call and have you meet me somewhere. I'm so sorry you've had to become part of this. Sometimes I wish I'd never told you about him."

"I'm very good at keeping the battery charged now. Also, don't ever apologize for that. It's how friends depend on and help each other."

When they arrived at the shop, Greg got out and walked her to the door, and once again hugged her before leaving.

As Greg walked toward the truck he noticed a strange shape close to the right front fender. He slowed his walk as he steeled himself for trouble. When he got closer he realized it was a familiar sight and said, "Hi Snapper, old friend, where've you been?"

Snapper stood up and started wagging his tail vigorously. When Greg opened the door the dog jumped in and sat on the seat as if to say let's go, so he fired up the engine, put the truck in gear and way they went.

***

One day when Greg and Bill were doing some paper work together, Bill said, "I almost forgot to tell you, Greg. There was a suit looking for you while you were out yesterday."

"What did he want?"

"He wouldn't say, so I told him I didn't know you. He obviously didn't believe me, because he left this business card and said to give it to you when I saw you."

"What did he look like?"

"He looked like he was in his fifties, a little shorter than me, but real stocky and solid looking. And, he had one of those military haircuts. He kind of made you feel he could walk through walls if he wanted to."

"His card doesn't say much, just his name, D.F. Harrison. His phone number, and the words, 'You Need It. I'll Find It'. That's weird. Did he say anything else?"

"Nope, that was it. What are you going to do?"

"I'll give him a call in the next day or so. Something else, I've been tossing around the offer you made the other day. I think I'll turn the attic into a living area for myself. That way even if I don't stay very long, the place will be set up for the next maintenance man."

"Great, I'll feel a lot better having you around to fix things. You make that stuff look easy. I'm good at paper work, and organizing people, but when it comes to home repair

I have quite a struggle. So, when are you going to start on the attic?"

"I've gotten everything else in the house finished, so I'll probably begin tomorrow."

CHAPTER TEN

Mindy told Greg that after several weeks, there hadn't been any sign of 'Sam', or his car, so maybe she was mistaken.

One Thursday morning, after finishing the attic, Greg decided to change his routine and have breakfast at Mindy's coffee shop. As he started inside he noticed that Snapper stopped and sat by the porch step instead of wandering off like he always had before. Cautiously he opened the door. Something wasn't right. It was almost like he could smell it in the air. Mindy greeted him as usual but she kept wiping the same spot on the counter. He headed for his normal counter stool, but he saw a steaming hot cup of coffee at the seat next to it, so he sat at the end stool where he could have his back to the wall. He said, "Hi Mindy. How are you?"

She put a finger to her lips, then came over to him and said in a whisper, "Greg, 'Sam's' in the restroom. Maybe you should leave."

It was too late, because at that instant 'Sam' came out of the restroom, so she served Greg a cup of coffee and a donut.

'Sam' is just under 6ft. tall and right at 190 pounds. He has very dark hair and a mustache. And, he's considered quite handsome. When the circumstances called for it, he can really turn on the charm.

When 'Sam' sat down he looked over at Greg and sized him up immediately. No words were spoken between the two men, and yet Greg felt the tension 'Sam' emitted, so he drug out his visit to the shop as long as he could, while he was being glared at.

As he felt 'Sam's' stare, he thought. *This is interesting, because last year at this time, I'd have sat here and tried to be invisible, or I would've left as soon as I could. Now, I'm hoping he'll wise off to me. I've got to keep my mouth shut though, till I find out what's going on with Mindy. Maybe I should go out and call her after while. If he's gone, she might fill me in.*

Greg finished his coffee and said, "I have to get going now, Mindy. I'll see you later."

After Greg left, 'Sam' grabbed Mindy's arm and screamed at her, "Who is that jerk? Don't even bother to tell me he's just a customer. I saw the way you two looked at each other. If you try to con me, you'll never see him again."

She replied, "Ted, he's just a homeless guy who I like as a friend and that's all."

Just then Greg walked back in the door and said, "I forgot to tell you I wanted a coffee to go."

She was glad for the interruption, so she could figure out a response for 'Sam'.

She said, "I'm sorry I didn't introduce you guys before. Ted, this is the neighborhood handyman, Greg. Greg, this is an old friend from years ago, Ted Padgett."

At that Ted said, "Honey, you shouldn't be so bashful. You need to tell him about us getting engaged."

"Well, I, uh, we didn't really have enough time."

Greg took the cue and said, "I was hoping I could turn her head in my direction."

"That's the way it goes, Greg. I guess the best man wins."

Greg got up and went over to wish Ted good luck. When they shook hands, Ted, who was very strong, squeezed Greg's hand as hard as he could. Greg knew that he could prevent Ted from having any leverage by placing his index finger against Ted's wrist. As they stood staring at each other, Ted couldn't understand why Greg was smiling and not grimacing in pain.

"Here's your coffee Greg."

"Thanks Mindy. I'll stop in Monday morning and take measurements of that vanity top for you."

"OK Greg, I'll see you then."

As Mindy watched Greg and Snapper walk away, she knew, when she turned back around and faced Ted, she didn't dare show any fear or hesitation. If she did, he'd sense it and move in and try to take complete control of her.

She was determined he would never do that again, so she jumped on the offensive. When Ted tried to grab her that time, she pulled away, spun around on him, got right in his face and said, "What the hell are you doing here?"

Somewhat startled he replied, "While I was in prison I saw the light, and became an honest man. So, I looked you up to see if we could work things out and start over again."

"I gave all of myself to you, and you drove off, leaving me out there alone. Not only did I have to fend for myself, but I also had to take the heat for all the crap you pulled.

Now, you show up here and want me to pick up right where we left off, like nothing ever happened. Do you have any idea where you can shove that B.S.? If you don't, I'll be happy to show you."

Mindy had always been so meek and mild with Ted that her aggression caught him off guard and left him momentarily speechless. That was something she had never seen out of him. Although he recovered quickly, she knew, when she looked into his eyes, he had lost some of his edge. He had flinched.

Now she was on a roll, and said, "Get out of here and leave me alone."

He retorted, "Don't think you can get rid of me. Try it and I'll tell the Portsmouth police chief where to find you."

"I hope you do, because Chief Hensley is looking forward to seeing you again."

"There's no reason for him to want to see me Mindy. You see, I made sure your fingerprints were all over that scam. Besides, the deal wasn't anything illegal. I used his greed against him,"

"As you know Ted, he has a huge ego and you really deflated it, so while you were running to avoid arrest, I learned how to re-inflate his ego, and stroke it. So, the chief and I had a few private, heart to heart, behind closed door meetings.

Now, who do you think he's going to believe, a tall nice looking blond with no record, who left him quite satisfied, or a cocky, arrogant felon, with a rap sheet the length of his arm?

Oh, by the way, he doesn't intend to take you through the court system. He has much better plans for you. I believe he said something about arranging a meeting between you and Jimmie Hoffa."

"There's other stuff I've set up that you don't know of."

"I've taken a lawyer through everything you thought you hung on me, and he's helped me clear my name of all of it, so you've got nothing to threaten me with. Now, get out!"

"OK. I'm going, but you haven't heard or seen the last of me. You'd better keep looking over your shoulder, because I'll be back, and when I come back I'll take care of your friend Greg, just for the fun of it."

As she watched him storm out, she knew it wasn't an idle threat. She also knew she had to tell Greg what Ted said about him. But, how could he defend himself against such a ruthless, unscrupulous con like Ted?

CHAPTER ELEVEN

"Stu, did you ever ask your dad about the woman in the picture, that your grandparents said, helped people?"

"Yeah, as a matter of fact I did. I was talking to dad the other night, and happened to mention her. He said people in the house called her a healer. They didn't know how she did it, but she carried a flowered bag every where she went, so they figured she had things in the bag that she used.to help people

He told me the only thing he ever saw her do was to help a little boy who looked to be around eight or ten years old. The boy had apparently been hurt by a falling limb from one of the oak trees out front."

"This was when you lived there, right?"

"Yes. Dad said one day while I was in school, he was doing some work in the master bathroom, and happened to look out the window as she was removing the limb from atop the boy who was lying there on the sidewalk. After the limb was out of the way, she picked him up and carried him to the house. The boy's head was bleeding and he appeared to be unconscious, because he was very limp. By the time Dad got out of the bathroom to the hallway she had already carried him into her room and was closing the door.

He said he went on about his work, and a short time later he heard some voices out in the hallway. He looked out to see the woman and the boy walking down the stairs toward the front door. The boy's head didn't have a mark on it that he could see, and he looked fine.

As she walked along with her hand on his shoulder, he heard her tell the boy, 'Yes this house is on top of the highest hill in town, but it isn't heaven.' She told him she knew it was very rough right now, so she'd take him back home and things would work out eventually.

Dad didn't know who the boy was or where he came from, and he never saw him again after that day."

"How long did she live here?"

"Dad said she left about a week after the incident with the boy, and he never saw her again either."

"That's fascinating, because it sounds vaguely familiar."

"Are you tied into this somehow?"

"No. Of course not, how could I be? We always lived in the south east suburbs. I was never in this area till I lived on the streets."

"OK. If that's true, how did you know what the inside of the house looked like the first time I met you here?"

"I don't know. I don't know what to tell you Stu. I wish I had a solid answer for you, but I don't."

"Well, there have certainly been a whole lot of strange things happening around here."

"Don't I know it. Oh, by the way, while I'm thinking of it, can I use your phone? Mine's in the truck being charged right now."

"Sure. Help yourself."

***

"Mr. Harrison, this is Greg Fetters. I understand you've been trying to get in touch with me."

"Yes I have Mr. Fetters, but first I have to verify that you are who you say you are. Would please tell me your birth date and place of birth?"

"I don't think so. I need to know why you've been looking for me and why you want that information."

"I'm not at liberty to say until I can be certain you're the person I'm looking for. If I may come to your residence and meet you, I believe we can resolve this impasse. I will bring all of the necessary credentials to verify who I am, and what I represent. I can assure you that I'm not seeking you for any criminal, or civil action leveled against you, and I don't want any of your money."

"It's a good thing you don't want my money, because I don't have any."

"I know that sir."

"Alright, since you put it that way, I can meet there with you. Say, next Wednesday, around three o'clock in the afternoon."

"That will be fine with me Mr. Fetters. Please have proper I.D. on hand. Once I verify your identity, you will know as much as I do pertaining to this situation. I will see you then."

***

"Thanks for the use of your phone Stu."

"You're welcome. What was that all about?"

"I don't know. Bill said this guy was looking for me and left this business card."

"Hm. I've never heard of him. Oh well, I guess you'll know next week."

"Let's hope so. See you later Stu."

CHAPTER TWELVE

"Greg, it's, Mindy. I hope you don't mind me calling."

"You know I don't mind. It's always a pleasure talking to you. Besides it's your phone."

"Are you going to be busy for a while this afternoon?"

"No I'm not. I'm in the truck right now, and I was thinking about heading to your place. I don't have anything to do for the rest of the day. Do you have something for me to fix?"

"No. The shop's OK. I have to get away for a while, so I'm closing the shop in a few minutes. There's something serious I have to talk over with you. Right now I'm badly in need of a friend. Could you come by and...?"

"Say no more. I'll be right there."

***

About a block from the coffee shop Greg saw her walking in his direction. She flagged him down, and before he came to complete stop, she opened the door and jumped in.

"You look like you've got the weight of the world on top of you. Is it Ted?"

"Let's go over to the park and sit by the lake. I'll explain it all then."

As they rode to the park she was very subdued, just sitting there and looking straight ahead. When he pulled the truck to a stop, she got out and quietly walked over to a park bench and sat down.

The park was beautiful. Many flowers were blooming and the trees had buds of spring on them. Most of the winter chill was gone from the air, but she didn't seem to notice. She sat and silently stared at the lake.

"You said you wanted to talk. The way you said it, sounded like you're going to tell me something I don't want to hear. Are you?"

"I really love living here Greg. I don't think I've ever enjoyed a neighborhood and its people as much as this one. But, I may have to leave."

"What's the hell's going on?"

"After you left yesterday Ted and I had it out."

"What do you mean had it out? Did he hurt you?"

She began sobbing and shaking. Between sobs, she tried to tell him what transpired with her and Ted. He couldn't understand what she was trying to say.

"Mindy, take your time. We're not in any hurry, so try to calm down and just tell me what's going on."

Finally she was able to get everything across to him. Even the threat he made about Greg.

"Why do you think you'd have to leave?"

"Because, I just think it would be better for everyone else if I did."

"It won't do any good to leave. He'll find you again. You won't be able to lose him."

"I know, but if I stay here, he'll harass everybody in the neighborhood."

"Everyone around here has been down the road to some degree. I think they can all take care of themselves."

"Before he went to prison the worst he ever did to people was to take advantage of their greed and weaknesses. Yesterday when I looked into his eyes I saw something different, and it scared me. I could tell he'd lost some of his edge, and I think he knows it, too. I believe, now he's capable of doing physical harm when he's angry. He's always kept himself in good shape and he really could hurt someone, because he used to be a boxer."

"He can't hurt all of us, but if you leave you'll be alone, and he can and probably will harm you. You need to stay, where you'll have friends around you to cover your back."

"I can't drag any of you into it. This is my fight."

"I think it's a little too late for that."

"Why?"

"He made it quite clear, he doesn't like me."

"But, that's the whole point. He dislikes you because of me. If I leave he'll follow me and leave you alone."

"No he won't. As long as I'm around I'll he'll consider me a threat."

At that point she started sobbing again and said, "Oh my god. I don't know what to do. Maybe I really am what he said I was."

"And what was that?"

"He always said it wouldn't work for me to try anything else, because before he found me, I was nothing, and the only thing I'm good for is to be a shill for him. And, he's the only one that would put up with me.

I thought all that was behind me, but I guess your past can catch up with you and be your present at any time."

"Do you still love him?"

"Oh no. I realized a long time ago, what I thought was love for him, wasn't. I was enamored by him, and felt I couldn't get by without him, but I certainly don't love him. I love y . . . er, ah, never mind."

Embarrassed, she turned away from him.

Without saying a word, he turned her around and hugged her. They stayed in that position for a long time. Finally he stood up, pulled her up by the hands, and said, "Let's go for a walk along the lake."

Silently she nodded, and they started walking. She didn't even notice Snapper walking along with them.

As they walked holding hands he said, "Please don't leave. I couldn't begin to imagine what it would be like around here without you. You are a part of us all now, and no one here would ever think badly of you because of your past. We all have some skeletons in our closets."

"It's just that I'm afraid of what he can do to you, all of you. I know what he's capable of."

"But, you don't know what your friends are capable of. Also, no argument, you are staying at the house tonight. You can at least relax, and hopefully get, a decent nights sleep."

"OK. You're right. I definitely need it."

"First, we're taking a little ride. I've got something to show you. Then, we're going out for a nice meal, and a little wine."

Snapper jumped into the bed of the truck, and down the road they went. For the first time Mindy realized he was with them. She opened the back window of the cab, and reached through to pet him. It was a surprise that he let her, because he had always avoided the touch of anyone but Greg.

After about an hour Greg stopped at the bottom of a hill. She looked rather quizzically at him. He just grinned at her, and said, "Trust me, I think you'll find what I'm about to show you very interesting. I've never shown this place to anyone, so you must feel appropriately honored to be here."

Finally laughing, she said, "If you say so, then I'm honored."

It was late afternoon, and it might be dark by the time they came back, so Greg grabbed a flashlight out of the truck, and holding her hand, led the way up an overgrown path.

Still laughing she asked, "Where are we going? I've never let a guy take me into the woods before. And, I'm not going to play hide-n-seek, or go snipe hunting."

"This place is called 'The Anthill'."

"Whoa! These must really be some huge ants."

"My grandfather built it when I was a kid, and after he finished it he was driving by one day and saw a bunch of motorcycle riders trying to ride to the top. He said from a distance they looked like ants, so he called it the "Anthill"."

"Did he build the whole hill?"

"No. Most of the hill was already here. He built something into the side of it, then, he added a lot of dirt to give it the shape he wanted."

When they neared the end of the path he stopped, and she watched, as a large door opened when he reached around and behind a rock. It looked like a big black cave in the side of the hill, until Greg went in and turned on a switch. In a short time a light came on.

"Wow, this looks like the front of a house."

Greg opened the front door, turned on another switch, and they went inside.

"You said your grandfather built this place. Why did he do it here?"

"Well, he was in Europe in the 1950's, right in the middle of the cold war, and he believed the communists would drop A-bombs on us, so he designed and built this as a bomb shelter. It is totally self contained, and can operate independent of the outside world for several years."

"What a fantastic idea. Are you going to show me around?"

"Do you really want to see it?"

"Oh yeah! Of course I do."

As they stepped inside she said, "It looks like a regular house in here. The furniture is beautiful."

"It's all hand made and although it's not padded, it's still very comfortable."

"How many bedrooms does it have?"

"Three large ones, and two baths."

"I noticed a fantastic picture of the outdoors on the living room wall. Where did that come from?"

"Each room has one wall with a picture of some natural scene that has been enlarged to mural size so it'll cover the wall. That way it makes you feel as though you are looking at the outside world."

"How can all this be self contained? Where does the electric and water come from?"

"The generator runs off of a natural gas well, and comes on automatically for ½ an hour every 2 months. The water comes from an artesian well, and the sewer is drawn away by a septic and leeching system on the opposite side of the hill."

"All food is dehydrated and vacuum packed. All trash is burned in an extremely high temperature incinerator that can recycle the heat through the furnace."

The air is drawn in through hidden supply ports and filtered through washable filters that clean it to better than 99.5 % pure. And the place has central heat and air."

"How big is this place?"

"The total living area is 2,800 square feet, with full laundry facilities, a sewing machine and material to make all kinds of clothing. Since this is a controlled environment the material won't rot."

"Your grandfather seems to have thought of everything."

"Now that you've seen it all, what do you think of it?"

"I think it's fabulous. Is it yours?"

"Yes. I inherited it when Pop, died."

"What a neat hideaway. Are you going to live here?"

"I could live here quite comfortably, but no. This is my escape. I can come up here and shut out the rest of the world till I get my head straight. If I lived here, I think that would change."

"What are you going to do with it?"

"I don't know yet, but I'll never sell it."

"As I said it's great. I'm sorry I never knew him. He must have been a cool person."

"I always felt he was. He was my hero. As far as I was concerned, he was the greatest man in the world.

"You said this place is self supporting, right?"

"Yes."

"Can we still eat the food?"

"Sure. It's dehydrated, but it's good when you add water and heat it. There's even dehydrated ice cream for dessert."

"Let's eat here. We can go out to eat anytime."

"You really want to do that?"

"I love this place. I want to stay here tonight."

"Alright, as you know there are three bedrooms. After we eat, pick the one you want."

She walked over to him, put her arms around his waist, and said, "You don't understand, Greg. I'm picking the bedroom you're staying in. I want us to stay here together."

"Do you really want to do this Min? We've never dated. We've never even kissed. You don't really know me."

"Oh, I do know you, and I love you. I think I have since the first day we sat and spent a whole afternoon talking over a big pot of coffee. I know we've never kissed. We're here together, holding each other, and I'd like a kiss now.

Oh my! Greg, I never waited to find out if you feel the same as I do. I didn't mean to put you on the spot by shooting my mouth off."

After a long romantic kiss, he said, "Mindy, the only spot you put me on is, trying to determine which room to spend the night in. The first time we hugged, it felt so good I didn't want to let go of you. This kiss took a long time to happen, but it was well worth the wait."

"I guess we do things when we're ready. I don't know about you, but I'm ready."

"Almost a year ago, (the first Friday in April), I woke up on that morning with the feeling my life was going to change, and change it has."

Not even thinking of an evening meal, they walked with their arms around each other into the master suite.

Following a wonderful night, Mindy woke up to the aroma of fresh brewing coffee. Just as she sat up, Greg came into the room carrying a tray with two mugs; cream, sugar, and a full pot of hot coffee.

"It's almost seven o'clock. You'll be opening the shop a little late today. I guess I should've set the alarm. I'm sorry I didn't think of it."

"I'm glad you didn't. I put a sign in the window that said I'd be closed for a few days on personal business. This wasn't what I had in mind when I made the sign, but the way I see it, spending the night with the person I love is as personal as it gets."

"I was always afraid to let myself even consider the possibility you'd be interested in a homeless nobody, so until last night, just having you as my friend was going to have to be good enough for me. Now that we're lovers as well as friends, I couldn't ask for anything more."

"From the day I met you, I knew there was a lot more to you than you let people see, and you weren't meant to spend your life aimlessly wandering the streets. I've had great pleasure watching you come out of your shell."

"I'm glad you saw something that I was certain was no longer there. I don't have any work lined up for a few days. If there's something you'd like to do, or someplace you want to go, we can do it."

"Other than going in to the store for some food or drinks, if you don't mind I'd like to stay right here with you. I want to make love with you until I can't anymore."

"You know it amazes me that you like this place so much. I've always been able to come here, get myself together, and by the time I leave here, have a better outlook on things. I never even considered the possibility of someone else feeling the same way I do."

"I do understand how you feel, because I really enjoy being here. This place is like Stu's house, it surrounds you with an, inviting warmth that very few other places have. As I look around, there's no doubt your grandfather built this from his heart. I know I'm not being realistic, but I don't ever want to leave."

"Min, we've got as long as you want. We can stay and enjoy it. I love you, and I don't care where we are as long as we're together."

"This is Saturday, and I don't want to think of, or talk about any outside problems or distractions until Monday."

After coffee, some talk, and more sweet lovemaking, they decided to take a shower. She had never seen a shower like it, and was thrilled.

They didn't close the bathroom door all the way, and as soon as Snapper heard the shower running, he came barging in and almost knocked them down as he ran around in the water. They hugged and laughed together as they watched him run back and forth through the shower streams.

Neither Greg nor Mindy had been this relaxed or content in a long, long time.

As all pleasurable times do, the weekend went by far too quickly. So, they decided to take Monday off as well.

***

Driving back to the shop after their beautiful stress break, they were both deep in thought when Mindy finally said, "You know he's going to show up again. What are we going to do then?"

He responded, "Look, we know it'll happen. We just don't know when. The only thing we can do is try to be ready for it. I have some ideas, so we'll see what happens."

CHAPTER THIRTEEN

Mindy opened the shop, and they both went all though the building, checking for any signs of Ted. Everything seemed to be OK.

For the rest of that week, and into Monday of the next, Greg stopped in the shop at least once a day. He came back every evening to help her close up and she spent the nights at "Annie's House"

Tuesday morning he decided to take his time with his coffee and donuts. For some reason he felt the need to stick around for a while

Just as he was about to take his last drink of coffee, Ted walked in. He turned the sign around so the closed side was facing out, and then he locked the door. He went over to the counter and sat next to Greg. He said, "Mindy, honey, I'd like a cup of coffee and a plain cake donut."

She said, "I'll get you coffee and a donut, but you need to get something straight. I'm not your honey. Frankly I'm nothing to you, so get used to it. The coffee and donut are on the house, and they're in a, to go bag. Those are the last things you'll ever get from me, so take them and get out."

"What happened to your loving attitude Mindy? I think you've been letting dumb homeless boy here, step on my territory. Did she forget to tell you she's mine? She's way far above a bum like you. I've been watching the two of you spending a lot of time together, and I think it's time to put a stop to it and take back what's mine."

Greg turned toward him and said, "She's already told you, she doesn't belong to you."

"Are you saying she's yours?"

"I'm saying she doesn't belong to anyone. She goes where she wants and does what she wants."

Ted stood up, and when Greg stood to face him, Ted said, "Listen homeless boy, you need to slink off and find your bedroll while you still can."

"Leave him alone Ted. He hasn't done anything to you."

"What's this? Are you protecting your new lover boy, Mindy? You really are scraping the bottom of the barrel with him. You need to make a move up and come back to me while I'm still in a loving mood."

Greg stood his ground, and while staring into Ted's eyes said, "Ted, have you ever heard of a company called FetLaw Concepts?"

"No I haven't homeless boy. Is that supposed to scare me?"

"You don't remember me do you?"

"No. I don't hang around with worthless bums."

"Well, I remember you Ted, or should I call you Terrence Plunket?"

At that point Ted took a step back, and all the blood drained out of his face. Suddenly the sneer disappeared and was replaced by raw anger.

Mindy stood behind the counter watching the confrontation between them, and shook her head, totally amazed at Greg.

Suddenly, Ted stuck his right hand in his pocket and pulled out a knife. When he pressed the button, a six inch blade jumped out.

After that, everything seemed to go into slow motion.

Ted made a lunge toward Greg with the knife in his hand. Greg sidestepped to his left, and with his right hand, grabbed Ted's knife hand, pulling him forward and off balance. At the same time, he brought his left hand down in a chopping motion on Ted's arm between his wrist and elbow, breaking his forearm, and causing him to drop the knife.

Continuing in one fluid movement, Greg stepped around behind him, wrapped one arm around his neck, and pushed his head to one side with his other hand. Within a few seconds, Ted was unconscious, and Greg let him slowly sink to the floor.

Mindy froze, staring for a long time. Finally she asked, "Is he dead?"

"No. He's just going to sleep for a little while."

"That's amazing. And to think, I was afraid he would hurt you. I didn't know you could do that. Where did that come from?"

"I learned it in Navy training almost twenty years ago."

"I've got a cousin who was in the Navy, and the only thing he learned was where to get tattoos and sex."

"I went through extensive survival training. Our trainers told us, once you've learned it, it's ingrained in you, and you never lose it. I guess they were right, because after I cleared my head of the alcohol fog it all became automatic."

"You certainly are full of surprises. Is there anything you can't do?"

"I'll quote a line from you. 'There are a lot of things I can't do. But I don't tell anybody what they are'."

"I guess I asked for that one."

Ted was beginning to come around. When he was completely conscious he grabbed his arm, yelling in pain.

Greg said, "You'd better get that arm looked at. It's going to have to be set."

"You son of a bitch. You broke my arm. I'll have your ass in court."

"I don't think so Mr. Plunket. You may have forgotten FetLaw, and me, but I have no doubt you remember the Two Hundred Thirty Thousand dollars you swindled from that company. In this state the statute of limitations hasn't run out yet, and I know the police would still like to know the whole story of what happened to the original inventor of those products you brought in. I can call them right now, so if you want to talk to them, and tell them what I did to you, stick around."

When Ted got to the door and opened it, Snapper jumped up, barking and snarling at him. He turned and said, "I'm not done with you, homeless boy. When you see my face again it'll be the last thing you and your dog will ever see. That goes for you too, Mindy." He then slammed the door and ran off holding his arm.

"Greg, I've never seen him so violent. He means it. I know him well. Once he sets his mind to something he follows it through. He's got a score to settle with us now."

"We're going to have to stay on our toes, and try to be ready for anything he throws at us."

"You are so calm and cool under fire, but that's not going to be as easy as it sounds. Frankly I'm kind of scared."

"I know. I'm concerned, too. We could hide for a while at 'The Anthill', and he'd never find us, but he could wait us out, because he knows you'll have to eventually cover your investment here."

"Greg, he's very cunning. He'll set traps for us."

"With you knowing him, it may help us to figure out how to make him fall into one of his own traps. Also he's angry and frustrated. When a person's in that state of mind, they don't think rationally."

"I hope you're right.

Oh, by the way. What's this about FetLaw, and a swindle?"

"Are you ready to listen to a long story?"

"Since the closed sign is facing out, I'm at your disposal, so fill me in."

"I was a half owner in FetLaw. It was almost seven years ago when this guy came in with, what was really a good idea for some new products.

We had several meetings over a three month period, and he presented a great plan for a new line of products. He had some parts, and showed us drawings.

He even brought in someone, he introduced as a patent attorney. The attorney had notarized papers showing patent searches, indicating that none of the products were patented, nor did they have a patent pending on them. As it turned out, that was the only part of the deal that was true.

The products were real, and they were good. The thing we didn't know was those products weren't his. They belonged to someone else, and he had no right to them. Ted Padgett using the alias, Terrence Plunket was the one who brought them in.

He told us, all his available money had been used on product development. But, he had a property in Florida to offer as collateral. We looked over the deed. We even had our attorney check it out, and he said everything looked OK, so we fronted the money to him.

Of course we never saw him or the products again. The whole scam hinged on timing, because we found out the property had been sold the day after we checked on it. When we tried to contact his attorney, his office was gone and his phone was disconnected."

"Did you ever learn who really owned the products?"

"Yes. He was on his way to an inventors trade show with his drawings, and products when he was carjacked, blindfolded, and taken to a motel room where he was held for a week. Then he was taken blindfolded to somewhere out in the country at night, then dropped off with enough food and water to last several days.

He finally made it back to civilization, somewhat shaken and weak, but other than that, he was unharmed."

"Was it Ted who kidnapped him?"

"He couldn't identify who they were. He was always blindfolded, and they never spoke a word for the whole week. The only thing he knew for sure was there were at least two of them, because as they led him around, there was one holding each of his arms."

"That would have been Ted and Phil Sparks."

"How do you know that?"

"They both do sign language."

"Wow. No wonder he couldn't tell who they were."

"How do you know all this stuff about the parts and the inventor?"

"When the police found out we were looking into the stolen products, they came around to us with a lot of questions. Once they realized we were victims, and not suspects we knew almost as much about the case as they did."

"Did the police have pictures of Ted?"

"No. They didn't have any way to identify him. And, I didn't know who Terrence Plunket was till I saw him come out of the restroom that day, right here in the shop. As I sat there watching him come to the counter and sit down, alarms were going off in my head. It took me a couple of moments to remember why, then, it hit me like a ton of bricks."

"Why didn't you say something then?"

"I wanted to see how this was all going to play out. Plus, I knew as long as I kept my mouth shut and didn't release that little bit of information I'd have a psychological edge, and that's very difficult to do with a con man. Today when he made that move with the knife he gave me the physical edge. Now he knows, not only do I have something on him that could send him back to prison, he's aware he can't defeat me physically one on one. He's desperate now. Desperate people do things they wouldn't normally do. Right now he's on the defensive, and he's not used to being there, because he's spent his whole life putting others there."

"So, exactly when did this scam take place?"

"It'll be seven years this coming August."

"That's interesting, because I was with him then, and we weren't in this state that year. Whoa! Wait a minute. There were four times that year when he and Phil took off, saying they were going to try some deep sea fishing. I knew better than that, because Ted didn't even like to be on a boat. But, I didn't dare question anything he did or said."

"Sometimes it's really strange how things come together when you least expect it. I mean, who would've guessed that I would know the same man you told me about."

"I remember when they came back from their last trip that year. They were laughing about the two hayseed idiots they had taken to the cleaners. As they were drinking to how smart they were, and their good fortune, Phil said, 'Mr. Plunket, you do such great work. I think I'll hire you'."

"Yeah, they did take us for a lot, but that's in the past, and I think we may have a winning hand now if we play it right. Hopefully we'll be able to use all of that in our favor."

"I hope you're right. This isn't anywhere near over."

"No, it isn't, but he won't be back for at least a few days, so it may give us enough time to work out a strategy. I'm going to have to go now. I'll see you this evening. I love you. Try not to worry, we make an excellent team, and we'll get through this."

"I love you too. Just be careful out there, because I'm sure he thinks if he can get you out of the way, I'll be easy pickings."

"I will Min."

CHAPTER FOURTEEN

"Mr. Fetters, this is D.F. Harrison. How are you sir?"

"I'm doing well. How are you?"

"That's what I need to talk to you about. Due to a death in the family, I'm going to have to cancel our appointment for tomorrow. Would it be possible to meet next week instead?"

"I don't see any problem with next week. Was it someone close to you?"

"Yes. It was my grandfather."

"I know how that feels. I'm very sorry for your loss."

"Thank you sir."

"When do you want to come by?"

"Would next Thursday at 11:00 AM be alright with you?"

"That'd be great. I'll see you then."

***

Since Greg didn't have to meet Mr. Harrison the next day he decided to take a walk down to what had been his home for the last five plus years.

He didn't want to be too conspicuous, so he put on some of his oldest and rattiest work clothes before he headed that direction.

As he walked through the thicket and wooded areas it brought back a flood of feelings and memories from those years.

When he approached his old lean-to, he saw someone sitting under it, eating what appeared to be a can of soup. He thought. *It, certainly doesn't take long for people to take over a spot that's vacant. I wonder what brought this one to the streets.*

It dawned on him that the person sitting there looked somewhat familiar. As he got closer he realized who it was, and said, "Larry, is that you?"

When he said it, Larry jumped, dropping his soup on the ground, and backed as far under the lean-to as he could, saying, "Please leave me alone mister, I haven't done anything wrong. I'm not hurting anything."

"Larry, it's me, Greg."

"Greg who?"

"Greg Fetters. We were friends at one time."

"Oh, yeah. I remember now."

"What happened to you? Why are you here?"

"I don't have any money, so I'm on the streets."

"Where's Delores?"

"Hah, she and some guy set me up. She had it all planned from the start. He knocked me out, and tied me up, and they left me at a rest area in Arizona. It took me almost 6 years to get back home, and I knew my parents didn't want me around, so here I am."

"What happened to all the money?"

"Delores took all my money and ran off with that other guy."

Greg moved quickly over to Larry, picked him up by the front of his jacket, and screamed in his face, "You piece of crap. You mean *our* money, don't you? Half of what she took was mine. You haven't gotten anywhere near what you deserve."

"Are you going to beat me up now? Maybe you can just kill me, and get it over with. Yeah, I guess that's what I've got coming."

With that Greg let go of Larry's jacket and pushed him back down.

"You'll never know how much I want to smash your face in, but you aren't worth the damage I'd do to my knuckles. I'm not going to end your misery for you. You'll have to do that yourself. I have no sympathy for you. If I don't ever see you again I'll be quite happy."

Greg turned and walked away, thinking of all the things he'd planned to do to Larry if he could get his hands on him. And, then, when the opportunity was finally in his grasp, he couldn't do it. He certainly wasn't going to do anything that might pull him back into the pity party he lived with for five years.

***

"It's good to finally meet you Mr. Fetters."

"Thank you. I hope after this meeting, I'll feel the same way about you. Now that you've confirmed I'm the Greg Fetters you've been looking for, it's time to tell me what this is all about."

"I'll be happy to. This is pertaining to the property in the Sheridan Hill neighborhood. I believe a lot of people call it Santos Hill because of the Santos Valley below it. And, there are also some monetary holdings your grandfather left you."

"What about that property? Is there something wrong?"

"Nothing's wrong. It's time for me to turn the deed for it over to you."

"I already own that hill."

"I'm not talking about anything you already own sir. These are holdings your grandfather wanted turned over to you, after you reached a certain age."

"Pop gave me the hill before he died, and Grandma had plenty of money to live on till she passed. I just thought that was all they had. Are you sure there's more?"

"Oh yes. There's definitely more. Here is an aerial photo that shows the property I'm referring to."

"OK. I recognize that. Right here in the center is the hill I already own."

"The parcel I'm talking about is this open land all around the hill you have your finger on."

"Wow! That's all mine. Are you sure?"

"I'm absolutely certain, Mr. Fetters."

"So, that's what he meant, when he said access to the hill would always be guaranteed."

"That's part of it. He put enough money into a trust account to hopefully cover the property taxes for the next 100 years. He figured that way no matter what happened in the future, the government couldn't take the hill away from his family for non payment of taxes."

"Alright that's the property you talked about. What are these holdings you mentioned?"

"See those houses just north of the woods?"

"Sure. Pop said it had been a wooded area and was sold off to be a suburban housing development."

"That's right. It was just short of 700 acres. Your grandfather owned it, and sold it to 'POP Inc.' which just happened to be his construction company. He took the money from the sale of that property and bought into some excellent municipal bonds and securities. Since his company was the developer of what became 'Santos Valley', that development also made a lot of money for his company.

As per the instructions in his will, his company was sold at a fair market price upon his death. The money from the sale of the company and its banking accounts was set into an interest bearing trust designed to take care of all your grandmother's wants and needs. Well, she only used some of the interest on that account, so it was still growing while she was alive.

The bonds and securities he bought were liquidated when he died, and that money was put into a similar trust set aside for you.

The figure on line 5 is the current balance of that trust account."

"Are you sure it's that much?"

"Yes. I'm absolutely certain sir."

"And it belongs to me?"

"Yes again."

"That completely blows my mind."

"When your grandmother died, all the money she left was put into yet another trust that was also set aside for you."

"You'll see that the balance on line 9 is nearly double the balance on line 5."

"I had no idea of any of this."

"The unusual part of all this is, most people turn trusts or other forms of money over to their heirs at age 21, 25, 30, or 40. Your grandfather wouldn't say why, but he didn't want the trusts and property turned over to you till after your 38th birthday."

Greg's eyes sparkled and he smiled and said, "I know why. At least part of his time in the military, he was in the

'38th' Fighter Group'. He felt it was quite an honor. That's why he always said I'd have a great year when I was 38."

"He loved you a lot Mr. Fetters. Because of him you are an extremely wealthy man. Not to mention the fact that you own 500 acres of some of the most valuable land in the county."

"Holy cow, I don't know what to say."

"Well, in order to facilitate the transfer of everything over to you, you'll have to say yes to coming to my office, and signing the papers I have for you. When would you like to come in?"

"Of course I'll be there. My schedule is open any time next week."

"Would you be able to come by a week from today at 1:00 in the afternoon?"

"That'll work for me. By the way, did you know my grandfather?"

"Yes I did. I worked part time for him while you were in the Navy. He was a great person to know and work for. He also talked about you a lot. He and your grandmother both were very proud of you."

"For the past five years, I don't think I was much to be proud of."

"You may have been down on your luck, and felt like you were at the end of your rope. But, I learned a lot of things about you in the time it took me to track you down Mr. Fetters. One of the things I learned was, all the people who knew you in the past, or know you now, like you, and they have nothing but good things to say about you. That alone would have made him very proud of you."

"Thank you Mr. Harrison."

"Many of the people I'm hired to find, wouldn't be the ones you would want as friends. Meeting you has been a refreshing change. It has been my pleasure sir. I'll see you next week."

***

After Mr. Harrison left, Greg walked around the house in shock. As he walked by the window in the office he saw Stu pull up in the driveway. He decided not to tell anyone of his new inheritance till he talked to Mindy.

"Hi Stu. What brings you by today?"

"I thought I'd see how you were doing."

"Everything's going well. I'm glad you came by. I wanted to talk to you about something."

"OK. What's up?"

"Do you remember the story you told me about the healer and the young boy?"

"Sure I do. Why?"

"I have a feeling, I was that boy."

"I thought you might be. What is it that makes you think so?"

"When you said the woman told the boy, this house isn't heaven, it triggered something in my memory banks that I had forgotten a long time ago."

"What was that?"

"When my father died, I asked, 'What happened to my dad, and where did he go?'

My aunt told me, he had gone to heaven, and that's where he lived now. I asked her, 'When will we get to see him?'

She said, 'When we go to heaven he'll be there waiting for us.'

I asked her, 'Where is heaven?'

She replied, 'Heaven is on high, and we will all go there some day.'

I asked, 'Why don't we go on high and see him now?'

She said, 'We have to wait till St. Peter is ready for us.'

Well, I missed my dad, and I didn't know who this Peter guy was, so I wasn't going to wait for him to tell me he was ready for me. The next morning, I got up early and left the house, determined to find heaven and see my father."

"How old were you then?"

"I was eight years old when he died."

"If you were that young boy, how did you get across town to here? That had to be twenty miles."

"When I left the house, I had no idea where to go, so I kept asking people where high was. People told me to go here and there, and finally, I found myself walking up this big hill, toward what is now your house.

The next thing I remember, I'm riding on a bus with the lady in your picture. When we got off the bus she took my hand and we walked from the bus stop to where I lived. When my mom saw us she started crying and ran out to grab me and hug me. I didn't know this at the time, but I'd been gone almost twelve hours.

The lady didn't say anything to my mom about an accident. She just told her, she found me wandering around looking for heaven. She didn't even tell Mom where she found me."

"You didn't remember any of this till now?"

"Not until you mentioned the boy looking for heaven. Everything seems to point to it being me, and yet, I still don't remember having an accident, so I can't be positive it is me."

"Oh, I think it's a safe bet that it's you. I'm also wondering how Mindy fits into all this, because it can't be an accident that the woman she drew in this picture is the same woman who helped you."

"I'll tell you, Stu, I have no idea. I don't know how any of this ties together."

"Alright, since we're speaking of the woman in the picture. Let's assume she was a healer. And, somehow she passed that ability on to you that would explain, Bill and me being healed after our accidents."

"If she passed it on to me, why did it take almost thirty years to take affect? Why haven't I been doing healing all my life?"

"Yeah, you've got a point. I guess you're right."

"Of course I'm right. I'm telling you, I'm not a healer."

"All this couldn't be a coincidence though, Greg."

"I agree. I just don't have the answers to it. Hopefully some day I will."

CHAPTER FIFTEEN

"Hi, Min. I really need to talk with you about something private. Is there any way I can convince you to go to the park with me this afternoon?"

"I'd love to Greg, but I'm pretty busy. It'll be a little while before I can get away."

"Bill said he'd come over and take care of the shop, then close it up for you."

"OK. When do you want to come over?"

"We can be there in an hour."

"I think I can get everybody through here by then. Why don't you just come alone? I don't want to put Bill in the middle of our problem."

"You're right. It's hard telling what Ted would try to do to him."

"You sound serious. Is something wrong?"

"No. Everything's fine. I'd just like to tell you what I found out today."

"OK. I'll see you in an hour."

***

After they closed the shop, they jumped into the truck and headed for the park. Of course Snapper wasn't going to let them go without him, so he was in the bed of the truck.

When they got to the park, they looked around at the beautiful flowers, and the fresh green grass. It was all so neat and well manicured. The air smelled clean.

The park was practically deserted. The only person they saw was a young girl riding her bike on the road that went around the perimeter of the park.

They walked silently, hand in hand for a long time. Snapper was right there by their side. The three of them seemed to be enjoying the scent and feel of spring in the air. After they had walked almost all the way around the park, and were nearly back to the truck, Greg looked down at Snapper walking beside Mindy and said, "I think my buddy deserted me for a beautiful woman. Nice going pal. At least you've got excellent taste."

"What did you want to tell me, Greg?"

"I think you're going to want to be sitting when you hear this, so let's go over to one of the benches by the lake. I'll fill you in then"

As they started to walk across the park road, Snapper froze, and let out his familiar low growl. Greg looked around and saw nothing, but he knew something wasn't right, and automatically stopped and said, "What is it pal?"

At that instant he heard the roar of a car engine at high speed. He grabbed Mindy and pulled her back off the road and toward the protection of a large tree that was nearby. As they ran to the tree, the car swerved, trying to run them down, but it was too late to get to them, and instead the car hit the young girl on her bike, throwing her high in the air, and onto the grass.

The car slowed slightly, then, the driver put the gas pedal on the floor, smoking the tires and sped off down the road.

The car was black, and had dark tinted windows, so they couldn't identify the driver. They didn't have to. They knew who it was even if they couldn't prove it. Greg was able to get the first three characters on the license plate (7Z3), but that was all.

Their immediate concern was the young girl lying on the grass. They ran over to her. She was unconscious. Mindy knelt down beside her and pushed her hair off her face. She had a large swollen, ugly, purplish knot about as big around as a baseball, on the left side of her forehead just below the hairline. Her left leg appeared to be broken in two places below her knee, and her breathing was very shallow and rapid. She also looked like she was going into convulsions.

"Mindy, you stay with the girl. I'll get the cell phone."

"Hurry Greg, she's in very bad shape."

When he got to the truck and grabbed the phone, he saw the bag with the box/block of wood in it, and picked it up too. As he ran back to Mindy and the girl, he kept thinking. *Please,*

please, be the box with the cloth in it. This little girl can't die because of us.

When he got there Mindy said, "She's fading fast. She isn't going to make it."

"She has to Mindy. We can't let this happen."

"What can we do?"

Greg opened the bag and almost cried. It was the box. As he opened it and retrieved the cloth, he said, "Quickly, touch all around the girl's torso until you find either a real hard, tight spot, or a sunken in area."

"My god, she's got a depression in her lower left rib cage I could put my whole fist into. No wonder she can't breathe."

He started wiping the cloth over the girl's rib cage. Mindy kneeled there trance like, watching in total amazement, as the girl's side began to take on its natural shape. Suddenly the indentation disappeared.

The girl's breathing became deeper and more normal. It looked as though she was still trying to convulse, so he took the cloth and wiped it over the huge bump on her forehead. While he stroked her head, the knot receded, and her whole body relaxed.

Mindy finally lowered herself into a sitting position on the grass and just sat there wide eyed and speechless, as he took the cloth down to her left leg, and started wiping. While he wiped her leg, each broken spot went back into place, and the skin color returned to normal.

"Mindy, you'd better call 911, just in case someone hasn't already done it. I think she has an injury that we haven't found yet."

After she made the call, she said, "Why do you feel she has another injury? She looks relaxed and comfortable."

"The cloth hasn't disintegrated yet."

"Wait a minute, Greg. Her right shoulder looks different."

"You're right. Let's try that."

When he wiped the cloth over her shoulder, they could see it go back into place.

116

Still, the cloth did not shred and disappear.

"I don't get it Mindy. The cloth is still intact."

"It looks like there's something written on it. What does it say?"

He read it and finally said, "I understand it now."

As the girl started to regain consciousness, Greg looked directly into her eyes and said, "Someday this opportunity to help will come to you. You must then help those who need it."

They both stood up transfixed as they watched the cloth shred and totally disintegrate.

Suddenly they were aware of several sets of emergency sirens blaring in the background. One siren kept coming closer and closer while the others seemed to stop somewhere off in the distance.

The girl on the grass looked at them and asked, "What's going on, and who are you guys? What happened to my bicycle?"

"My name is Mindy, and this is Greg. You were hit by a car, and that's why your bike is messed up. We think you're going to be alright, but you can't get up yet, because the ambulance is on its way, and they need to check you out first."

The girl started crying and Mindy asked, "What's wrong? We think you're OK."

She said, "My mom's going to kill me for getting hit. She's always telling me I'm not careful enough."

"It wasn't your fault. We saw it happen. The driver came up on the sidewalk and hit you. What's your name, and how old are you?"

"My name's Carla and I'm 14."

"Do you live around here?"

"Yeah, I live just outside the park, over there."

Greg said, "We'll go to your house with you and tell your mom what happened."

"OK. You know what mister? I had a dream about you."

"You did? What was it about?"

"I dreamed you were wiping my head with this really soft and cool wash cloth, and it felt wonderful. Then I woke up."

"When did you have this dream?"

"I don't know for sure. Maybe it was just now."

Just then, an ambulance and a police cruiser pulled up, and stopped beside them.

Mindy said, "Greg, we've got a lot of talking to do when we're alone."

"Oh, we certainly do, and you don't know the half of it yet."

"What I just saw cleared up a lot of things, and at the same time it created a whole new set of questions. Now you're telling me there's more?"

"Yep, and don't forget. We also came here to talk about something."

"Oh yeah, that's right."

The female E.M.T. asked, "Is this the girl who was hit by a car?"

"Yes it is. She seems to be alright, but we made her stay on the ground till you've had a chance to check her out. She said her name is Carla, and she's 14 years old."

"OK. I'm Melissa and this is Jason. Carla, Jason's going to hook you up to a heart monitor and look at your blood pressure while I'm checking everything else out on you. Is that alright with you?"

"I feel OK. These people helped me. They said I was hit by a car, but I don't remember it. All I remember is riding my bike, and then I woke up here on the grass."

"That's pretty normal after a trauma like this. Do you remember where you live?"

"Sure, 714 Rosewood Dr."

"Good, that's just on the other side of the park. So far, you seem to be OK. And, looking at your bike, I'd say you are a very lucky young lady. Anyway, after we're done here, we'll have to take you home."

"Folks, I'm Officer Ed Thomson. While they're checking her over, I need to get some information from you, if you don't mind."

"Of course. What can we do to help?"

"Tell me how it all happened."

"We were starting to cross the road, when we heard a car coming at a high rate of speed. It looked like the car was heading right for us, so we ran back to the safety of that tree behind you. When we were running, the car appeared to swerve in our direction. I don't know if the driver lost control or not, but the car went onto the sidewalk and hit the girl. Then he or she just sped off down the street."

"Do you have a description of the vehicle?"

"Yes. It was black and sporty. Like a Mustang or a Camaro. I couldn't see the driver, because the windows had a very dark tint. I did get the first three characters on the license plate though. They were 7Z3. That's about all I can think of. Did you get anything else Mindy?"

"No. I was so scared I was just looking for something safe to get behind."

"That sounds like the car we had a call on while I was coming over here. Dispatch said the car went through a red light and was clocked doing 80 in a 35mph zone. I haven't heard the outcome yet."

"Officer, she's fine and we're ready to take her home now."

"We'll put her bike in the back of our truck and follow you there. We told her we'd let her mom know it wasn't her fault that she got hit."

Greg put the bike in the truck bed with Snapper, and they trailed behind the ambulance and cruiser to Carla's home.

After Officer Thomson gave her mom the police report, Mindy, and Greg filled her in on what had happened.

As they walked outside Officer Thomson was waiting for them.

"I've got some updated info on the hit and run vehicle. They were definitely chasing the same vehicle you two saw hit the girl."

"What do you mean, 'were chasing'? Did the driver get away?"

"No. It was a male driver. While he was trying to run from us, he lost control and wrapped it around a huge tree, eight blocks from here."

"So, you caught him then?"

"Sort of. When he hit the tree his car burst into flames. By the time they got to him, it was too late. He was dead, so we have no idea what he was trying to do, or what was going on with him. Perhaps an autopsy will show us something."

"And, you're sure he was the one we saw hit Carla."

"From what you told me, it had to be him, because the car fit the description, plus the first three characters on the license plate match what you said.

Both the car and the license plate were stolen, by the way."

"Well, is there anything else you need from us Officer Thomson?"

"No. I've got your phone numbers and addresses. If I need anything I'll let you know."

"OK. We're going to go then."

"Greg, and Mindy, hold on a minute."

"What's wrong Jason?"

"Does this bag belong to either one of you?"

"It's mine. Where did you get it?"

"Melissa picked it up. She thought it was Carla's, but she said it wasn't hers. We took the liberty to open it up and look inside for some ID, but the only thing in there is a piece of wood. Most people don't carry a piece of wood around with them. If I'm not being too nosy, what's with the wood?"

"Uh, well, I've started to take an interest in wood carving, and it looked like a good piece to practice on."

"Oh. OK, see you guys, and thanks for staying with Carla till we got there. She is so lucky, not to have even a scratch on her anywhere. I'm sure she'll be sore in the morning."

A knowing glance passed between Greg and Mindy. Finally Mindy said, "I think we need to go back to the park."

***

When they sat down on the park bench, Mindy turned to him and said, "I thought I was going to lose it when you told Jason you were taking up carving."

"Well, could you see him believing the real story?"

"Certainly not. It's amazing they weren't really suspicious about Carla's lack of injuries."

"I know. I heard them agree that the bike had to have taken all the blunt force from the car, and it had thrown her onto the soft grass."

"My mind is still reeling over what happened right here, just a little while ago."

"I'd love to ask you what's on your mind, but I think I already know. So let's start there and get that out of the way first."

"OK. I know I saw it, but seeing, isn't always believing. I saw you take a box out of that bag and a cloth out of the box, and use it to heal a young girl, who was for all intents and purposes, going to die right there in front of us. Then you put the very same box back into that bag.

When Jason opened that bag I saw the same block of wood I saw the day Snapper was healed. Now, would you please open the bag and take out whatever is in it?"

"Alright, here it is."

"Just as I thought, it's a box again. What the hell is going on, Greg?"

"You know as much as I do. I woke up one morning about a year ago, and the box was beside my bedroll. I have no idea where it came from, or how it got there. I do think I know now why I have it, but I don't know what I'm supposed to do with it now that the cloths are gone. Do I keep it or what?"

"Why do you think you have it?"

"What I said to Carla, is the same thing the woman in my dream said to me."

"Is that what was printed on the cloth?"

"Yes. And, that makes it more than a dream."

"I don't understand?"

Greg told her what Stu's father had said about the young boy who was injured in front of the house.

"It sure seems like you're the boy in that story. But, what happened in the period of time between when you were injured and when Carla got hurt? Where has the box been?"

"I don't know. I'm surprised that you were able to see the transition from block of wood to box and back more than once. That is completely confusing, considering that the last time I tried to show it to you, it was a block of wood."

"How many cloths were in the box when you got it?"

"Five"

"OK. I know about the ones for you, Snapper, and Carla. What is the story on the other two?"

"One was used to heal Stu, when he got hurt, and one healed Bill."

"So, they got to see the box with the cloths, right?"

"No, just like Carla, they had a vague memory of the cloth, but never saw the box."

"Wow, this is really confusing. Do you think I saw the box because it was the last cloth?"

"It could be. But, I think it was because Carla would have died before the EMT's got here, if I couldn't have gotten to the cloth."

"There are still a lot of questions, Greg."

"I know. It seems like the more we learn, the more questions we have. And, I don't know if we'll ever get any of the answers."

"Maybe the answers aren't as important as the results."

"Now, here's something else. We both know it was Ted driving that car, but is there any way we can verify it?"

"We could call Officer Thomson tomorrow. I'm sure he'd tell us."

I'm almost afraid to bring this up, but you still haven't told me why we came out here."

"Ahh, yes. Well, you know that Harrison guy I said I was going to meet today?"

"Yeah. What was that all about?"

122

"It appears; my grandfather left me a whole lot more than 'The Anthill'."

"Something you didn't know about before?"

"OHHHH, yes, I think you could say that."

He filled her in on all the details. As she sat there listening, she kept shaking her head, and finally said, "Oh my god. That means you're a multi millionaire."

"I know, and I'm still in a state of shock."

"What are you going to do now?"

"I have no idea. I don't think it has sunk in yet. I'm going to have to take this stuff one step at a time. I still have to figure out the box thing first."

"Just for the hell of it, let's see if it's still a box."

OK. Here it is, and it's a box, and it's still empty."

"Doesn't that look like some kind lettering on the inside bottom?"

"Yeah, it does. When I first got this box I took all the cloths out of it, and I didn't see that before."

"What does it say?"

"It says, 'Someone you know needs this box. As you think, so goes the box'."

"Holy cow! This is getting stranger all the time. What are you going to do with it?"

"I'm not sure. I don't know what it means by someone needing it. How would I, know who needs this box?"

"Do you feel like all that's happened in the past year seems to point in the direction of several of us being tied together in some way?"

"I sure do. Maybe sometime in the future we'll find out how."

"Is there anyone in our group who would need it?"

"I don't think so."

"You've got a lot of things to get your head around. Perhaps I should leave you alone, and let you sort it all out."

"I don't want to be alone. Actually, I'm asking you to stay with me from now on. I love you, and if you don't mind, I'd like for us to spend the rest of our lives together."

"She grabbed him in a big hug, and said, "I was hoping you'd say that. So, what would you like to do now?"

"I hadn't given it much thought."

"Why don't we go to the 'The Anthill'? I love it there."

"You definitely are a woman after my own heart. This is Thursday, and I don't want to come back till Monday, so do you need to stop and pick up anything on the way?"

"I just need to put a closed sign in the shop. Get some cosmetics, a toothbrush, and an outfit to wear when we come back. I always have my birthday suit with me, and that's the only thing I'll be wearing while we're there."

"Let's pick up a pizza and some thing to drink after we go to the shop."

"Sound good to me."

As they walked toward the truck, Snapper ran ahead of them, jumped into the truck bed, and looked back at them as if to say hurry up, let's go.

***

When they walked into the shop the phone was ringing.

Mindy answered it and listened for quite a while, and finally said, "Are you are certain that's who it is? Yes I did. I'll be happy to see you Monday morning and fill you in. Thank you and you have a nice weekend too."

She turned toward Greg with a sad look on her face, and said, "It was definitely Ted. They found his I.D. and checked his prints in the data base. Also, Officer Thomson said his right arm was in a cast, and had been broken between the wrist and elbow.

He asked if I knew Ted. I said I did, and would see him Monday and clear it up for him."

"Although it's a relief to know he won't bother us again, it still isn't something you can feel happy about."

"No, it isn't. He was such an intelligent man, and he could have done so many good things with his life, but he always had to be putting something over on people.

Well, I'm not going to let it ruin our weekend. I'm ready. Let's go."

Greg and Mindy had a lot of things to toss around, so they felt the best place to do that was "The Anthill".

With Snapper in the back of the truck, that's where the three of them went to contemplate their future.

On the way there Mindy had a thought and said, "Look Greg, I've got a friend who owes me a favor, so after I to go to see Officer Thomson Monday, I can give her a call and see if she can fill in for me at the shop if you want to take more time."

***

After dinner, a shower, and some wonderful lovemaking, Greg went out to get the coffee pot ready for the next morning. As he walked by the dining room, he noticed the bag containing the box setting there on the table.

He sat down, pulled the box out of the bag, and studied it for a long time, trying to sort it out in his mind. *Who should I take this box to?*

After setting up the coffee pot he walked back through, and looking at the box he said, "I know who needs the box, and I'll take it to him tomorrow."

***

The next morning, Greg went into the kitchen to start the coffee and stood staring at the table.

The empty bag was there, but the box was gone.

CHAPTER SIXTEEN

"Where did this thing come from? Hmm, it's about the size of a shoe box, and it's made out of a dark wood that could be mahogany. The fantastic carving all over makes it a real piece of art. Hey, the top opens up. It's a box. I think those are hieroglyphics of some kind on the inside of the lid. Wait a minute! What are those strange looking things inside it? They remind me of the jacks that young girls used to play with, but they really sparkle. They are so bright they look like they have lights in them."

Larry found the box beside his head when he woke up that morning.

A thought occurred to him. *I don't know where this box came from, but it's mine now.*

This is Friday, April 19th. The flea market opens today. I'll put the box in my back pack so no one knows what I've got, and take it to Ray's booth. He can probably tell me what it is and where it came from.

Well, here we go again, because we aren't anywhere near the end of THIS story!

Episode 2-Larry's Friday

CHAPTER ONE

Picking up his ratty looking backpack, Larry put the box inside, zipped it shut, putting his arms through the straps, he headed for the flea market.

"If I'm lucky this box is a one of a kind antique worth a lot of money, and I can get enough money out of it to find Delores and kill her for what she did to me."

***

"Hey Larry, long time no see. What've you been up to?"

"Nothin much, I just found this neat box, so I brought it to see if you'd be interested in it."

"Where is it?"

"It's in my backpack. Here, I'll turn around, so you can open it and take the box out, and let me know what you think of it."

Ray opened the backpack pulled the item out and said, "Is this one of those puzzle things? If it is, you're going to have to show me how it works, because it just looks like a plain old piece of wood to me."

Larry turned back around, and couldn't believe his eyes.

"OK, what'd you do with the box?"

"What box? This is the only thing in your backpack."

"This isn't funny Ray. Where's the box?"

"You're welcome to look around. This is what I pulled out of your backpack. I wouldn't do that to you."

"Just put it back in there. I'm out of here."

With that, Larry stormed out of the flea market. As he walked along the sidewalk he was only vaguely aware of the man walking toward him. He was a clean shaven, elderly gentleman with salt and pepper hair; very important looking, about 6ft. tall, and dressed quite well; wearing a tailored navy pinstripe suit with a white shirt and red tie, expensive wing-tip shoes, and all topped off with a classy looking dark blue felt hat. He was carrying a cane with an engraved handle made of eighteen karat gold. As he approached Larry, he stuck the cane in his path and stopped him saying, "You have the box. Does it contain stars?"

"I don't know what you're talking about old man."

"You do have the box."

"I told you, I don't know what you're talking about, and I don't have your damned box."

"It is not my box. At the present time it is yours. I'm going to give you my business card. You will know when to summon me."

"I don't have your box, so why would I want to call you?"

"Please take my card because sometime soon you will need my help. When you do I will be there to help you."

He made a fist and drew back as if to hit the gentleman, but as he looked into his eyes something made him stop and drop his hands to his sides.

"I can take care of myself. I don't need your help. I don't need anybody's help, so butt out old man."

"I'm aware that you are self sufficient mister Lawter, but with the box you will need direction, so, please take this card. It won't hurt you to carry it. If I'm wrong and you never need it, then nothing is lost."

"Alright, if it'll make you shut up and leave me alone, give it here."

He took the card and without looking at it stuck it in his shirt pocket, and started to walk away. After taking several steps something the man said occurred to him, so he stopped to ask the man how he knew his name, but by the time he turned around the man was gone.

"Where the hell did he go? He couldn't have run off that quickly."

He stood for several moments staring down the street, then, continued on his way looking for the nearest trashcan. As he got to one he took the business card out of his pocket and looked at it.

"What the...? All it says is, 'A star can make it right'. What's that supposed to mean? This thing's going in the trash. And, that hunk of wood's going with it."

He unzipped the backpack and pulled out the...box... with carving all over it.

"Whoa! This is really getting weird. Oh, man. Something's not right. How'd he know I had that box? Is he the one who left it there? I don't know; something's really strange. I'd better hang on to this box and card long enough to see what this is all about."

With that, he took the card and put it in the box and then placed the box back into his backpack.

"At first, I thought Ray was just jerking my chain. But, now I don't know. I was thinking he's just like all the rest of them, always acting like they're my friends, then when my back's turned they stick a knife in it and try to screw me over. That's what that damned Greg did. I knew he was lying when he said he was trying to talk to me about Delores. He just wanted her for himself, but I wasn't about to let that happen. I got her away from him. I just wish I'd kicked his ass before I left."

Every time Larry got into a fight that he couldn't handle, Greg would step in and save his butt, so thinking he could whip Greg didn't make sense.

***

Walking through a field on the way back to his lean-to, he noticed a couple of boys playing in a large maple tree about thirty feet away. As he approached the tree one boy lost his grip and fell, landing on his head on the hard ground. Larry raced over to him and saw he was unconscious, so he told the other boy to run to a phone and call 911.

As he tried to make the boy comfortable it occurred to him that he looked to be about the same age his brother was when he died.

Oh my god, he's Danny's age. He even looks like him; same build and hair color. I can't stand it. I've got to get out of here!

He felt like he was starting to hyper-ventilate.

I don't know if I can make it. It feels like everything's closing in on me. But, I can't leave till the paramedics get here. I feel like I'm coming apart. What can I do? Oh my god! Oh my god!

He sat there rocking back and forth holding the unconscious boy. After what seemed like a lifetime, the boy started to come to. As Larry was trying to comfort him and keep him calm, he finally heard the sirens. By the time the paramedics arrived Larry, was frantic and shaking uncontrollably. As they were placing the boy in the ambulance one of them noticed Larry and tried to check him over, but he wouldn't let him touch him.

"Sir, please let us at least check your pulse and blood pressure. I'm afraid you're going to have a stroke or heart attack."

"No. I'm fine. I'm out of here. Leave me alone."

"Sir, can I just get your name?"

"No! Leave me alone! I don't care what you say! I didn't do it! It wasn't my fault! My name is none of your business."

"We know you didn't do anything sir, we just want to be sure you're alright."

He said, "I told you to leave me alone.", and ran off as fast as he could. When he reached his lean-to he sat cowering in the corner in a fetal position shaking and crying.

After a couple of hours he finally settled down, and sat there staring, way into the past of many years ago. It had been almost 20 years since the last time he allowed himself to think about his brother. Twenty three years ago Danny had died tragically at the age of 9… and; it was Larry's fault.

"I really loved Danny, but sometimes he was a pain in the ass. I couldn't go any where without him hanging around. He could just piss me off. He wouldn't leave me alone. I just wanted him to go away. That's why I told him what I did. It's my fault he's dead. He wouldn't have ridden his bike down that gully in Hilson Woods if I hadn't lied to him.

Oh, Danny, I'm sorry. I miss you so, so much. If I could take it all back I would, and if I could die in your place, I would. That way, Mom and Dad could have the son they always wanted."

Larry didn't feel he deserved to be alive, that's why he constantly got into fights. It was almost like deep inside he wanted someone to end his life for him, because he didn't have the guts to do it himself.

"Danny, I wish there was some way I could talk to you one more time and tell you how sorry I am for what I did to you. I know I can't ask you to forgive me. I can't forgive myself, but if I could talk to you just one more time and tell you I'm so sorry. I didn't mean for it to happen."

He sat staring at nothing for a long, long time. Suddenly, he turned and looked quizzically at his backpack. He could here a voice coming from it. The voice was calling his name. Almost like he was in a hypnotic trance he reached over picked it up, unzipped it and took the box out of it. After sitting and holding it in his hands, he finally opened it. One of the stars was glowing rhythmically and changing colors. As he picked it up and held it in his hand a voice spoke to him.

"Larry, it's me, Danny. What do you want to talk to me about?"

Astonished and wide eyed, Larry jumped, and almost threw the star.

"Who is this? Danny's dead. Why are you messing with me?"

"I'm not messing with you. You don't have anything I'd want to take from you. You said you wanted to talk to me."

"That's a crock of bull. You can't have a conversation with dead people."

"If that's true, why are you talking to me?"

"Because, whoever you are, you aren't Danny, and you're not dead. Dead people don't talk."

"Nobody really dies, Larry. When our bodies stop functioning, the essence of what we are makes the transition to a different level, or plane of consciousness. Sometimes it's referred to as the other side."

"I don't know how or why you're doing this, but it's sick. I'm throwing this star and the box away."

"It won't do any good. You've opened this line of communication and it won't close until we've resolved the issue you have. You asked to talk to me; I didn't ask to talk to you."

"The things you're trying to tell me aren't possible."

"Oh, yeah? Well, tell me this then. How did the bee get in the teapot?"

"How did you know about that? I never even told Danny about it."

"I am Danny. I watched you through the kitchen window when you put that bumble bee in Mom's teapot. That was funny, because Mom really freaked out when she saw it."

"If you're Danny, why didn't you tell Mom then? Danny always told her everything I did."

"I knew if I didn't tell Mom I could have something to hang over your head. That's why I told you I wanted to see you when you got back from Eddie's."

"This whole thing is unbelievable. It has to be a dream. I just hope it's not a nightmare."

"It isn't either one. This is all real and it's happening right now."

"If you are really Danny, then what was thing you valued the most?"

"The scale model of the race car of my favorite driver Marc Danson."

Larry hung his head and started sobbing.

"What is it? Why are you so upset? I thought you wanted to talk to me."

"It's my fault you died. I killed you."

"What? Where'd you get that idea?"

"I told you I threw your model car down the gully in Hilson Woods. When you went there to get it you hit that tree, and that was my fault."

"It didn't happen that way."

"What do you mean? The police said you rode your bike down into that gully, too, fast and when your chain came off you hit that tree, and that's what killed you."

"Well, for starters, I saw you hide my model car in the garage, so when you said you took it to Hilson Woods, I acted all mad and left. Then after you went to Eddie's house I went in the garage and got my car, and hid it in Dad's old footlocker up in the attic, because I knew you'd never look in there for it."

"No wonder I couldn't find it when I looked in the garage. That doesn't make sense though. Why did you go to the woods then? You know… this is getting weirder by the minute. I still can't believe I'm talking to a glowing star."

"You aren't. You're talking to me. Do you feel strange talking on a telephone?"

"No."

"Ok then. Consider the star the same as you would a phone. It's just a device that allows us to bridge the communication gap between us."

Larry sat there shaking his head in disbelief.

"Ok, but its still nuts."

"Someday you'll understand it all. Till then, let's get back to your question. I was riding my bike to River Park and my chain broke. While I was stopped along the side of the road, a guy in a green pick-up came by and said he'd help me and take me home. I was relieved cause I wasn't looking forward to that 3 mile walk back home. He tossed my bike and chain in the bed of the truck. I jumped into the cab and we drove off. I told him where I lived and that he was going the wrong way. When he didn't turn around I got scared and started crying. He told me if I shut up he wouldn't hurt me, so I did. He drove to the woods and when we got to the edge of the gully he drug me out of the cab. I started crying again, so he said if I did what he wanted I wouldn't get hurt. After I did what he said to do, he grabbed my bike and threw it down the gully. Then he turned around, picked me up and threw me after my bike. When my head slammed against that oak tree, it fractured my skull and broke my neck, killing me instantly.

The next thing I knew, I was looking down at myself lying beside to my bike."

"What happened to the chain? The police said they never found it."

"After he got to his home he realized the chain was still in the truck bed so he put it in an old coffee can and buried it next to his garage."

"How can I know if any of this is real?"

"It's all real. What I told you, is exactly how it happened."

"How can you prove it's really you?"

"The next time you're home, go into the attic. If you look in Dad's footlocker and under his uniform you'll find my race car. It's still there, and Dad doesn't know it, because he's never opened it in all these years."

"You mean on the left side under his Army uniform?"

"Nice try, Larry. You know as well as I do; his 'Navy' uniform is folded so that it takes up the whole length of the footlocker."

"For 23 years I've been beating myself up because I just knew I was responsible for your death. If this is all true, I won't know what to do. I've spent all that time on useless guilt and anger. Man, I've got a lot to think about."

"I didn't know you felt that way, Larry. You never let on. Nobody ever knew that you blamed yourself. You kept it all bottled up inside. No wonder you've been so angry."

"There's something I don't understand."

"Ok."

"If you've known I've been angry all these years, why didn't you know the reason for it?"

"When we pass on to this level, or side as some call it, we can move back to yours and observe what goes on, but we can't get into your heads unless you invite us in, so I could see by your actions you were angry. I just didn't know what you were angry about.   Why didn't you talk to somebody about it?"

"Yeah, right. You can't begin to realize how ashamed I've been. It was all I could do to admit it to myself let alone anyone else."

"You said if you were dead and I was still alive, Mom and Dad would have the son they always wanted."

"Yeah, so?"

"It isn't true, Larry. They love us both a lot, and they miss you so much."

"You'd never know it by the way they act when I go to see them. They give me the feeling they don't want me around. But, then I guess I deserve it by the way I act."

"You have so much anger in you, it scares them. They're afraid of you. After you leave Dad mopes and Mom just sits and cries."

"Am I really that bad?"

"Most of the time you hide your anger fairly well, but when you go home it's like the gloves are off and you cut loose. Watching you, it's almost like you want them to hate you."

"I do love them, and miss them. Although I want them to love me, I guess I tried to make them hate me because I felt like I didn't deserve their love after what I had done."

"They need to know that they can love you without reservations. You are all they have. They want you by their side when they pass from this life."

"Wait a minute! Are you telling me they don't have much time?"

"I don't know if you can understand this or not, but time doesn't exist on this side. We go by events. No past, no future, only now. Consequently I have no idea how much time they have."

"I don't know how to change things. I've spent so much of my life wallowing in this attitude, I'm not sure I can get out of it. I don't dare tell anyone I've talked to you, because most people already think I'm nuts, so if I tell them I've talked to my brother who's been dead for 23 years they'll be convinced of it."

"I can't advise you on what to do. You'll have to look inside yourself to figure that one out. I do feel that a good place to start would be to tell Mom and Dad you love them. Also, if it would help you; they definitely believe in reincarnation."

"It's scary, Danny, because this anger is what they've seen of me for most of my life. What if they won't believe the different me?"

"It's not going to be easy, but you can do it. Maybe some humility and a slice of humble pie would help. When you tell them how you feel, they'll have something to tell you about."

"What is it?"

"It's something that'll make you feel a little better about yourself."

"What do you know about the box and the stars?"

"I only know you need to keep them with you."

"Why? What's going on with it?"

"I don't know what'll happen, but if you find yourself in a situation where you don't know what to do, take the card out of the box and hold it while you look at it and the gentleman who gave it to you will find you."

"Who is he, and where did he come from?"

"That's something that I really don't know about."

"Where do you and I go from here?"

"If the issue you needed to talk about has been resolved we probably won't be in contact till I see you here."

"Does that mean I'll see you when I die?"

"I'll always be around you Big Brother. If you'll relax and believe in this conversation, and everything I've told you, you'll even sense my presence sometimes. I love you and you're still my hero."

"I love you, too, and I miss you terribly, Danny."

"Till then."

Larry opened his hand and watched mesmerized as the star slowly began to lose its bright glow and the color faded. When the light finally went out, the star became snow white, then floated off into the sky and vanished. He opened the box and pulled the card out. As he read the words "A star can make it right", aloud, he wondered what was in store for the rest of the stars, and what if any part he'd have in it.

"What's going on? Where did this box and stars come from? And, why do I have them?"

A lot of confusing things were swirling around in his mind, so he fired up the propane stove and made a pot of coffee for himself. Sitting silently and sipping coffee for a while he finally said, "I've alienated everyone around me with all this anger. I don't even have one friend. The only friend I did have was my business partner, Greg, and what did I do? I just decided to screw up a great business and take our money, and run off with some damned gold-digger who cleaned me out. I'm still going to kill her if I ever see her.

How do I go back and undo the things I've done to turn people away? I really don't know. Maybe the first place to start would be with Mom and Dad, like Danny said, but what do I tell them? Will they ever believe in me?"

CHAPTER TWO

The walk to his parent's home wasn't really that far, but it was the longest walk he'd ever taken. When he got there, he stopped on the opposite side of the street and just stared. Looking at the grey two story house with the large porch across the front brought back a flood of memories involving Danny. The most vivid one was when his mom brought Danny home.

At first I didn't want him there, and tried to get her to take him back to the hospital, but as time went on I learned to love him and wanted to be his protector. As soon as he started talking he made it clear he wasn't having any part of that.

Then, looking up at the large second story dormer he remembered when he fell out of that window and rolled off the roof to the yard below.

While I was lying there, dazed, and confused, Danny kept crying and screaming hysterically that his big brother was dead. At the hospital, when he found out I was OK, he frogged me on the arm for scaring him. I wonder why it's our nature to not know how much we love and appreciate something or someone till they're gone.

Standing and remembering that and many other things brought a smile to his lips. He was beginning to realize how important his parents were, and he desperately hoped it wasn't, too, late to make amends with them.

Wow! On the way here I almost turned around and walked away at least a half dozen times. The only thing that kept me going was Danny saying the best way to start would be with Mom and Dad.

If in fact it really was Danny. He still had some questions about that, but he was glad he didn't back out.

His hand was shaking as he knocked on the door. He was afraid of their reaction. The door opened and he could see the anguish on his father's face. He had been back in town almost a year, but he hadn't seen his dad since the day after he cleaned out the business accounts, so he was surprised to see how much he had aged since then.

Will Lawter, is 6ft. 2in. tall, about 220lbs; a handsome, distinguished looking man in his late 50's, and his almost snow white hair and piercing blue eyes give him an air of importance.

Larry's mom is in her mid 50's, a very pretty woman with natural red hair; and beautiful green eyes. She's the type of person who reaches out to everyone, and will help others at the drop of a hat. At the same time, she has an extremely sharp sense as to when someone is being straight up with her or trying to pull something. When you meet her, you instantly like her.

The casual observer wouldn't pick Larry's mom and dad to be a couple, because at 5ft. 2in. tall and 140 lbs.; she's very close to half his size. But, once you see how they react to one another, and the way look at each other, it's very obvious they belong together.

"What do you want Larry? We can't take any more trouble from you."

"I'm not here to give you any grief, Dad."

"We don't have any money to give you."

"I'm not here for money. Is Mom home?"

"Of course."

"Can I come in and talk to both of you?"

"Your mom isn't up to any more fights with you. The last time, she sat and cried for days."

"I know, Dad. I'm not here to fight. I'm changed now."

"We've heard that before."

"I swear to you, I won't argue or fight with you. I'm so sorry for what I've done to you and Mom. You've never deserved the way I've treated you."

"OK, but if it starts, you're out of here for good."

"It won't happen, Dad. It'll never happen again. I promise you. I just really need to talk to you and Mom."

"Come on in. Go sit down in the living room. Your mom's in the kitchen I'll see if I can get her to come in and talk."

"OK."

As he walked by the clock on the mantle Larry was surprised to see it was already 6:30 pm.

***

"Jeanie, Larry's here, and he says he wants to talk to us."

After a long deep sigh she said, "Will, I can't take it again. I just don't think I can survive it."

"I don't know why I think so, but there's something different about him. He said he knows we didn't deserve the way he treated us and he apologized. He promised he would never fight with us again."

"That is different. He's never apologized before. I'm just not sure I believe it. Why don't you go out and sit with him while I make a pot of coffee and think about this."

"OK."

As she watched Will, walk toward the living room she felt tears well up in her eyes. Tears brought about mostly by fear, but also just the tiniest bit of hope.

***

"Your mom's making us some coffee, but I don't know if she'll sit down and talk."

Dad, we've got to get Mom in on this. Please. I need your help. She's got to be here. What I have to say is for both of you. You have to get her in here. After I'm done, if you don't ever want to see me again, I won't blame you. I'll leave you alone. I promise you.

"Are you going to tell us you're sick or dying or something?"

"Who's dying?"

Larry didn't realize she was standing behind him listening to them, so when she spoke his head snapped around and he watched as the tears flowed down her cheeks.

"I'm not talking about anybody dying, Mom. Will you please sit with us? I've got something very important to tell you."

"Larry, I can't just stand back and watch any more of your terrible displays of anger. I love you, so, much. I can no longer watch as you destroy yourself."

"It's all over, Mom. I've learned some things about my self today."

"Oh my god. You are dying."

"No I'm not! Please sit down with us. I need to tell you what's going on."

"Alright."

She went over to the couch and grabbed Will's hand as she sat beside him.

"Mom, Dad, I'm not sure where to start, so I'm just going to blurt some things out and we'll go from there. OK?"

"Before you start, Larry, we need to tell you, we've never stopped loving you, and all we ever wanted for you is the very best. It's just that the last time you were here we knew we couldn't take your abuse and rage any more."

"Mom, I can't say I know how you feel, because I don't. I just know you and Dad didn't deserve all those things I did to you. I've had an experience that made me face the fact that the reason I treated both of you with such anger, was simply; I felt it was necessary to make you hate me because I had done such a terrible thing, that I had no right to accept your love."

"What could you have done to make you feel that way? Wait a minute. Does this have anything to do with Danny? You've been this way since Danny was killed. That's 23 years now. Are you saying that, that has something to do with all this?"

"Mom, until this event, I was convinced it was my fault Danny died."

"We never blamed you for that. We always wondered if you blamed us, and that's why you hated us."

"No, of course not. I was convinced it was because of me, so I didn't need your help to feel guilty. I was doing a real good job all on my own. Now I know better, because I know how he died."

"We both knew you didn't have anything to do with it, so why would you blame yourself?"

"I told Danny a lie, Dad, and I always thought he went to Hilson Woods because of my lie. I found out today that wasn't the reason."

"Larry, he was kidnapped and taken to the woods against his will. The kidnapper threw him down the hill, and that's how he landed against that tree, and died. You didn't have anything to do with that. You said you just found that out today. How?"

"I'm not sure I can explain it now. How long have you and Mom known that? And, how did you find out?"

"I think it was around 6 years ago, about a week after the last time we saw you. Detective Fleming called to tell us that a career criminal in state prison had requested to see him. When he got there the man, whose name was John Carpell, was in the infirmary, on his death bed. Detective Fleming said the man knew he didn't have much time left and needed to get something cleared up before he died. He told Fleming he was the one who killed Danny Lawter. He gave details of the crime that, only someone who was there would have known. He said although he wasn't bothered by any of the things he had done to other people; killing that little boy had haunted him from that day on. He said there wasn't one day since, that he didn't visualize that boy lying by the tree. He said he knew he owed it to the boy's family to tell the truth before he died. He also said he didn't plan to hurt Danny he just wanted to throw him down the gully so he would have enough time to get away. Detective Fleming said the real clincher was when Carpell told him if he went to the back yard of the house he was living in when he was arrested for robbery, he could find the broken bike chain in a coffee can, buried in the back yard by the left front corner of the garage, and that's where it was. It was all rusty and corroded but it was identifiable."

"Wow! That's what Dan...uh, never mind."

"What were you going to say about Danny?"

"Nothing, Dad. Was there anything else?"

"Fleming said Carpell told him he didn't know why, but for some reason he just couldn't seem to throw the chain away.

Fleming said he was relieved after finding the truth, because something had always bothered him about the accidental death ruling."

With a bewildered look in her eyes, she asked, "What lie did you tell Danny that made you think it was your fault?"

"I told him I threw his race car model down the gully in Hilson woods, and I thought that was why he went there."

Openly sobbing, she ran over to Larry and wrapped her arms around him saying, "My poor son. I just wish you could have told us how you felt, and yet I know why you were afraid to. I know we can't make up for lost time, but we don't dare waste any more."

Tearfully, Will, asked, "Where are you staying? Would you like to come back home?"

"I can't do that just yet, Dad. I have other people I've hurt and I have to work things out with them."

"Son, I hope you know that we'll always be here for you, and we always wanted to be, but you wouldn't let us. At least now we know why. I just wish there had been some way I could've known what was going on."

"I know you'll be there, Dad, and how could you have known if I didn't tell you?"

"Larry, you said you lied about Danny's race car model. We've never seen it. What did you do with it?"

"I put it in the garage. Danny got it and hid it in Dad's footlocker under his Navy uniform."

Larry's mom sat silent for a long moment, and then finally she asked, "If you thought he believed you and went to the woods to get it; how do you know he put it in the attic?"

Larry took a deep breath and let out a long sigh before responding with, "Mom, Dad, let's go up there to see if I'm right."

As he was going up the stairs to the second floor, Larry looked around and realized that for the first time in a lot of years, it felt good to be back, home. Stepping into the attic, he remembered how Danny used to like to go there and read his comic books, so he'd hide there in the dark and scare him when he came in with his arms full of comics.

Will, reached up into the rafters, got the key and unlocked the footlocker. He slowly lifted the lid and gently pulled his old uniform back. The three of them just stood there staring at the race car model, exactly where Danny had said it was.

Any doubt Larry had about his conversation with Danny being real, evaporated in that instant.

"How was he able to put it in there? I've kept it locked."

Chuckling, Larry, said, "Dad, we always knew where you hid the key."

Larry's mom finally changed the subject with, "The coffee should be ready, let's go downstairs and have some coffee and cake. I don't know why, but for some reason I had the urge to make you and your dad's favorite cake today; milk chocolate with fluffy white icing."

Back downstairs as they sat around the dining room table Will, said, "All these years I kept wondering what happened to that little car, and it was right there under my nose. I'll never stop wishing there had been some way we could've helped you through this."

"I could see the pain on both of your faces because of the loss of Danny, and I guess I figured the last thing you'd want is to love the person responsible for his death."

"You never answered the question, Larry. How did you know that car was there?"

"I don't know how to explain it, Mom. I'm not sure I understand it myself."

"You also said you finally learned today that you weren't responsible for Danny's death. How did you learn it? There must be something you can tell us about it. Won't you please try?"

"Maybe I should start with what's in my backpack."

"What's in your backpack?"

"I'll get it and show you."

Will and Jeanie looked at each other quizzically as he went into the living room to get his backpack.

Larry brought it into the dining room, unzipped it and pulled out a block of wood the size of a shoe box. He placed it on the table, and the three of them sat there staring at it.

Will shook his head and said, "I don't get it. What's a block of wood have to do with all this?"

"I had a feeling this would happen. Mom, Dad, I really don't understand it either. I know I've not been a good son to you, but I'm definitely different now. Please believe me. I'm not asking for anything, and I'm not pulling anything. If I can ever get to the bottom of this I'll let you know."

Looking at Larry, Jeanie said, "It's obvious something has happened to you. You're different. I can see it in your eyes. Danny has come to you somehow, hasn't he?"

"I guess you could put it that way."

"How? Did it have something to do with this piece of wood?"

"I can't explain it, because I don't understand it myself. I don't know what to say. I'm going to try to find out though."

"Something I was wondering about. We haven't seen Greg since you left. Do you know what happened to him?"

"I saw him about 2 weeks ago. He was so pissed, he grabbed my shirt and I thought he was going to kill me. Suddenly, he let go, pushed me down and walked away. I don't know what he's doing now or where he lives."

"Are you going to try to find him?"

"Oh, yes. Next to you and Mom, he's the one I hurt the most. Someday I hope I can tell you what I did."

"Any time you're ready, just let us know."

"Thanks, Dad. I will someday when I get things sorted out in my life. I guess I'd better get going. I'll stay in touch; I promise you, and you'll never have to doubt my love again."

"We know it, and we love you too."

***

Walking back to his lean-to, Larry thought about how the events of the day had completely blown him away, *I wish I knew where that box/block of wood came from, and why I have it. I just hope everything else that happens with it is as positive as today's events.*

For the first time in as long as he could remember, Larry realized, as he drifted off to sleep he was totally relaxed.

The next morning he woke up in a very rare good mood. He was thinking about shaving while his coffee was brewing, but when he moved his shirt to get to his razor, he felt something in the pocket. He reached in and pulled out 5, $20 bills.

"What the...? Dad must have put it in there when he patted my chest.

I think I'll go out for breakfast. I saw a little coffee shop a few blocks from here the other day. The sign in front said they serve excellent breakfast sandwiches, and pastries, and the best coffee and tea in town. I'm going to try it."

***

"Good morning, sir. My name is Cindy. May I help you?"

"I'd like coffee, and 2 bacon egg and cheese sandwiches on an English muffin."

"Yes sir. Coming right up."

"I don't get to eat out much, so this is my first time here. Have you been here long?"

"This isn't my place. It belongs to a friend of mine. She called this morning and said she was going to be out of town for at least a couple of weeks, and asked if I'd run it while she was gone."

"You must be a good friend. Are you from around here?"

"I have my own kitchen over in Largo."

"Who's running your place then while you're gone?"

"My kitchen is different. I have large commercial kitchen, and I rent out kitchen space on a timed basis to chefs and other professional cooks so they can market or cater their food specialties. That way I don't have to be there all the time. As long as I can stop by for a couple of hours each day I can keep it going."

146

"I've never heard of anything like that before. It sounds pretty interesting."

"Well, it is unique. I have the only one in the state. What about you? What do you do? Are you from around here?"

Her question caught him off guard, because in the last six years no one showed any interest in him, so he fumbled with his response.

"Oh, I kind of float around right now. I…I…don't know if I want to talk about it."

"I'm sorry. I didn't mean to be, too, nosey, I was just making conversation. If I upset you I apologize."

"No. I'm not really upset. I'm just not used to people wanting to know anything about me. Usually they don't want me around."

"Why?"

"It's probably because, for most of my life I've not been easy to get along with, but I recently discovered some things about, myself, that make me want to work as hard as I can to change that."

"Good for you. I hope you can do it."

"At this point it isn't an option. Which reminds me, I've got an old acquaintance to look up so, I'm going to have to run."

"By the way, what's your name?"

"I'm Larry."

"Nice meeting you Larry. Hope to see you again."

Well, if you're going to be around for a couple of weeks, I'll probably be back in before you leave."

Watching him walk out the door she couldn't help but wonder what was troubling him so much.

***

While he was wandering around somewhat aimlessly he was thinking about yesterday's events and at the same time, also wondered where he could find Greg.

It's not likely he'd still have the building we had our business in, but I don't know where else to start Both of his parents have passed away, and as far as I know he doesn't have any other family around.

If there is someone in our old shop maybe they'll know where I can find him. It's worth a try, so I'd better get moving, because it's a long way from here and if I don't leave soon it'll be dark by the time I get there.

Heading for the shop he couldn't get his mind off Greg.

"How did he know where to find me? Is he some how involved in all this? I don't think so. I have a feeling this is something much bigger than both of us. Obviously there are still a lot of unanswered questions, and I think this is just the beginning. I hope this isn't a hallucination, because I don't remember ever feeling this good."

As he walked along, he didn't know why, but he felt the urge to look behind him, and when he did, he noticed a woman about 50 feet back. From that distance she appeared to be quite young. It didn't seem significant, so, he continued to walk toward the old business, deep in his own thoughts. After about thirty minutes he had occasion to glance back and noticed she was still there. She didn't look dangerous, but her presence made him a little uneasy, so he picked up the pace a little. Suddenly someone crossing the street ahead of him caught his eye. It looked like the elderly gentleman in the blue suit he had encountered yesterday.

He started running toward the figure and hollered for him to please wait. The man either didn't hear him, or was ignoring him because he kept walking till he disappeared around the corner of a building. As Larry hurriedly rounded the corner of the building he almost ran into the man. He was standing there waiting, blocking his path.

He said, "She needs what you have. You must wait here for her."

"Who are you talking about?"

"The young lady behind you."

"I don't have anything. Why is she following me?"

"You'll know when she gets here."

Larry looked around the corner of the building and saw her moving up fast. When he turned back to say something to the gentleman, he was gone.

He was standing there in disbelief and felt someone tapping him on the shoulder.

"What?"

"Why have you been calling my name?"

Up close, he realized she looked to be about his age. She was about 3 inches shorter than him; with a petite figure, a pixie like face, brown eyes and coal black short hair. As he stood there studying her, he replied, "I haven't called your name. I don't even know you. Who are you?"

"I'm Lori-Ann Mills. I've been hearing you call my...Wait a minute! It's your backpack."

"What about it?"

"That's where the voice is coming from."

"I don't think so. There's nothing in there that'll help you."

"Yes there is. Would you please open it?"

He found himself thinking maybe she wasn't as harmless as she looked.

"OK. But, I'm afraid you're going to be disappointed. It's just a block of wood"

He took his backpack off, sat down on the bus stop bench, unzipped it and pulled out a...beautifully carved box?

"I don't believe this. What the hell's going on?"

"That's a beautiful box. Something inside is calling me. Don't you hear it?"

"No."

She opened the box and Larry sat awestruck as one of the stars was glowing rhythmically and changing colors just like the one he'd held in his hand while talking to Danny. Suddenly he could hear the voice. It was calling Lori-Ann's name.

"I can't believe you don't hear that voice calling my name."

"I do now."

As he sat with the open box on his lap, she sat down beside him, and reaching in, she took the star in her hand, then, held it out in front of her. The voice said, "Lori-Ann this is your best friend, Judy.

"That's impossible you can't be Judy. She died last year. I went to her funeral. I saw her in the casket."

"It's really me Lor. I have to explain something to you and I think this may be the only chance I'll have, so please believe me."

"This isn't true. When we die that's it, we're done. This afterlife stuff is a bunch of bull. There's no such thing. I don't know who you are, but if you don't stop it, I'm calling the police."

"You need to think about that. How are you going to convince them that a glowing star is talking to you?"

"There's no such thing as a talking star."

Although, Larry knew from his own experience that what the voice was saying was true, he decided to keep his mouth shut and stay out of it.

"Look, the star in your hand is like a phone or a two way radio. It's just a device for us to communicate with each other."

"Just leave me alone. Crooks like you find people who have lost friends and relatives, and take advantage of them because they're grieving. Well, the jokes on you, because I don't have anything to take advantage of. I'm flat broke. As a matter of fact, I'm so deep in debt I don't know how I'll ever get out of it."

"That's why I'm here, Lor. What I have to tell you can help you get financially straight, so you can keep the house."

"This is nothing but a big scam, and the two of you aren't going to get anything from me."

"What do you mean when you say 'The two you'?"

"You and this guy that gave me the star."

"I don't know him. I've never met him. He's just the one carrying the connecting line for us to talk to each other."

"Yeah, right."

At this point Larry became quite agitated and said, "Hold on a minute. I didn't ask to be involved in this and I'm not out to get anything from you or anyone else, so, don't accuse me of any scams."

"What's your name, and why are carrying that box around?"

"My name's Larry, and I'm not sure why I have it, but what I do know of it, is a long personal story. And, one more thing, you followed me for 30 minutes. I didn't follow you."

"I'm sorry. You're right I don't know you and I don't have the right to accuse you of something crooked, but what that voice is saying, is not possible. Dead is dead, and that's all there is to it."

"I know what my experience is with the box, but I'm not going to try to influence your thinking either way, so, I'm leaving and you can figure it out for yourself."

"So, in other words, you're going to run off and leave your partner to face possible prosecution."

"Alright, I've had enough of this. I'm not going to repeat what I just told you, but look around. Do you see anyone else here? Who are you going to prosecute? Now! If you'd like to let me know how this works out for you, I'll be in a little coffee shop on the corner of 4th & Welton, Tuesday morning around 9:00. I promise to be there, and if you show up, I'll buy your breakfast. If you still think this is a scam, then bring the police with you. Either way, I hope to see you there."

With that Larry put the box in his backpack, strapped it on his back, and walked off. Lori-Ann sat there in a state of total confusion, and watched him leave.

"Lor, you've got to listen to me. I can help you, but you have to believe me. It won't cost you anything, because we have no use for material things on this side, especially money."

Lori-Ann started crying and yelling, "Stop calling me Lor. Judy was the only one I ever let call me that. You can leave me alone now, because I'm throwing this star thing in the trash can."

"It won't do any good. Once you responded to me, you completed the line of communication and it'll stay open till the issue is resolved. In other words, I can't go away."

"You mean I'm not going to get rid of you?"

"That's right."

"How many times do I have to tell you? Judy is dead and gone."

"There is no such thing as dead. When we pass, we pass to another level of consciousness."

"Ok. If you really are Judy, then you'll know something about me that no one else knows."

"I know you're about to default on the loan you took out on the house I left for you, and they're going to foreclose and evict you if you don't come up with a minimum of 6 back payments."

"That's public knowledge. You're going to have to do better than that."

"Alright, how about what you and your cousin Jamey did the night before she passed away."

That stopped Lori-Ann dead in her tracks. She sat there wide eyed, staring at the star in her hand, and kept repeating over and over, "Oh my god."

"Do you believe me now Lor?"

Letting out a big long sigh she said, "I never told anyone but Judy about that night." With tears rolling down her cheeks she said, "It is you, isn't it? I miss you so much. I wish you were here with me."

"You have no idea how many times I'm with you. I guess I'm the lucky one in that respect. I can stop in and see you whenever I wish, even though you can't see me and don't know I'm there."

"I don't understand how this can happen."

"I don't either. I just know that I was made aware of the opportunity to talk to you one more time."

"I can't believe I'm really talking to you. I've always been so certain there was no such thing as life after we die."

"I know. That's the way I felt, until I got here."

"What do you want to talk to me about?"

"Well, just for starters, you not only used up all the money you had, but went over $100 thousand in debt trying to save me, and pay my medical bills.

"It's no more than what you would've done for me."

"That's true, but it's more than my own mother did."

"I know, and I never understood why she didn't see the really good things that I saw in you."

"Well, you know she was pissed because my grandparents left their house to me."

"Yeah, I know. She really believed what your dad said about his parents stashing money in the house, didn't she?"

"Yep. Even though she had her own home paid for, and a tidy sum in the bank after Dad passed, she was still upset. She felt like the house should've been hers."

"Boy, she really went berserk when she found out you had turned the house over to me. She was convinced they had money hidden in that house, but since I took it over, I've looked, and I can't find a nickel anywhere."

"That's the biggest reason I'm talking to you now."

"What do you mean?"

"My mom was right."

"What?"

"There's a lot of money hidden all over the house."

"Where?

"Do you have some paper and something thing to write with?"

Checking her fanny bag she replied, "Yeah."

"Good let me know when you're ready, this gets a little detailed."

"I'm ready. What do I do?"

"Go to the pull-down stairs that lead to the attic over the garage. You remember them don't you?"

"Of course I do. You and I used to sneak up there and play when nobody knew it. I've already been all over that attic, and I couldn't find anything."

"It's not in the attic. Pull the stairs down and go up the steps till your eyes are even with the ceiling joist. Then, turn around like you're going to go back down. You'll see three

153

knots in the wooden cross support in front of you. If you press real hard on the knot on the far left side, it'll release a spring loaded latch and the wooden joist will pivot so you can see into the right side. Reach in and to the right, and you'll find a metal box. Take the box out and open it. Inside there's $97,000 in cash; all in100 dollar bills."

"Are you serious? Really?"

"Ohhh, yes. And there's a whole lot more. It's your money, but you have to get it before they take over the house or you won't have any rights to it."

"When are they going to do this?"

"I don't know. We have no concept of time here, only events."

"Ok. How do you figure it's my money? It belonged to your grandparents, so it should be yours."

"Uh, think about what you just said. I have no need for money over here."

"I know, but why didn't you get it while you were still alive?"

"I didn't know it was there till I got to this side."

"You mean, you're able see those things now?"

"No. Of course not. Being over here doesn't give us the ability to see through solid objects. My grandparents are here, since they know what good friends we've always been, they want you to have the money and keep the house, so they told me where they hid it."

"Wow, I still feel guilty. If I'd known there was more money, I might have been able save you."

"It figures you'd think that way. No amount of money was going to prevent my passing. That was set in motion the day I was born."

"Is that the way it is with everybody?"

"Not always, but that's for another discussion. Let's get back to the money."

"I'm still not sure I feel right about taking it."

"Listen to what I'm telling you. If you don't get it, someone who doesn't deserve it will. The only way you can keep the house is with the money that's hidden in it. Plus, there's enough extra to get you back on your feet. So, let me finish telling you where the rest is."

"Ok, go ahead."

"You know the old stereo radio and record player in the den?"

"Yes."

"Pull it out about 3 feet away from the wall."

"OK."

"You'll see an electrical outlet in the wall behind it with 2 cords plugged into it. Unplug the bottom cord only, and a small door in the paneling will open. If you unplug both, the door won't open. When the door opens and you reach inside, you'll have to reach up almost as high as you can, and as you do, you'll feel a small shelf. Sitting on that shelf is another metal box. Get the box and when you open it, you'll find $84,000 inside, mostly 100 dollar bills, with some 50's thrown in."

"If my math is correct, that's $181,000, so you're right, that's more than enough money for me. Why did they hide all that money in the house instead of investing it?"

"They told me that early in their marriage they had invested everything they had with a man who conned them out of all of it.

After that happened, they decided they would never invest their money with anyone again, so they started their own business and invested in themselves.

Oh, by the way there's more money hidden on the property."

"There's more? How much and where?"

"There's another box hidden in the garage with $28,001 in it. These bills are all 20's and 50's."

"That's an interesting amount. Why the odd dollar?"

"That dollar is a coin that was minted the year my grandfather's grandmother was born, and it was a sentimental keeper for him."

"So, where in the garage is the money."

"When you walk into the garage; go to the workbench on the left. On a wooden shelf above the workbench you'll see a bunch of old coffee cans. Most of them have things like; screws, nuts, small hinges, picture hangers or other odds and ends in them. Find the one that says Chase and Sanborn on it. That one has 12, 6 inch long metal rods that look like they are all 1/2 inch in diameter, but they are slightly different, only one will do the job you need done. Do you remember the big saw that Grandpa would cut all those neat shaped pieces of wood on?"

"Do you mean the tall one over by the window, with the long skinny blade?"

"That's it. Grab a hammer off the wall over the workbench, and take it and the can with the bars over to that saw."

"OK."

"There's a cutting guide on the saw table. Pull it up off the table and set it aside. You'll see two holes in the groove where the cutting guide was, one toward the front of the table and one toward the back. Take each metal bar; one at a time, and place it in the hole toward the back, then tap down on the exposed end lightly with the hammer. When you've used the right bar you'll hear a click, and a panel under the right side of the table will drop open. Inside you'll find the final metal box and the rest of the money is in it."

"Is that all I need to know?"

"There's nothing else I can think of. What about you? While this is still open, is there anything you need to ask me?"

After Lori-Ann folded the paper she had written instructions on and put it in her fanny pack, she asked, "Will I ever talk to you again?"

"I don't have an answer for that. But, you need to know that, whenever you think of me I'll be with you. Also, when you pass to this side I'll be here waiting for you."

"What's it like there?"

"Perceptions and thoughts are so much different here that I don't think I know how to explain it to you. I guess you'll just have to see for yourself when you get here. I love you my friend"

"I love you, too. Tell your grandpa he doesn't have to worry, I'll keep his coin."

"No! He wants you to sell it! His grandmother is here and he has no need for you to keep it."

"Oh. I hadn't thought of it that way. Ok. I'll look into it, and see what its worth."

"Well, I don't have anything else to take care of, Lor, so I'm going to have to go."

"I know. I've missed you so much, and it seems I've been in nothing but a blue funk since you've been gone."

"I'm not really gone. Although I'm in a place where you can't see me, sometimes when you feel calm and peaceful you'll sense my presence, and you'll know all is well. One last thing I have to tell you. You have so many wonderful things that are yet to happen in your life. Be positive, and look forward to what life brings you. Live your life with no anger, no fears and no regrets, and remember, when you've finished all the things you are there to do I'll be waiting here for you."

"What wonderful things are you talking about?"

"You'll see in your own time. Be happy and fill your life with every experience you can."

Lori-Ann watched intently as the star in her hand gradually began to lose its bright glow, and the color started to fade. When the light finally went out, the star became snow white, then floated off into the sky and vanished.

At first she felt unhappy and depressed because her friend had left her once again. Then, she went over things in her mind, realizing that, "She's right. I've been angry, resentful, and afraid since she first got sick two years ago, and I haven't allowed myself to let go and move forward. Everything that just happened isn't possible, and yet it did happen, didn't it? Or, is this some sort of illusion? I don't know how to find out. Wait a minute! Yes I do."

She jumped up and practically ran all the way home.

"It's a good thing I had that paper and pencil with me. I never would have remembered all that."

Once inside the house, she locked all the doors, pulled all the drapes, and opened the piece of paper with the instructions written on it. Following the first set of instructions, she went out to the garage, placed her instructions on the workbench, and pulled down the stairs to the garage attic. She suddenly realized how much the anticipation was affecting her. On very weak and shaky legs she carefully went up the steps till her eyes were even with the ceiling joist. She was so nervous she nearly fell as she turned around. Holding the small handrail to steady herself she closed her eyes tightly, then gradually opened them and looked straight ahead. She couldn't believe what she was seeing. It was there. The cross support with the three knots in it was right there in front of her. All the times she and Judy had gone up and down those steps when they were kids, and she hadn't even noticed them before. Her hand was shaking so much she had difficulty putting her finger on the knot to the far left. She pushed and pushed with her finger, but nothing happened. She was getting discouraged. Finally she placed the thumb of her other hand over her finger and pushed with both hands. When she did, she heard a distinctive click and watched as the right side of the support swung out of the way, leaving an opening on the right just like Judy said.

"So far so good." She started to reach into the opening and stopped. "What if it's a trap? What am I saying? The voice was Judy, and she wouldn't lead me into a trap."

Yet she very cautiously reached in and to the right. Feeling around, her hand struck the metal box, and grabbing it she slowly pulled it out through the opening. Within seconds of pulling the box out, the support piece snapped shut.

Her hands were shaking so badly she almost dropped it, and she was afraid she'd fall before she got down the steps. Slowly she made it down, and wobbled her way to the workbench. She set the metal box on it, and sat on the stool, taking slow deep breaths in order to get herself calmed down. After several minutes she felt like her heartbeat was starting to return to normal.

"Oh my. Can this really be happening? I'll go inside and get the second one, and count the money after I get all of them out."

She picked up her instruction sheet and started back into the house. "Wait a minute. I'm already out here, so I might as well get the box that's in the saw."

She found the Chase and Sanborn can and took it over to the saw. Following the instructions exactly, she tried all 12 of the rods. Nothing. She turned all the rods around and tried the other end in the hole. Once again, nothing. She stood there totally confused. She put the can of rods back on the shelf, grabbed the instruction sheet, and went back inside. She realized she was getting nervous again. "What if I screwed everything up and I'll never be able to get the rest of the money?" Going into the den she pulled the old stereo out. Again, she followed the instructions exactly, and the panel opened. She reached inside and pulled out the metal box. As she set the box down she heard the panel close.

"I don't get it. How could Judy only be right about 2 out of 3?"

She walked back out to the garage, picked up the can of rods, and followed the instructions again. On the 4th rod the panel opened. Breathing a long sigh of relief, she pulled out the final box. Once again within seconds that panel clicked shut as well.

Somewhat confused she grabbed all three boxes and went in, and sat at the dining room table. Seeing the boxes setting there in the light she noticed they were sequentially numbered, 1,2,3.

She opened the boxes one at a time and counted out $209,001 in 100, 50 and 20 dollar bills, and a $1 coin. The coin was in a velvet pouch, so when she opened it she didn't touch it. She let it slide out onto a soft cloth. It was a silver dollar dated 1889, and it was very shiny. It didn't look like it had ever been used, so without her fingers touching it directly, she slid it back into the pouch.

Getting up from the table, she turned the stove on, and filling the tea pot with water, she set it on the stove. Waiting for the water to heat she stood there studying the boxes. Just as the tea pot began to whistle it hit her. Whoa! I think I get it. Everything was set up so that if someone found out about the money, the only way they could get it all, would be to open the hidden areas in the right order. Man! What a genius idea.

The whistling tea pot finally got loud enough to bring her back to reality. She made a cup of tea, and sat back down at the table, slowly sipping it until she got herself calm enough to decide how she was going to set everything up with the money. She knew if she put all that money in her account at one time it would definitely raise a lot of questions. She would use enough cash to bring the loan up to date, put a couple of thousand dollars in her checking account, and put the rest, along with the $1 coin in her safe deposit box. That would give her time enough to figure out how to handle it. "Also someday when I have the time I'll have the coin checked, and see what its worth."

***

Larry's long walk to the old business site turned out to be a dead end. The building was empty, and there was a large for sale sign in front. The property was all overgrown, and as he walked around looking in windows, he recognized some of the old office equipment he and Greg had used, so it was quite obvious there hadn't been any business activity going on there for several years. It made him sad to know he had been the cause of all that loss.

"No wonder Greg was so angry."

Walking back to his lean-to, he kept going over the events of the last 2 days. "Wow. Nothing in my life has been the same since I woke up yesterday. It's kind of scary, because I've always believed, if it looks too good to be true, it probably is, so I can't help but think that there's going to be a high cost in the end.

Where the hell did those stars come from? Does each star have someone's name on it? Why me? Where's this all going, and what's my roll in it? I've got nothing but questions. When do I get some answers? I guess I'll take it as it comes. Yeah, like I've got a choice.

I wonder if I'll ever find out what happened with Lori-Ann. What the hell am I thinking? It's not likely I'll ever see her again and if I do, she'll probably want to tear my head off. Well, I guess maybe with a little luck I'll have my answer Tuesday morning."

***

Sitting at the table the next morning after breakfast, Will and Jeanie were discussing the recent encounter with their son.

"I'm not sure just yet. How do you feel Jeanie?"

"Will, I know what he's been like all these years, but there is definitely something different about him. I can see it in his eyes, and the way he carries himself. I don't know how to explain it."

"I can see a difference, too. I think we need to give him the benefit of doubt."

"I do, too, Will. After all he is our son, and he's the only family we have left."

CHAPTER THREE

"Good morning, Larry. How are you this wonderful day?"

"Hi, Cindy. I'm Ok. How about you."

"I'm good. What can I get you?"

"I think I'll just have a coffee for now. There's a slim chance someone will be meeting me in a little while, so I'll order food later."

"OK. One coffee coming up."

Sitting at the counter sipping his coffee, Larry was so deep in thought he didn't realize someone had come into the shop.

Suddenly he felt a tapping on his shoulder. When he turned around on his stool, he found himself face to face with a very pretty woman with a pixie like face and short coal black hair. At first he was confused, then it dawned on him, he was looking at Lori-Ann.

"I've seen you twice, and both times I had to tap you on the shoulder to get your attention. This could turn into habit if it continues."

Looking all around Larry said, "Well, I don't see any policemen, and you don't look angry, so I guess I owe you a breakfast."

"No. I owe you."

"Why? I didn't do anything."

"Let's go over to that table in the corner, and talk."

"Sure. What happened after I left?"

"Before you two go hide in the corner would you like to place an order?"

"Yes. What would you like Lori-Ann?"

"I don't know. What are you having?"

"I'd like 2 bacon, egg and cheese sandwiches on an English muffin."

"I'll have just 1 of the same with just the coffee to drink please."

"Coming up."

As they walked to the corner table Larry asked, "Would you like for me to call you Lori-Ann?"

"Just, Lori is fine."

"OK, Lori, do you want to tell me what happened?"

"First I have to apologize for my behavior Saturday. I realize I was wrong about you, because if it hadn't been for you I'd soon be heading for a home on the streets."

"It wasn't me. Like the voice told you, I just happened to be the person carrying the item that allowed the two of you to connect."

"But, I've got so many questions. The first of which is, how did you find me?"

"First tell me how things worked out for you. I don't expect you to get real personal, so just tell me what you're comfortable with, then, I'll try to fill you in on what I know. OK?"

"Alright. I'm not sure how to explain it, or where to begin, because I'm afraid you're going to think I'm nuts. But, after everything that happened last Saturday I'm beginning to believe it myself."

"Why don't you just start with what happened after I walked away? You never know, I just may not believe you're nuts at all."

She gave him a raised eyebrow look, and proceeded to tell him what took place, but since she didn't really know him, she had already made up her mind, she was not going to tell him exactly how much money was involved, so she carefully danced around that subject as she filled him in on the other details.

"I know it all sounds wild and beyond belief, but that's what happened. Now it's your turn to tell me what you know."

With a smile he said, "Just one more thing and I will."

"OK. What is it?"

He reached down, picked up his backpack. Setting it on her lap, he asked Lori to unzip it, and look inside and tell him what she saw.

Doing as he asked she said, "It's that beautifully carved box you had Saturday."

"OK. Zip it back up, I won't touch it. You hold on to it till Cindy brings our food."

"Why? What's going on?"

"Just humor me. Here she comes now."

"Here's your breakfast, you two."

"Cindy, while you're here, Lori would like to show you something and see if you can tell us what it's made of."

"Sure. I'm not an expert on a lot of things, but I'll try. What do you have?"

"Lori, would you please show her what's in my backpack?"

With a questioning look, Lori, unzipped the backpack, and was astonished at what she saw. She was looking at a plain block of wood.

"Like I said, I'm no expert but it looks like a block of wood. Maybe pine but I'm not sure. Is it something special?"

"No. Not really. I just wanted to see if you knew what kind of wood it is."

As Cindy walked away, Lori sat with her mouth hanging open and kept looking back and forth between Larry and the block of wood.

She finally gathered her wits enough to ask, "How did you do that?"

"How did I do what? After I sat it in your lap I never touched it. Now, will you please zip it shut, and when Cindy can't see it, unzip it again and look inside."

She did what he asked, and, as he watched her reaction to what she saw inside, he sat there unable to hold back a big smile and a chuckle.

"It's the box again. You knew that was going happen, didn't you? Who are you really? Would you like to tell me what this is all about?"

While they sat eating their breakfast, he filled her in on all the things that took place from the time he woke up the previous Friday morning.

"Now you know why I didn't think you were nuts."

164

"Where did the box come from, and why do you have it?"

"I don't have answers to those questions. I do know that my life has done a complete turn around since Friday morning."

"How?"

"Well, since I had blamed myself for my brother's death, I guess deep down inside, I felt I didn't deserve to have anyone be nice to me, so, I treated everyone like hell. That way, I was guaranteed to turn them away. I even betrayed the only true friend I ever had. But, after talking to Danny,on Friday, I realized I had been, and was continuing, to waste my life by being a horse's ass. Now, I've got a lot of making up to do."

"Would I be, too, nosey if I asked how you betrayed your friend?"

Larry hung his head, and with tears in his eyes, explained, "We were partners in a very successful business, and one day about six years ago I decided to embezzled all the available funds and run off with our secretary's daughter. I didn't even care or consider when I did it, that it would cause him to lose the business. Now, I've got find him and make things right, even if I have to go to prison."

"You don't know where he is?"

"No. I was heading for our old business, hoping to find him when I met you."

"Did you ever make it there?"

"Yeah. But, when I got there the building was empty and it was obvious that it had been for a long time."

"What are you going to do now?"

"I really don't know. He doesn't have any family in the area, and if he has family anywhere else I wouldn't have any idea where to find them."

"Do you know for sure he's alive, and, if he is, how do you know if he's still around here?"

"He was, when I saw him about 2 weeks ago."

"Why didn't you talk to him then?"

"Well, for one thing, that was before I talked to my brother, and for another, when I saw him I thought he was going to kill me."

"Because of what you did?"

"Yeah."

"Did he come after you?"

"Yes, and I don't know how he knew where to find me."

"What did he do?"

"He grabbed me by the shirt, said a few nasty words, then pushed me down, and as he walked away, he said I wasn't worth the damage it would do to his fists if he beat me up."

"Could he beat you up?"

"Oh, yes. He could take me out in, probably just seconds with his bare hands."

"Is there anything I can do to help you find him?"

"Are you serious? You don't even know me. Why would you help me?"

"I don't know. I just know I feel good about you. I think you've been kind of sidetracked, and inside you is a good person that could use some help to prove it."

Once again he had tears in his eyes as he looked at her.

"That's something a friend would do. Are you sure you want to trust me? You know what happened to the last person who did."

"I'm not worried about that. That's not you anymore."

"How can you say that? This is only the second time we've seen each other, and the first time you threatened to call the police on me."

"I know, but I had a lot on my mind Saturday. Today I've had time to sit and talk with you, and I'm usually a very good judge of a person's character. I have a feeling you'll put far more effort into being good to people, than you did to hurt them in the past."

"It's nice to be able look at someone and want to have them as a friend. Thank you."

"You're welcome. Well, I've got some things I have to do, so I'm going to have to go now."

166

"Ok. How will we meet again?"

"I can call you. Do you live around here?"

"Well, I don't have a phone, and I'm kind of in between places right now."

"Ok. I'll tell you what. How about we meet here one week from today, same time?"

"Alright. You're on, I'll see you then."

"Oh, by the way, breakfast will be on me. It's my turn."

"Gotcha."

As he sat watching her walk out the door, Cindy came over to clear the plates off the table.

"Is she the old acquaintance you had to look up?"

"No. she's a new acquaintance."

"Boy, when you decide to start making friends, you sure know how to pick em."

"What're you talking about?"

"Well, for starters, she's beautiful."

"Yeah, she is isn't she?"

"And, it's obvious by the way she looks at you, she really likes you."

"I don't think, so, I just met her last Saturday."

"Where did you meet her?"

"I was on my way to a place where my old friend and I used to get together when I...we...our paths crossed."

"What was it you were saying about the police?"

"Oh, we had a slight disagreement, and I told her if she didn't believe me, she could meet me here today and bring the police."

"I didn't see any cops, so, she must believe you."

"I think we worked out our differences."

"The way she looked at you, I'd have to agree. Did you find your friend?"

"No, the old place was all closed up."

"What're you going to do now?"

"I'm not sure, but I've got to find him, so I'll figure it out eventually. I won't quit till I do."

"I wish you luck."

"Thanks. I need all the luck I can get. Well, I'd better go. Apparently I'll see you next Tuesday morning."

"Sounds like it. Nice seeing you again, Larry, take care."

"You, too, Cindy."

CHAPTER FOUR

For the next several days Larry tried to figure out how to find Greg. He even went to the places he and Greg used to frequent when they ran around together. Not coming up with anything, he decided to go over to his parents late Saturday morning. Perhaps his dad might be able use some of his business connections to help locate him.

"Hi, Larry, it's good to see you, Son. Come on in. What's on your mind?"

"Well, I need a little help with something Dad."

"Sure, if I can help I will. Have you had lunch yet?"

"Not yet. Where's Mom?"

"Do you remember George Turner?"

"Yeah, he works in your shop."

"George died 4 months ago, and every Saturday, your mom picks up his wife, Linda, and they spend the afternoon together shopping or going to the movies, or whatever they want."

"George died? He wasn't really that old was he?"

"No. He was my age."

"What happened?"

"One day when he finished work, he walked out to his car, started it, and before he could put it in gear, he had a massive heart attack, and died."

"Wow. I'm sorry, Dad. Wasn't he the first one you hired?"

"He was, and he was also my best friend. I really miss him."

"I can only imagine."

"Come on back to the kitchen, we'll have something to eat, and talk about what I can help you with."

After a couple of lunchmeat sandwiches and sodas they settled back to talk.

"What can I do for you?"

"Dad, I can't figure out how to find Greg, and I don't feel like I can move on till I do. I've exhausted all possible leads I might've had. I even went to the house he lived in when were growing up. It's gone and a bank was built in its place, so I don't know where to go from here."

"Ok. Let's check on the computer and see what we come up with."

For the first time since he was a little boy, Larry and his dad worked on something together without it ending in a dispute.

At the end of a long and fruitless search, they finally decided to sit back and relax with a cup of coffee.

"Larry I don't want to cause any problems or get, too, nosey, but…"

"Dad, you can ask me anything you want. I won't go off on you or anybody anymore. I know it's going to take some time getting used to it, but I really am different. I don't know what it is or why, suddenly all that anger that was inside me is gone."

"I was just going to ask you what you're doing, what kind of work."

"I'm not doing anything right now."

"Where are you staying?"

"Well, I…um, I'm not sure exactly where I'm going to…"

"You're living on the streets aren't you?"

Larry sat there looking at the floor and responded, "Yeah."

"Why don't you come back home? You can stay as long as you want and no questions."

"I know I can, Dad. I can't explain it, but I've got some things to work out, and I need to be off by myself. I'm ok for now."

"I guess it probably sounds pretty strange coming from me, but I understand what you're saying, and I respect it."

"Please don't tell Mom. She'd be a nervous wreck over it."

"I won't tell her, but I won't lie if she asks."

"I know, Dad. I wouldn't expect you to."

"Look. I'm going make you an offer. I know for a fact it'll help me, and hopefully you, too. I want you to really think about it before you answer."

"What've you got in mind?"

"George kept the equipment in excellent working order, and since he died I've had to go back into the shop and stay there to keep it all running. Right now, I'm kind of neglecting my customers. I need to get out of the shop and back in touch with them so I can bring them up to date on the new landscape designs. They're getting very impatient."

"Are you saying what I think you are?"

"Son, you're the only one I know who could fill in for George."

"Wow. I don't know what to say."

"I'll still do everything I can to help you find Greg, and I'll pay you the same as I paid George."

"I sure could use the money, no doubt about that. When would you want me to start?"

"Well, I'm going to need time this week to set some appointments with my clients, so how about if you come in next Friday. I'll have keys for you and reacquaint you with the shop, because I've got some new machinery you'll need to familiarize yourself with. Then, you can officially start the following Monday. How does that sound to you?"

"That works fine for me."

"Also, on that key ring will be a key to the house. I'll say it just one more time, and I won't bring it up again. You're welcome to come back home any time."

"I know, Dad. Who knows, I may do it sometime. I'm just not ready right now."

"OK. One other thing; from time to time I may have to call you in on your time off, so will you let me get you a cell phone?"

"Sure."

"The company will pay for it, but you can use it for personal calls, too. This is Saturday and the phone store is still open at the mall, so let's go get one now."

"Ok."

***

That evening as he walked back toward his lean-to, he saw a sign on the front window of the local tavern stating that they were going to be closed the following day in order to serve a free home cooked, walk in Sunday dinner at 1:00 PM for the homeless and needy in the neighborhood, but they would reopen for regular business on Monday.

***

The next day at exactly 1:15 PM Larry walked through the front door of the tavern, and was greeted by a medium height, wiry middle aged man in blue jeans, a plaid shirt and a John Deere cap. The man smiled, stuck out his right hand, and said, "Welcome to Charley and Barb's Tavern. I don't believe I've ever seen you here before. I'm Charley, and I hope you've come to have dinner with us."

"Hi Charley, my name's Larry. The food sure smells good. How much is it?"

"No charge at all."

"I have some money. I can pay for it."

"If you come in here tomorrow you'll pay for what you get, today you can't."

Larry looked around at the tavern full of people and said, "You're in business to make money. How can you feed all these people and stay in business?"

"Barb and I didn't buy this place with the intention of getting rich. We want to be solid citizens in the neighborhood by helping all the people we can, and as long as we can take care of ourselves and pay our bills at the same time, we're happy, so on holidays and some other select Sundays like this one, this is what we do for the needy in our neighborhood."

"What do you do if someone who doesn't need it comes in and eats?"

"Well, if they can sleep with it so can I."

"You and Barb are some special people."

"Thanks. What about you, Larry? Are you new in the neighborhood?"

"No. I've been around here about a year. I'm pretty much a loner. I've just kind of kept to my self."

"Well, it's nice to meet you and as I said you are always welcome to join us. Since this is your first time here, I'll fill you in. Today the strongest drink you can get here is coffee or iced tea, and all the refills of it you want. You can go back for seconds on the food if you feel the need, but in fairness to the others please don't take anything out. Also when you're done please place your tray and utensils on the rack by the dishwasher."

"OK."

"Well, you'd better get a spot in line so you can find a seat."

Larry thanked Charley, and as he walked around talking with the other diners, it suddenly dawned on him how relaxed and comfortable he was. This was definitely a new sensation for him, since all his life he had felt sort of over shadowed, and threatened among such a large group of strangers.

After getting a tray of food he found one empty seat at a 2 person table, and upon sitting down, he introduced himself. "Hi, I'm Larry."

"Hi, my name's Bob."

Bob's about 6 ft. tall and slender built with straight brown hair. The look in his grey eyes give you the idea he is very serious and all business, and he looks to be about Larry's age.

"Are you from around here?"

"Yeah, but I've been away for a while. I just came back about a month ago."

"The reason I asked, was because you look familiar."

"So do you. In my mind it seems like some years back, but I just can't put my finger on where."

"I can't either, but, given enough time we'll probably think of it, because it seems like time is what we've got the most of."

"I think... that's one of the things I'm running out of."

Larry could tell by the look on his face that Bob regretted saying anything, but he still asked, "Why? What's going on?"

"Nothing. Forget what I said. I'm just down in the dumps. Let's enjoy this nice hot meal. OK?"

"Sure."

They ate quietly. After finishing, they placed their trays on the rack, and on their way out thanked Charley and Barb for their kindness.

As they were walking away from the tavern together, Bob finally broke the silence.

"I apologize. I didn't mean to shut down the conversation. I've just had some things going on that aren't very good."

"I'm sorry to hear that. Is it anything I can help you with?"

"I don't know what it would be."

"Would you be OK talking about it?"

"I might as well tell you, about it. I don't have anyone else to talk to."

They walked along and Bob began telling Larry about his illness, when suddenly Larry realized they were right around the corner from his lean-to.

"We're close to my camp, so why don't we go back and have some coffee while we talk."

"OK."

While they sat and talked through the remaining afternoon and well into the late evening, Larry was feeling quite comfortable with Bob.

"I sure wish I could remember where I know you from."

"Yeah, me too. I feel like I worked with you somewhere, but in the last twenty years I've had so many jobs that I couldn't begin to count them."

"Well, maybe we'll figure it out before long."

"Yeah, if I'm lucky."

"Have they given you any kind of timeline with your illness?"

"The last time I talked to the medical people, they said I'll be lucky if I get six months. That was about two months ago."

"So, did you come back to die at home?"

"Well, that and I've got to get something worked out before it's, too, late."

"What's that?"

"Nothing. Never mind, It's something I'd rather not talk about."

"Ok. I know where you're coming from. Say, I've got an extra bedroll. You can stay the night if you want."

"Thanks, but I have to go now, maybe some other time. Nice meeting you, Larry. See you around, maybe."

With that, Bob got up and walked out.

Larry sat there for several minutes totally stunned.

Finally saying, "What the hell just happened? Did I say something that pissed him off? I don't know what it could be. Oh well, nothing I can do about it now."

He finished his coffee, climbed into his bedroll and drifted of into a fitful nights' sleep.

***

When he walked into the coffee shop Tuesday morning, Larry was surprised to see Lori-Ann sitting at the counter.

"Good morning Lori. How are you?"

"I'm good, how about you?"

"Great."

Cindy came over and poured coffee for them.

"Good morning, you two. Are you both having the same breakfast you had last week?"

"We are."

"OK. I'll be back with it shortly."

"Have you had any success finding your friend?"

"No, but I found a job."

"I didn't know you were looking."

"I wasn't really, but it was offered, so I start Friday."

"What kind of work is it?"

"I'll be taking care of tools and machinery, for a landscaping business. How about you? Do you have job?"

"I work out of my home. I'm a freelance writer."

"Wow. No kidding. What do you write?"

"Journals for magazines."

"That's fascinating; I've never known a writer before. I'm honored to be in your presence. Oh, by the way, I got a cell phone. Here's the number."

"Good, I can call you then?"

"Only if I can call you."

"Of course you can, silly. Here's my number."

After breakfast they sat and talked for a while. Then, Lori asked, "Larry would you like to go for a walk with me?"

"I'd love to."

Lori paid the bill and they left

***

After they walked for a little while Lori reached over and put her hand in Larry's. Finally realizing what she had done, she apologized to him and started to pull her hand away. Gently squeezing her hand he told her he enjoyed walking together that way.

"What are you going to say to your friend when you find him?"

"I don't know. I just hope I can say what I need to, before he beats me to a pulp."

"Would you like me to be with you when you meet him?"

"I'd love for you to, but it's something I'll have to do by myself."

"Well, if you change your mind let me know and I'll be there."

"You really are something. You know that?"

"No I'm not. I just consider you a friend and that's what I would do for a friend."

"I don't understand it. I'm not anyone special. I'm homeless. I don't have anything to offer anyone, so why would you do that for me?"

"You've been honest about yourself right from the start, and I feel you not only need a good friend, you deserve one.

Plus, I certainly know I need a friend and I believe you'd be a good one for me."

"After the way you've treated me, how could I not be?"

"You just said you were homeless."

"Yeah, that's right."

"How did that happen?"

"Well, the whole story is a long one, but, to make it short; the woman I ran off with lied to me, and when we got to San Francisco this guy was waiting in the motel room. As we walked in he jumped me, knocked me out, and tied me up. Then they took all the money I embezzled, and after he beat me severely, they dumped me out in the desert in California, and left me for dead."

"Wow. How long were you there?"

"Three days."

"How did you survive?"

"After laying there for a while I was able to rub the ropes on some rocks and got them worn enough to break them. I wandered around for a couple of days and I guess I passed out, because the next thing I knew I woke up in a hospital. They said I'd been there, unconscious for four days."

"In high school our science class went on a three day survival study to a desert in Arizona. The first day we went six hours without any water, and it was unbelievable how dehydrated you can be in such a short time. You're lucky to be alive."

"I think the only thing that kept me going was the determination to find Delores and kill her. I spent several years in California looking, but couldn't find a trace of her there, so I decided to work my way back here, hoping she had come home as well. Now almost six years later here I am"

"Did you ever find her?"

"Thankfully, no. Because, if I had found her before I talked to Danny, I would've killed her, and basically my life would be over now."

"What would you do if you found her now?"

"Well, I still think it was really rotten the way they beat me and left me to die, but I don't have the right to be upset over the money because I have to face the fact that I deserved that one, so I wouldn't do anything to her."

"Are you sure you feel that way?"

Larry paused, looked very seriously at Lori, and said, "Oh yeah, I've become a firm believer in the fact that what we give in life is what we get back. I know since I've had this change in my life I feel better about the people I meet, and I get a better response from them. Take you for example. If we had met before this you would not have wanted me for a friend."

"In that case I'm glad I didn't know you before."

"Yeah, me, too, I don't think I would've been very much fun to be around."

"Well, I like being around you now."

"It seems we've just been talking about me. What about you? Are you from here?"

"Yes. I was born in Montana but we moved here when I was two years old, and I grew up here."

Where are your parents?"

"I never knew my mother, and Dad passed away when I was sixteen."

"That had to be kind of rough."

"It was. I loved my dad a lot, and I was at quite a loss with myself when Judy's grandparents took me in so I could finish high school. Dad and I didn't have much and when he died I had no place to go, because we rented the house we lived in, and I had no money or a way to get any."

"How did you get into writing?"

"It's something I always enjoyed doing, so after high school I got some grants and student loans in order to get a degree in writing."

They spent most of the day walking together and talking, finally it was late afternoon when Lori said she had to get back home. They agreed to talk over the phone and get together again sometime the following week.

CHAPTER FIVE

In the middle of the night, Larry was jarred awake with the feeling that someone was there. After laying there for a while, listening he didn't see or hear anything, so he finally drifted back off to sleep.

The next morning he woke up with the feeling, something was different. It took him a few moments to realize that his backpack and the carved box were gone. He was getting frantic as he looked everywhere in his lean-to, then searched all around the outside. They were nowhere to be found. He was getting upset. "Now, what the hell's going on? What if there were more things I was suppose to do with the box? The old man's business card is in the box, so I can't even contact him to tell him it's gone. Damn-it, if more people need the stars, I can't help them."

As he sat there he started to calm down, and said, "I don't know where the box is from, or how it came to me. Maybe it wasn't stolen. Maybe its' business with me is done. There were three stars left, so they could be for someone else and it's moved on to the next person who needs them."

***

The following Friday Larry went into his dad's shop and began his orientation for the new job. This shop was in a new building, and in a different area of town than the one his dad had when he was growing up. As Will, was showing him around, something caught his eye. "Dad, there're shower stalls in the restrooms."

"Yeah, and on the other side that door is a locker room. That way when the employees come in to clock out they can shower, and change clothes before they go home."

"Wow, this is great, I can take a shower and shave everyday after work. I'll be glad to go back to just having a mustache. I'll bet Lori won't even recognize me."

"Lori? You've never mentioned her. Who is Lori?"

"Oh, she's a friend. I met her the day I walked over to our old business looking for Greg."

"Just a friend, huh? Oh, I almost forgot. Your mother is packing lunch for you, and I've been given strict instructions to bring it to you everyday. Also you have an open invitation from her to please join us at least once a week for dinner."

Standing there grinning and shaking his head he just said, "Why am I not surprised. OK"

***

With his first paycheck he purchased two things; a used bicycle to make it easier to get back and forth to work, and a new backpack in order to carry toiletries and clothes for personal cleanup at work.

"I can't believe how easy it's been to slip back into work mode, and how good it feels to be doing something positive again."

Meeting Lori for the first time after he started working was interesting.

"It didn't work. I knew you immediately. Why did you shave?"

"This is the way I used to look when I was working before."

"I like it. You look great."

***

For the next few weeks he and Lori talked on the phone and met a few times at a little restaurant in her neighborhood. Finally, one day she said, "Why don't you come over to my house for dinner tomorrow night?"

"Are you sure you want a homeless bum in your house?"

"Just get your butt over here by 6:00 tomorrow evening."

"Uh, you're going to have to tell me where you live first."

"Oh, yeah."

She proceeded to give him directions on how to get there.

The following evening he was there at 6:00 right on the dot.

After the meal she gave him a tour of the house. It was a two story, with a large attic, that was remodeled and converted into a nice sized third floor, fully furnished apartment. The main house was laid out quite similar to the house he grew up in.

"This is a very nice house. Is this the one you said you inherited from your friend?"

"Well, she actually turned it over to me when she knew her illness was terminal, so I wouldn't have to pay any inheritance tax on it. While she was ill, I stayed here in one of the bedrooms on the second floor so I could take care of her till she passed."

"This is the one you said you went deep in debt with, in order to try to save her, right?"

"Yes. I just couldn't believe money wouldn't make her well. So I had to do what I could, and I'd do it over again. It's also the home her grandparents owned and let me live in after my Dad died. The apartment I showed you on the top floor is where I stayed till I graduated high school, and moved into the college dorm."

"So, Judy told you where there was enough money in here to bring the mortgage up to date."

"Yeah, it's ok now. Oh, by the way, are you still homeless?"

"Yes."

"I'll be happy to rent you the apartment. It has its' own entrance on the other side of the house, so you can come and go as you wish without bothering me, and I won't charge you very much."

"I appreciate your offer, I really do, but for some reason I feel I have to find my old friend and take my lumps, or work things out with him before I can get my life out of this quagmire and move on. I know we can never be buddies again but I have to get this cleared up between us.

I hope you realize it's nothing against you. I enjoy having you as my friend, and I hope we will always be friends.

I know I'm not good at expressing myself, so I hope you understand what I'm trying to say."

"I do. I just hate the fact that you're living outside and fighting the elements, but I understand what you're saying and I give you a lot of respect for feeling that way."

"I also want to stay where I was the last time I saw him, because he knows where to find me, and I don't even begin to know where to look for him. Speaking of being there, I'd better get going. Somebody in this friendship has to have a real job, and I guess it has to be me."

She grinned at him, slugged him on the arm and said, "You'd better believe it, cause its not going to be me."

Riding back to his lean-to he thought about the positives in his life since the box showed up that Friday. *I've met Lori, Cindy, Bob, Charley and Barb, and best of all; I'm on real solid ground with my parents. If I can just get things worked out with Greg, it'll round out my life.*

That was the first time he had given any thought to the carved box and the stars since they came up missing.

***

"How was supper, Larry?"

"Wonderful, as always, Mom."

"It sure is nice to have you with us like this. You'll never know how much I've prayed for it."

"Mom, Dad, you've never asked and I've never told what I did to hurt Greg."

"And, you don't have to tell us now. It won't make any difference how we feel about you."

"I know it won't, Dad, but the shame I feel is so overwhelming to me, that if I tell you, what I did, maybe you'll understand why the most important thing in my life now is making it right. Even if I have to go to prison."

"Prison sounds pretty harsh, but go ahead."

"We had some new products to develop, but we needed more money. So we decided to look for some investors. We were very busy in the shop, so Greg left it up to me to find them. Well, to make a long story short, I convinced the investors to set the checks up so they were available to me, then I embezzled that and all the money I could get out of our business accounts and ran off with our secretary's daughter."

"Did she know where the money to run off, came from?"

"Of course she did. As a matter of fact she encouraged it. She was smart. She recognized my pent up anger and fed it, knowing she could use it to her advantage."

"Greg was your best friend. Do you think he'd file charges against you?"

"I don't know. If he did I couldn't blame him, besides it may not be up to him."

"Hmm…I hadn't thought of that. What happened to the girl?"

"Well, that's a story for another time."

"Is that why the business is closed?"

"I don't know for sure, but I have a feeling he was so far in debt that he couldn't survive it."

"Hell, no wonder he was so upset. And, I can understand why you feel your life is at a stand still, until you get this behind you."

"You do know I'd never do that again don't you?"

"Oh, sure. Most of your life, it was obvious you were very angry, and you pissed a lot of people off, but till that time, you never took anything that wasn't yours."

Will and Jeanie looked at each other and when she nodded, Will said, "Son, we have some extra money, if it'll help you."

"So many times in the past, the both of you have jumped in and tried to help me, and I brushed it off. I'm not doing that this time. I really, appreciate it, Dad, but this time I have to follow this through from beginning to end on my own."

"Ok, just let us know if you need us."

"I will. I'd better get going. I don't like to ride at night if I don't have to."

"You know you can use the work van if you need to."

"I know, sometimes I will. Ok, I'll see you next week, Mom. I love you both. Goodnight."

"We love you, too."

***

As summer approached, Larry found himself getting so busy at work, some weeks he had to work six days, which was a good thing for him, because even though he was still determined to find Greg it helped to take away some of the desperate need to do it immediately.

***

Sunday morning, Larry woke up to see someone sitting on the other side of his lean-to. He wasn't expecting anyone so it startled him.

"Who are you? What do you want? If you're looking for money or valuables you've struck out here."

The person sitting there responded, "Don't you recognize me?"

Larry, looked long and hard, and finally said, "Is that you Bob?"

Hanging his head and looking at the ground, Bob let a long sigh and said, "Yeah...and I need to talk to you."

"Would you like something to eat and some coffee?"

"I'll have some coffee. I can't eat anything."

Larry fired up his propane stove and got the coffee pot going. They sat in silence while they waited for the coffee to brew. When it was ready, he poured a mug full and handed it to Bob. Reaching for it, Larry, noticed that not only was Bob's hand shaking, his whole body was.

"Bob, you look like hell. Are you getting that sick? Is there something I can help you with?"

"No. I'm not sick right now. Don't make this worse by being nice to me. I feel bad enough about it as it is, and, I don't usually feel bad about anything."

"What in the world are you talking about?"

"I'm the one who stole your backpack and that thing in it."

"You took it? Why?"

"I was desperate, and I figured I could make a lot of money on it.

184

"Why would you think you could make money on my backpack?"

"I knew what you had in it, was really valuable."

"Where did you get an idea like that?"

"I don't know why I'm telling you all this… I guess it's because, I'm at the end of my rope and I don't know what else to do. You know, I even tried to bring it back and leave it here when you were gone but by the time I got back to my camp it was there waiting for me."

"I'm still totally in dark. What the hell's going on and what, are you talking about?"

"Look…here I go again. I'm not a nice person. Usually, when I've seen something I wanted I just took it. I didn't care who was affected by it. After I took your backpack though, it didn't take me long to realize this was going to be different."

"Just what was it that made you think my backpack had any value to it?"

"The day you met a pretty girl named Lori-Ann Mills, I saw and heard what happened."

"How did you do that?"

"Well, you probably didn't notice it, but there is a lot of overgrowth behind that bus stop where you met her."

"You're right, I didn't really see it. So?"

"My lean-to is in that overgrowth and I've got it trimmed so I can see out at anybody around the area before they can see me. That way, if I have to, I can make a quick exit in at least two other directions."

"I still don't know what you think you saw or heard."

"I was back there laying down on my bedroll that Saturday afternoon when I heard some people talking at the bus stop. Just as I looked out the girl (named Lori-Ann) told you she heard you call her name. You said you didn't know her name. Then she said the voice was coming from your backpack, and asked you if you heard it. You said no."

Then she asked you to open your backpack."

When you told her there was nothing in there to help her, she told you there was, and asked you to please open it."

"How can you be so sure that's what went on?"

"From where I was, I could see and hear everything clearly. And, I have an excellent memory."

"Ok, go ahead."

"You took your backpack off, sat down on the bench and pulled a very expensive looking, carved box out of it, and set it on your lap. She opened the box, and when she sat down, she reached into it and took out a glowing thing that looked like a little star. How am I doing up to this point?"

"You're right on, so far."

"Now, this is where it gets real dicey."

Bob picked up the backpack, and upon opening it asked, "What do you see in there?"

"A block of wood, why?"

Pulling the piece of wood out and setting it down, he asked, "How did it get there?"

"I can only tell you I didn't put it there."

"Who did?"

"You can do what ever you want, but the answer's still the same. I don't know."

"We both agree that's not what was in there that day with Lori-Ann, right?"

"That's right."

Larry noticed, the more Bob talked, the calmer he became, even though he was on his third mug of coffee.

"OK let's get back to that day. As she held the star in her hand, a voice came from it and said she was Lori-Ann's best friend who had died. After an exchange of words between you and the girl, she accused you of trying to con her out of money and she said she didn't have any. So you got pissed, stuffed the box, into your back pack and left. As you walked off you said something to her about calling the police, but I couldn't get the rest of it, because you were to far from me by then."

"Why did you think it would be valuable?"

"I figured it was a con, and I had never seen one that good, so I wanted it."

"Did you hear what the conversation with her dead friend was about?"

"No. I stayed and heard a little bit about a house, and her mom, and grandparents, then it dawned on me, you had the major key to the whole thing and I needed to follow you. My plan was to catch up with you, beat the hell out of you and take it from you, because if this was a con, I knew I could make hundreds of thousands of dollars, and, if by some very slim chance it was real, I could make millions."

"There was quite a time span between the day I met Lori and when my backpack came up missing. What took you so long?"

"When I finally headed in your direction, you had gone around a corner and by the time I got there you were out of sight. So I turned and doubled back to the bus stop. When I got there she was gone, too. I didn't know where to look for either one of you at that point, so I was sure I blew it, and just gave up."

"What changed it?"

"I was sitting in Charley and Barb's eating, and I couldn't believe my eyes when you came over and sat down in front of me. Before that happened I had no idea you were a streeter like me."

"Ok. Now it's starting to make some sense, but you haven't explained why you're telling on yourself like this."

"Look, this whole business is about to put me in a rubber room."

"I must be missing something, because I just don't get it."

"When I stole your backpack I took it to my lean-to and opened it. The box wasn't in it. Instead it was a solid piece of wood. I thought you'd taken the box out and put the wood in it, so I went back to your camp the next day and searched for the box. I couldn't find it anywhere, and I was really getting frustrated. I didn't know that was just the beginning of my frustrations and problems."

Bob, who was somewhat quiet and withdrawn the first time they met, seemed to be on a roll today, and there wasn't any stopping him.

Having a pretty good idea of at least one of his problems, he had a hard time hiding a grin when he asked, "What kind of problems, are you having, Bob?"

"Things started getting weird that night after I came back and searched your place. Sometime in the middle of the night I woke up hearing my name being called. At first I thought someone had found my camp, but I flicked on my flashlight and...nothing. Thinking I must have imagined it, I laid, back down and went back to sleep. A little while later it happened again. Once again, nobody was there. This went on several more times that night. The next night it happened again at least a half dozen more times. By this time I'm thinking someone's pulling something on me, or I'm losing my mind. The third night, I laid there for a long time pretending to be asleep and it didn't happen...until I finally drifted off, then it happened again, and kept happening."

"How in the devil were you getting any sleep?"

"That's just it...I wasn't getting any at night and only little bits during the day. For a while I thought maybe it was you, paying me back for taking your stuff."

"What would make you think that? I've never been to your camp. I didn't even know where it was till you told me just now."

"Well, I've since realized you aren't doing it."

"Then, who is?"

"This is the kind of scary part. One night while I was still thinking it was you, I decided to put the block of wood in the backpack and sleep with it in my bedroll. That night I discovered the voice that woke me up was coming from inside the backpack, so I opened it and the voice was coming from the block of wood."

Larry, was finding it difficult not to laugh openly at that, "That doesn't make sense. How can a piece of wood talk?"

"That's what I thought, so the next day I went out and stole a magnifying glass, and I sat all day studying that piece of wood. I couldn't find a flaw or a crack or opening in it anywhere. Then, to make matters worse, the voice started calling me during the day. Now I can't even get any sleep day or night."

"I guess my real question is. Why are you here. What do you think I can do?"

"Being the type of person I am, my first impulse was to come back and work you over till you told me how to make this thing work, but on the way over here I kept having the feeling, that doing that wasn't going to help me. Plus, if I ended up killing you I could be stuck with this for the rest of my life"

"I'm glad you decided not to do that. But, why do you feel you'd be stuck for life? And, aren't you running out of life anyway?"

"I'm not sick; that was just BS. We'll talk about it some other time."

"I'm all ears, I can't wait for that, but let's get back to why you think you'll be stuck with it"

"After about a week of listening to that thing calling my name I took it to the nearest trashcan, backpack and all, and threw it away."

"And?"

"In the middle of the night I woke up hearing my name being called. When I turned on my flashlight, there it was. Next day, I carried it down to the river, took the piece of wood out and threw it in. I stood and watched as it floated toward the bay till it was out of sight."

"I'm betting I don't have to ask what happened then."

"Same old story again. So, next I put it in a dumpster and stood watching while the trash truck driver emptied the dumpster and compacted all the trash. Guess what? That night, it's back."

"Finally I built a fire and threw the piece of wood in it. It wouldn't burn."

"So, now what?"

"I'm here to see if I can give it back to you and hope this will all go away. If it doesn't I don't know what to do.

"OK let's try it."

Bob put the piece of wood in the backpack, zipped it up and handed it to Larry. They sat silently as they drank their coffee. When they finished Bob got up, apologized to Larry and as he started to turn away, he stopped and said, "Son of a...it won't quit."

"What are you talking about?"

Bob stood in obvious anger with his fists tightly clenched.

"I don't know how you're doing this, but if you don't stop it right now I'm going to tear you apart."

Standing up so he could run if he had to Larry responded, "I'm not doing anything, and I damned sure don't know what you are talking about."

"Don't stand there and tell me you can't hear that."

Larry's thinking, *He's going to kill me and I don't even know why. Wait a minute.*

Reaching down and picking up the backpack, Larry said, "Stop just a second." He then unzipped it and pulled out the...box.

"Are trying to say you can't hear that, Larry?"

"I do now, but who is she calling?"

"That's right it is a woman's voice isn't it. She's calling me."

"Martin Timmers? I thought your name was Bob."

"Robert's my middle name, and I've always gone by Bob. Open the box."

"The call's for you. I think you have to open it."

As Larry, held the box, Bob opened it. One of the stars inside was glowing rhythmically and changing colors. Bob and Larry looked at each other and when Larry nodded Bob reached in, took it in his hand and held it in front of him with his hand open.

A very serene and calming voice coming from the star said, "Robby, it's wonderful to talk to you again. I've wanted to so many times."

"This is not possible. You can't be Mary."

"There are things between us that were left unsaid. Now we have the chance to correct that."

"This can't be happening. Larry, what are you trying to pull?"

"Tell me what I could gain by pulling something, Bob. Do you have some hidden properties, or bank accounts, or investments in foreign countries?"

"No."

"You're a big man and could beat me to a pulp, so I'm not stupid enough to try pull a sick joke on you, it doesn't make sense that I would do anything against you.

Now, even though this is my place, I'm going to take my box and leave for a while. That way, you and the person you're talking to on the other side, can have some privacy. If you want to talk about any of it later, Bob, you'll probably be able to find me right here."

Larry put the box in his backpack, zipped it up, and walked out carrying it over his right shoulder.

"Ok. Who is this, and what are you up to?"

"Just like your friend said, what would be the point of trying to put something over on you? Other than the ring that was your grandfather's, and that note from your mom, you have nothing anyone could get from you. And, you don't have to ask who I am, you already know."

"You sound like Mary, and you know two things about me she knew, but Mary died almost seven years ago, so, talking to her is impossible."

"I always felt that way, too, till I passed over to this side."

"If this is all real, and you know I don't have anything that you can get from me, why are you here? Why is this happening?

"I'm with you a lot, Robby, and I've seen how you've become a different person than the one I knew when I was on that side. You used to care for people and you wanted to help them. Now all you do is take from them and you don't care how much you hurt them. You don't seem to do anything just for the fun of it, and deep down inside, that's not the real you."

Bob was starting to get angry and he responded with, "I don't have friends. I don't have anything, so tell me what there is to have fun about."

"The man who had the box with the stars would be your friend if you'd let him. The time the two of you met he wanted to help you then, and you lied to him and wouldn't let him."

He was on the edge of real fury at that point.

"I don't believe you. None of this is real. You're nothing but a con artist."

The voice in the star responded very calmly, "I'm sure you remember the scar on the right cheek of your butt. You know, the one you wouldn't tell me how you got it."

"What about it?"

"Who was the only one who knew how you got it?"

"My mom."

"Your mom passed before we met, and I've never met her, right?"

"Yeah, so what's your point?"

"You snagged it on the barbed wire fence when you tried to jump it getting away from the calf that was chasing you. You asked your mom not to tell, because you didn't want anyone to know you were afraid of a calf."

"If you know so much why, don't you know why I hate people?"

"I can't read your mind, Robby, so that's why I'm talking to you now."

Tears of rage streamed down Bob's cheeks as he screamed, "I hate people, because every time I love them, they tell me they love me, then, they give up and leave me."

"Please calm down and explain what you mean. I don't understand what you're saying."

"When I was a fifteen my mom got sick. She was sick for a long time, and I tried to do whatever I could to help her and make her feel better. Nothing worked."

"What did she pass from?"

"You never saw the note she left me did you?"

"No. You wouldn't even tell me what was in it."

"She told me she loved me more than anything, but she couldn't take the weakness and the pain any longer, so she was giving up. Then, she took an overdose of her pain pills, and died peacefully in her sleep. I understood why she did it, but I've missed her so terribly since then."

"I'm so sorry that happened to you at such a young age."

"When you and I met it was wonderful. It was all I had hoped for in my life. We seemed to make a perfect blend. Almost from the beginning, you always told me I was the most important person in your life."

"Ohhh, you always will be the most important part of me. And, yes we were the perfect blend."

"But, then you got sick and stayed sick for a long time just like my mom. Finally the doctors said it looked like you were going to get well, but I guess by that time you'd had enough, and just gave up and died. The two people I loved the most in my life left me alone. If my mother loved me so much how could she give up and leave me? If you loved me so much how could you leave me, too?"

"Oh, my gosh, Robby! I didn't leave you! I was murdered!"

"What? How?"

"Someone I didn't recognize came into my hospital room, I couldn't see his face but he was dressed like a doctor. He studied my chart, then stuck a hypodermic needle in my intravenous tube and shoved the plunger down. Almost immediately I started gasping for my breath, and before he got out of the room I knew I was dying. I don't know who it was, or why he did it."

Openly sobbing, Bob stopped long enough to say, "I don't know why he did it either, but I know who he was."

"How do you know?"

"I was heading to your room that night, and when I got about twenty feet from the door, it opened, and the male nurse we liked so well, from the cardiac floor, came out of your room. I didn't think about it till just now, but I remember, he was acting kind of nervous, and I don't think he knew that I saw him coming out of your room. When he finally saw me, he said he stopped in to see you and you were having a hard, time breathing so he was going after a crash cart. I ran into your room and you weren't breathing, so I went to get a doctor. By that time it was, too, late. Afterward, the doctors said you had been out of the woods, and if you could've held on overnight, you would have made it, but you must have been, too, weak. That's why I thought you gave up just like my mom."

"I never would have given up, Robby. I love you, too, much. Unfortunately I didn't have a choice."

"All this time I blamed you for leaving me. Can you ever forgive me?"

"Of course I forgive you, Robby, I love you, and I always will. I take it you now believe I'm not a con artist, and I'm really Mary?"

"Oh sure. I know it's you, Mary. I'm just trying to figure out how this is possible."

"I don't know any more than you do how it works. I was just made aware that I could talk to you. I'm just so glad it happened. As often as I'm here with you, I still miss us talking like we used to."

Bob sat, staring at the star in his hand and sadly said, "You aren't going to be able to stay and talk with me are you?"

"Once the concerns we've had to talk about are taken care of, this will probably be the last time we'll speak until you pass to this side, and when you do, your mother and I will be here to meet you."

"I really miss you Mary, and tell my mom I'm sorry for being upset with her."

"She knows, and I miss you, too, just remember; anytime you think about me it's, because I'm near you."

"It's really interesting; how I feel now. It seems like all the anger and irritation is gone."

"That's great, because you have a lot wonderful things ahead of you, Robby. Embrace them, and enjoy them."

"Things like what?"

"I don't really have details; I can only see brightness and laughter, and warmth surrounding you."

"Well, one thing I feel I need to do is to find the man who killed you."

"Don't do anything rash. It isn't worth it."

"I won't. I'm not looking for trouble. No matter how sick or twisted his thinking is, he had to have some reason in his mind for killing you. Maybe you weren't the first or the last."

"I hadn't thought of it that way."

"It's obvious I can't go to the police and tell them that you came back from the other side and told me he killed you, so I've got to see if I can find him and hopefully figure out how to put some things together."

"Just be careful, Robby, I love you."

"I love you, too, Mary, and I'm sorry I doubted you."

"It's ok. Don't worry about it. You have to let me go now. I'll see you when you get here."

Bob held his hand out and watched as the star slowly lost its' bright glow and the color began to fade. When the light finally went out, the star became snow white, and floated off into the sky till it vanished.

He sat for a long time and stared after the star, then stood up straight, and with a calm easy smile on his face, walked away.

CHAPTER SIX

That evening When Larry got back from Lori's place, there was no sign of Bob.

Settling into his bedroll he wondered if he would ever see him again, and if he did would Bob tell him what happened?

The following morning as he was sipping coffee and waiting for time to go to work, he pulled the carved box out of his backpack, opened it, and looked inside, "Three stars gone, and two left, along with the gentleman's business card. "So far, the box and stars have been life changing for Lori and me, and, from what little I saw, Bob as well. This has been really interesting so far, and I can't begin to imagine what's yet to come."

***

When summer went into full swing, Larry found himself working a minimum of six days a week, and some weeks seven. At that he was just barely able to keep up. One Saturday, Will, stopped in the shop before going home. "Larry, you're getting swamped in here, and I don't think you're going to be able to do all this."

"I don't know what else to do, Dad. I'm working as much as I can."

"I think we need a change."

Larry's heart dropped as he responded, "Like what?"

"We just took on three new major accounts, and it looks like two more are going to sign on soon, so this is only the beginning. You need to hire someone to help you in the shop."

"Why do you want me to hire someone? You're the owner, shouldn't you do that?"

"Son, since you've been here I haven't had to give one moment of concern about this shop, and that's why I was able to pick up those new clients. As far as I'm concerned the shop is yours. You know what you're doing and what it takes to make it run like a fine watch."

"Thanks for the confidence. When do you want me to do it?"

"As soon as you can. If you know someone you can depend on, get them in here. Like I said, you're running the shop, you hire the people you need."

"Ok, Dad. I do have a guy in mind, his name is Bob. It's almost noon and I'm getting ready to leave, so I'll take the van and see if I can find him, and thanks again."

***

Larry got in the shop van, and as he started to pull out of the lot it dawned on him, he wasn't sure of the exact location of the bus stop where he met Lori, so he stopped and called her.

"Hi Lori, am I interrupting anything?"

"Fortunately, yes. What's on your mind?"

"I need to go to the bus stop where you and I met, and I'm not sure I can find it. Can you tell me how to get there?"

"Sure. I'll never forget that place; it was a life changing day for me. Why do you have to go there?"

"I need to hire someone to help me in the shop, and the guy I'm looking for lives there."

"That's a pretty long ride on a bike."

"I've got the shop van today."

"Would you like for me to ride along and show you where it is?"

"I don't want to pull you away from anything you're into."

"I've got to get away for a while. I'd love to go with you."

"Alright, I'm on my way; I'll be there in a few minutes."

When Larry pulled up, Lori was standing at the curb waiting.

"Wow, you must really need to get out of the house."

"Sometimes I pour myself so deeply into my writing that I lose track of everything else, so when the phone rang it jerked me back to reality and made me realize I'd been at my laptop almost 12 hours nonstop. It was time to take a break."

"You mean, you've been writing all night?"

"Sometimes if I can't sleep I'll sit up and write till I get tired. This time I didn't get tired."

"Well, it's nice to know I'm able to create a diversion for you."

"Well, just don't think you can make a habit of it, or I'll have to slap you around."

"You wouldn't do that, because you're afraid I'll like it and you'd have to do it all the time."

"Yeah, I can see that happening. Ok, now, getting back to the subject at hand. As I remember it, the area we're going to is all businesses. Does he live in an apartment above one of them?"

"He lives on the street, and I'm hoping he'll want a job."

"He's someone you know from the streets?"

"Yeah. But, there's more to it than that."

He proceeded to tell her how he met Bob, and what prompted him to steal the backpack with the box in it.

"Let me see if I understand this correctly. He watched us at the bus stop then stole something from you and you're going to offer him a job?"

"That's not the end of it."

"You mean this gets better?"

Larry continued to fill her in on the rest of the details about him bringing the block of wood back, and how it became the carved box and then someone named Mary, called Bob through one of the stars.

"Then he's like us; he knows it's not just a block of wood?"

"Yes."

"Who's Mary, and what did she want?"

"I don't know. I didn't stay around to listen. I figured it wasn't any of my business, and if he wanted me to know, he'd come back and tell me."

"You know; this might be real interesting if we find him, since the three of us are the only ones who have seen it as a box."

When they got to the bus stop all the overgrown brush was cleared away, and it was a vacant lot with a for sale sign on it.

"Now what're you going to do?"

"I don't know. Hmm...I wonder if Charley would know where he is."

"Do you want to go there now?"

"Sure, I might as well; you can ride along if you want."

"Of course I do. This is getting better all the time. I wouldn't miss it for the world."

***

"I don't know where he is Larry. I didn't see him at the last dinner. Why do you want to know?"

"I want to see if he'd be interested in a job."

"Give me a number where you can be reached, and I'll give it to him if I see him."

"Ok. Here it is."

"Aren't you going to introduce me to your girl friend?"

"I'm sorry Charley. Of course I will. Charley, this is Lori-Ann Mills. Lori, this is Charley. He and his wife Barb are the great people I've been telling you about."

"I've heard a lot about you Charley. It's a pleasure to finally meet you."

"It's my pleasure as well, Lori."

"I'm going to give you my number, too. I work out of my home, so I can come in and help with your dinners if you need it."

"Thanks, from time to time my regular volunteers aren't able to make it so if I call it could be on short notice."

"That's fine with me. If you call, I'll get here as soon as possible."

"The same goes with me, Charley."

"Thanks Larry. Someday I'll hold the both of you to that."

"Just let us know, Charley. We'll see you later."

Climbing into the van, Lori said, "Ok, Mr. Detective, what now?"

"Well, why don't you let me buy you lunch, and we'll talk about it?"

"OK. Do you have someplace in mind?"

"I was thinking about the little coffee shop where we met for breakfast the first time. Is that alright with you?"

"I'm good with that. Did you know that I'm now your girl friend? I was surprised when you didn't correct Charley."

"Well, you really look like a girl; a very pretty one at that and you are my friend, so what could I say?"

"You're a smart aleck, but you're kinda cute, too, so I guess I can live with that."

***

"Hi, you two, how can I help you?"

"I'd like an unsweetened iced tea, and a beef and cheese wrap."

"How about you sir?"

"That sounds good. I'll have the same."

"Here're your iced teas. The wraps will be ready in a couple of minutes.

"Ok. Thank you."

"I don't believe I've ever seen you two in here before. Are you new around here?"

"We're not from this side of town, but we came in a few times when Cindy was here."

"That must have been when I was on vacation last spring."

"As a matter of fact it was. Are you the owner?"

"Yes. I'm Mindy. Who are you?"

"This is Lori-Ann and I'm Larry"

"It's a pleasure meeting both of you."

"Thank you, and nice meeting you, too."

The shop was getting pretty busy, so they took their drinks and food to one of the tall tables by the window and had a leisurely lunch. By the time they had donuts for dessert, and were ready pay and leave, the shop had cleared out.

As Larry paid, Lori said to Mindy "We've walked around the neighborhood before, but I was wondering if there's a nice city park close by where we can go to walk off this good lunch?"

"Yes there is", Mindy told her about the park she and her fiancé go to often.

"Thanks Mindy, we'll stop back in again sometime."

***

They spent the afternoon strolling around the lake in the center of the park, and finally as the sun was getting low in the sky they got in the van to head for Lori's house. Just as he was about to pull away he had to slam on the breaks in order to avoid hitting a teenage girl on a bicycle.

"I'm sorry mister. I didn't mean to ride in front of you. I wasn't paying attention to what I was doing."

"It's ok young lady, but please try to be more careful in the future."

"I try mister, but my mom says I'm kind of accident prone, so she teases me and calls me AP."

"Does that upset you?"

"No. I think it's funny. I know she's just kidding me."

"What is your name?"

"It's Carla."

"Nice meeting you Carla. This is my friend Lori-Ann, and I'm Larry. Maybe we'll see you when we come back to the park."

"I'm glad to meet both of you, and the next time I'll try to look out for you."

Laughing, Larry put the van in gear and headed for Lori's.

***

"Why don't you come on in and have supper with me?"

"OK. What're we having?"

"Yesterday I made some chicken noodle soup, and we'll have that and ham sandwiches."

"Sounds good."

After eating, they sat and talked while working on a jig saw puzzle she had started a month earlier.

"We haven't talked much about this before, but how do you like being back in the working groove?"

"It feels good. Although we're so busy, sometimes I get so tired I don't think I'll be able put one foot in front of the other."

"Will that help if you can hire someone?"

"Oh yeah, it'll give me chance to catch up on paper work."

"What makes you think you can trust Bob to give you an honest day's work, and not screw you over?"

"Well, do you remember what you told me when I asked you why you trusted me though you didn't know anything about me?"

"Yeah, I do. Even after you told me what you did, I knew deep down you were a good person."

"That's the way I feel about him."

"You certainly don't sound like a guy who spent most of his life with a chip on his shoulder."

"Sometimes I'm still surprised that I don't have that nasty attitude anymore."

"Were you really that angry?"

"It seems like everything I did for 23 years was motivated by it. Greg seemed to be the only one who could keep me at least partially, grounded."

When they finished the puzzle he sat back, and glanced up at the clock on the wall. "Holy cow! It's after midnight already, I'd better get going."

"Why don't you just stay here? I've got extra tooth brushes, and the bed in the spare room is made and ready, and the adjoining bathroom has towels and wash cloths for you to take a shower."

"What will your neighbors think?"

"I don't remember caring what my neighbors think about anything."

"I am tired, so I think I'll take you up on that."

The following morning Larry woke up to the smell of coffee brewing and bacon and eggs frying.

Lori looked up as he walked into the kitchen and said, "You're just in time, breakfast is about to be served."

"This is nice, I could get used to it real quick."

"Don't expect this to become a habit. You are a guest now. If you live here, you're on your own."

"Are you planning on us living together?"

"You know what I mean; if you move into the apartment upstairs."

"OK. I just wanted to be sure what you were saying."

"You knew exactly what I meant."

"Of course. I just thought I'd jerk your chain."

"One of these days I'm going to pop yours."

Finishing breakfast, Larry thanked her, and said his goodbyes.

***

On the way to taking the van back to the shop Larry decided to stop by his camp. As he stepped into his lean-to, he was surprised to see someone sitting there. It was Bob.

"What are you doing here?"

"As it turns out, right now, I don't have anywhere else to go, because when I got back in town my camp was gone. If you're not, too, pissed at me, I'd like to take you up on that offer to use your extra bedroll."

"Sure, you can use it for as long as you need to. Speaking of your camp, I went by there yesterday and that whole area was cleared, and had a for sale sign on it."

"That's on the other side of town. What were you doing over there?"

"Looking for you. I'd like to offer you a job, if you're interested."

"What kind of a job?"

"I need a helper in a small machine shop."

"Wait a minute. You live on the streets, and run a machine shop?"

"My dad owns a landscaping business and I run the shop for him. It's gotten to the place where I'm swamped and he told me to hire the help I need."

"There are a lot of things that don't add up about you."

"I don't think you have any room talk. What about that terminal illness you told me you had?"

"Yeah, you got me there. That was just a con to make people feel sorry for me. Most of the time it worked."

"You had me convinced, but I've spent enough time out here to know that sometimes we have to do things we wouldn't normally do just to survive. Getting back to my first question, are you interested in a job?"

"I could definitely use the money. What would I have to do?"

"We have to keep the machinery in good running order and all the tools ready and sharp."

"I've done a lot of work on small engines, so I think I can handle it."

"Ok. Can you start tomorrow?"

"Sure, but where is it, and how do I get there?"

"You can stay here tonight if you want, and ride in with me."

"After what I did to you, why would you offer me a job?"

"Look, I used to think I was a real mean bad-ass and some thing came along and changed my attitude. I don't know why, but I have the feeling if you get the right break it'll help change your attitude, too."

"My attitude has already changed since the last time I was here."

"Well, if you're interested in the job, why don't you ride over to the shop with me, so I can show you around and fill you in on what you'll have to do. Then you can decide for sure if you want it."

"OK. When do you want to go?"

"We can go now."

For the first few minutes in the van, they were both quiet. Suddenly Bob said, "There has to be more to this than what you're telling me."

"I don't understand. There has to be more to what?"

"Well, for one thing, what's the deal with the box that turned into a block of wood and back into a box again, and where did you get it? Also, I'm still not sure I believe your explanation about why you trust me after what I did to you."

204

"If you'll tell me about your experience with the star after I left, I think I can clear some of this up for you, and hopefully put your mind at ease."

"I don't know if I can. That was a pretty personal thing."

"Sure it was, and I'm willing to bet it was life changer, too, or you wouldn't have been able to talk to someone through the star."

"You're going to laugh and think I'm crazy."

"No I won't, I need for you to trust me on this."

Bob proceeded to tell him about how his mother had died, and, how he thought his fiancé did the same thing when she died, and what it had done to him emotionally. Then after he talked to his fiancé through the star, and found out she had been murdered, it started changing his outlook on everything.

"As it turned out I knew the guy who murdered her, so I went to the library and used the computer to track him down."

"Wow. How did you do that?"

"He was a male nurse who specialized in working with people who were going through life threatening illnesses, so it was pretty easy to find him, by going through the employee lists of hospitals. You aren't supposed to be able to do that, but if you know your way around a computer, it can be done."

"So, did you find out why he killed your fiancé?"

"Yeah, by the time I caught up with him, he had been arrested for killing patients in other hospitals. When I told the police about Mary dying in the hospital here, they questioned him about it and he confessed to killing her, too. He said he watched the patients who had been sick a long time, and if they looked like they had already suffered, too, much, he did it to put them out of their misery."

"Did you want to beat him to a pulp?"

"I thought I did, but when I saw him I kept remembering my conversation with Mary that day, and all I could feel for him was pity."

"Man, what a thing to learn."

"Now, do you see what I mean about it being crazy? I have to admit to myself that sometimes I think I just imagined it all, and yet my life is different now."

"You aren't crazy, Bob, and now maybe I can explain why.

I not only don't know where the box came from, I don't know why I have it. I woke up one morning and it was setting right there beside my bedroll. Little did I know it that morning, but that was destined to be a day that changed my life forever, and here's why."

Larry told him about his brother dying, and how he spent the next 23 years being a real ass because he blamed himself for his brother's death, until he talked to him through one of the stars.

"Why is it happening to us?"

"It's a question I've been asking since that Friday last April, when it first happened to me, and I still don't have an answer."

"How many stars did it have in it when you got it?"

"Five."

"After I took mine there were only two left. If you got one and I got one, then the third one is the one that Lori-Ann got, right?"

"Yes."

"What was her story in this?"

"I don't think it would be right for me to tell you. If you'd like, I'll introduce the two of you, and you can ask her. Then, if she wants you to know, she'll tell you. If she doesn't, she won't hesitate to say so."

"OK. Do you know who's going to get the other two?"

"I have absolutely no idea, who, where, or when."

"Do you know what's going to happen when the stars are all gone?"

"No."

"Wow. This is all amazing."

"You're preaching to the choir, Bob."

They were quiet till Larry pulled into the parking lot, then he showed Bob around, and explained what his job requirements would be.

"Here is a list of benefits and what you'll be paid. The restrooms have showers and lockers in them, so the employees can clean up and change clothes after work. So, what do you think?"

"I think I can handle it, and I'd like to do it."

"Alright, you're hired. We start at 7:00 AM, and you can ride in with me. When Brooke, our secretary comes in at 8:00, she'll give you the necessary paperwork to fill out."

"There's still something I don't understand."

"What's that?"

"I believe you when you say you're in charge of this shop, but why are you living on the streets?"

Larry told him what he had done to his business partner, and how he was determined to do what ever it would take to make amends for it.

"OK. But, why do you have to live on the streets?"

"I don't have to, but the last time I saw him he came to my camp, and I thought he was going to kill me, but he didn't. He just walked away, and that makes me believe I may be able to straighten this out with him. Also, he knows how to find me, but I don't know how to find him."

"So, you're afraid if you move he won't be able to find you?"

"At this point it's the only chance I have."

"Could he kill you?"

"Oh yeah! He could do it with his bare hands and never break a sweat."

"Man, that's determination."

"Talking to my brother through that star changed my attitude and outlook, so that's why I feel your experience with a star changed you as well. Now you have the answer to your question, about why I feel that if someone would give you the break you needed, you wouldn't let them down."

"Yeah, I guess I do now."

CHAPTER SEVEN

For the first week Bob stayed in Larry's camp and rode to work with him.

At the end of that week Larry was able to get him an advance on his first paycheck, so he bought a used bicycle and some equipment to set up his own camp.

By Sunday afternoon he informed Larry he had found a spot for a new camp, and told him where it was located.

As the weeks passed by it became clear that Bob was a great employee. He was punctual, showed up for work everyday and he handled with ease, everything Larry threw at him.

Anytime Larry had to go out to a job site he knew he could depend on Bob to do what ever was necessary to get the work done.

***

Larry continued to go to his parent's house once a week for dinner. Finally one time he decided to bring Lori-Ann with him.

"Well, hello Son, who is this with you?"

"Dad, this is my friend, Lori-Ann Mills."

"It's a pleasure to finally meet you, Lori-Ann. Welcome to our home, I'm Will Lawter, and this is my wife Jeanie."

"I've heard some really great things about both of you, and it's a pleasure to meet you as well."

After a great meal of chicken and home made noodles, followed by a milk chocolate cake made from scratch, the four of them retired to the living room for coffee and some relaxing conversation.

"What motivated you to go into freelance journalism, Lori?"

"Well, Mrs. Lawter, as long as I can remember, I've wanted to be a writer, so I wrote a couple of novels, and submitted them to publishers, but they weren't interested.

Finally one day I saw something happen on the street that I thought was fascinating so I wrote about it and submitted it to one of the major magazines. They not only liked it, they printed it, and paid me for it. Since then I've written several articles for other magazines. Now I'm just about to the point that I'm going to publish my novels on my own."

"Please, don't be so formal. Just call me Jeanie."

"I'll try, but that'll take some getting used to, so I may slip once in a while, because I was always taught to put Mr. or Mrs. in front of the name of someone the age of my parents."

"Ok. I understand, but please try."

"I will."

"I know it's none of my business, but I'm going to ask anyway. How long have the two of you been going together?"

Lori and Larry looked at each other in surprise to the question, then Lori's face got red and she looked down at her coffee cup.

A move that Jeanie picked up on immediately, and said, "I'm sorry I didn't mean to embarrass you Lori."

"That's OK, I'm not embarrassed."

"Uh…Mom, we're not going together, we're just friends."

"Oh, my mistake," said Jeanie with a nearly imperceptible smile. "Usually when a man brings a very nice woman home to meet his parents it's pretty serious. So, how long have you two known each other?"

"Do you remember the day I came here to apologize, Mom?"

"Of course I do, why?"

"Well, the next day I was walking over to our old shop, and I met her on the way there."

Their conversation led well into the evening, suddenly, "Mom, Dad, I hate to break this up, but even though tomorrow's Saturday I have to go in to the shop for a while."

"I'm going to have to go in tomorrow myself and finish some drawings, so I'll see you then, Son."

"Goodnight Lori-Ann. It has been a real pleasure to meet you. I sincerely hope we'll get to see a lot more of you in the future."

"Thank you Mrs. Law… I mean Jeanie. I really enjoyed meeting both of you, and anytime your son invites me I'll be here."

Larry poked her on the arm and said, "Boy! That's a heavy load on my shoulders. Now every time I come over here, if I don't bring you along I'll have Mom on my back."

She looked at him, batted her eyes, flashed him a big grin and said, "Yep. They're nice to me."

He just walked away shaking his head and saying, "No matter what I do, I can't win. I don't know how you put up with it all these years, Dad."

***

In the van on the way back to Lori's, she said, "You've got great parents. I'm glad you were able to get things worked out with them."

"Me, too. I wasted what could have been a lot of great years with them because of my anger. That won't ever happen again."

"I wonder why your mom thought we were going together."

"My mother has always been a romantic. She feels like everybody needs somebody, and there's someone for everyone. Boy, she sure caught you off guard. I've never seen you speechless before."

"Just don't think you can get used to it."

"I have no doubt you'll make up for it."

"Thanks again for taking me."

"You're welcome. I'll see you sometime next week."

"You don't have to go, you can stay here tonight. As a matter of fact you have an open invitation to move in."

"I know, but you know why I can't right now."

"Sure. See you later."

***

"How're you doing Son?"

"I'm great Dad, How about you?"

"I'm good. Say! Your mom and I really like Lori. She's well read and has a sharp wit. It's nice to talk with someone who can keep up with what's going on in the world. And, it certainly doesn't hurt that she's beautiful."

"Yeah, she sure is."

"See you later. If you need me, I'll be in the design room to finish some layouts."

OK, Dad. I've got to finish putting this Bobcat back together so it can be ready first thing Monday. I'll see you later."

Larry had about two hours of work left before he could leave for the weekend, so he jumped in to get it done. He'd finished the job and had just dressed after showering when his dad came into the shop and asked, "Who wants me?"

Larry glanced up with a surprised look on his face, "What are you talking about Dad?"

"Someone's calling my name."

"I don't hear anything."

"I hear somebody calling my name."

Larry sat there thinking, *This has to be interesting.*

"That voice is coming from over there by your desk."

"I still don't hear anything, Dad."

Will walked over to the desk then just stood and listened, "It sounds like it's coming from your backpack. Do you have a phone or recorder in there?"

I guess I might as well go over and take it out. Once the voice starts it won't go away.

"I'm not hearing anything Dad, but I'll take a look anyway."

He got up, walked over to his backpack, unzipped it, pulled the carved box out and laid it on the desk.

"That's a beautiful box, where did you get it?"

"I'll fill you in on that later, Dad."

"The voice is coming out of the box. Don't you hear it?"

"No I don't."

"Why don't you open it and see what the source is?"

"You said, it's calling your name, I don't hear it."

Standing there with a big grin on his face, Will said, "This is some sort of joke, isn't it?"

"If it is, I don't know about it."

"Then why won't you open it?"

"It's not calling my name."

"But it's your box, so you should open it."

"OK. I'll try it."

Larry pulled and pulled, but the box wouldn't open.

"Dad, I know you think this is a prank of some sort, I promise it isn't. I might play a joke on you sometimes, but this isn't one of those times, please trust me on this."

"Well, I know you wouldn't do anything to hurt me, and I've got a change of clothes in my closet, so here goes."

As he very slowly opened the lid on the box, he said, "I can't believe you don't hear that."

"I hear it now. Do you recognize the voice?"

"No."

With the lid open all the way, they watched and listened while a star like item inside the box was glowing rhythmically and changing colors, and the voice kept repeating Will's name. They both looked up at the same time, and their gazes locked. Finally, when Larry nodded; Will reached in and picked up the star, cradling it in the palm of his open hand.

A woman's voice came from the star, "Will Lawter, my name is Ruthie Taylor. You don't know me, but I met your father shortly before he died."

"What's this all about? What kind of a scam is this? What are you trying to pull?"

"This is not a scam Mr. Lawter. I'm not pulling anything. I have something to tell you about your father."

"Larry if this is some kind of joke it's a sick one. I'm throwing this thing away."

"It won't do any good to throw it away, Mr. Lawter, because once we communicate I'm here till the issue is resolved."

"Larry, what's going on?"

"Dad, I don't have any idea what the voice is going to tell you, but, I can guarantee the star in your hand is real, and so is the voice coming from it."

"If you don't know what she's going to say, how do you know it's real?"

"Do you remember me telling you about Danny?"

"Of course, I do."

"Ok. Please see this through, and once it's done, we can sit and talk about it."

"Ok, Son, I'll try."

"I'm going for a walk Dad, so you can handle this privately."

"If you don't mind, I'd like for you to stay here with me."

"I'll stay if it's alright with the voice in the star."

"You can stay if you'd like, Larry, it won't make any difference to what I have to tell your father."

"I have to admit I'm still skeptical, but I do trust my son. If this is a prank he'll owe me for as long as I'm alive."

"I assure you, this is not a prank. I have some very important information about your father's military service when we were at war in Korea."

"The information my mother got wasn't very complimentary, so if it's more of that I don't want to hear about it."

"What I have to tell you will hopefully answer all your questions, and settle any doubts, once and for all about the type of person he was."

"I know you said your name is Ruthie Taylor. We are obviously using this star to communicate. Am I correct?"

"Yes."

"Where are you Ruthie?"

"I'm on the other side."

Larry had to stifle a laugh when his dad said, "The other side of what?"

"I've passed on."

"What! You mean you died? How are...? This can't be real."

"It's all very real."

"Uh…I don't understand any of this. If you died, how can you be talking to us?"

"I was informed that if I still wanted to, I could have the opportunity to talk to you about your father, so I took advantage of it. It's something I always wanted to do, but I promised I wouldn't do, while I was on that side."

"How did you meet my father?"

"I was the charge nurse in a field hospital in Korea, when they brought him in. He was very badly wounded."

"If what you say is true; how was he wounded?"

The color drained out of Will's face as he listened to the voice describing the damage.

"He was shot in the back three times. One shot severed his spine right at his waist, so if he had survived, he would have been paralyzed from the waist down. Another shot hit one of his kidneys, destroying it, and a third hit his liver doing damage that we couldn't repair, so he was mortally wounded. At that point the best we could do was to try to make him comfortable until he passed. He was conscious and in a lot of pain; and all the other nurses and attendants under me were busy, so I stayed alone with him until that happened. It was while I was tending to your father that I learned the most important single lesson I had ever learned in my lifetime."

"How, so?"

"Well, back in those times, when a soldier was brought in to the hospital with entry wounds in his back, it raised some questions, about his bravery. The medics carrying him on the stretcher had already made up their minds, because they weren't very gentle with him. My first inclination was to feel the same way about him. Until…I really studied him. He had to be in unbelievable pain, yet the most I heard out of him was an occasional grunt, and he would tighten his face when it hit hard."

"My mother said, when she asked how he died, the military's response was kind of vague."

"I asked him how he got wounded, and although it was struggle for him to speak, he told me he was scared and was running away when they shot him.

As I wiped his forehead, I looked deeply into his eyes, and I knew he was lying. There was no fear in his eyes. I told him I didn't believe him.

Just as he was about to say something, a Captain came in, and asked him, "Sarg, why did you do it?""

"He responded by, "I just got spooked and ran.""

"The Captain said, "I know better. You did it to keep me from leading the company into a trap that was certain death. Why did you give up your life for me?""

"He said, "If I had let you die in that trap Captain, your family wouldn't be able to have the medical help they need, and I knew that running out there was the only way to stop you.""

"The Captain then said, "What about your family?""

"Your father didn't know, your mother was pregnant, and said, "I don't have children, and my wife and I aren't doing well together""

"The captain said, "This can't end like this. You are a hero!""

"Struggling even more to speak, your dad said, "You can't say that to anyone Captain. I'm going to die, so there is nothing to gain for me, but if you tell that story, you risk your military career, and the welfare of your family. Captain, for your wife and daughter, you have to promise, you won't tell anyone""

"The Captain tried to protest, but your dad wouldn't hear of it. Finally he promised not to say anything."

"After the Captain left, I looked over at your father and knew it wasn't going to be much longer. Fighting through tremendous pain, he squeezed my hand, and made me promise him that as long as I lived I wouldn't tell anyone about that conversation. All that time…I kept my promise."

"So what was the lesson you learned?"

"No matter what things look like, don't ever make a decision about a situation until all the facts are in front of you, and even then, look again before you decide. Your father was a very caring, and extremely unselfish man, and the thing that made it even more important, was the fact that if he could've done it without anyone knowing it, he would have. If I hadn't witnessed the scene between your dad and the Captain, he probably would've died a coward in my eyes, and I wouldn't have had the honor of holding the hand of real hero while he passed to another life."

"My mother always said he was a good person, and she never stopped caring for him, but she said she just couldn't see spending her life as a career military wife, and they were going to get divorced when he came home."

"How did your family come to have questions or concerns about how he died?"

"The questions came when my step-father ran into some guys he knew that were in the same company in Korea with my father."

"What did they say?"

"Nothing really bad; they just said it was never explained why he was shot in the back.

Do you know why my father was so concerned about the Captain's family?"

"Yes. After the Captain left, your dad told me that his wife and daughter both had contracted Polio; also the Captain had been somewhat of a renegade and if he didn't get in line and do things the military way, they were going to wash him out, and that command was his last chance. Your dad knew if they washed the Captain out, his family wouldn't get the best medical help."

"Do you know what happened to the Captain and his family?"

"Yes. He got his military life together and went on to become a full Colonel. His wife and daughter survived the Polio, although his wife had to wear a leg brace, his daughter was left with one leg slightly smaller than the other and a barely noticeable limp.

After he retired, the Captain formed an organization in his home town to help veterans arriving home from active duty.

His organization's goal is to get them re-acclimated into civilian life. His volunteers work with vets from the time they set foot in town till they are settled into whatever life they aim for. If they need emotional help, they are led to it. His people help them cut through the government, and V. A. red tape, to get them where they need to be, financially or educationally. They also talk to local business owners in order to encourage them hire the Vets. He named his organization "Harry's Vets", using you father's first name."

"How did you find out about me?"

"After your dad passed I looked up his records and took down your mom's name, and when she applied for survivor's benefits I had a friend look it up and he informed me that Harry Lawter had a son that was born nine months after his last leave at home before being sent to Korea."

"How do you know so much about the Captain?"

"He and I became good friends, and I helped him organize Harry's Vets. I remained as his assistant till I passed 3 months ago."

"Wow! What else can you tell me?"

"There is one more thing. The Captain's very ill, and would like to meet you before he passes. He has pictures of your dad and has written a diary about their times together. He wanted to contact you so many times, but was afraid to because he didn't know what you would think of him."

"I'd really like to meet him, and see the pictures, and read the diary. He sounds like a good person."

"He's a wonderful person. He never forgot the sacrifice your dad made for him, and he dedicated his life to trying to repay it. If you have a pen and paper I'll give you the Captain's address and phone number."

"I do, and I'm ready when you are."

After giving him the address and phone number, she told him, "You should see the Captain at your earliest convenience; he is very ill."

"Do you know how long he has?"

"On this side, time has no meaning, so I have no way of knowing."

"OK. I'll get a flight out Monday."

"I have accomplished what I needed to by talking to you. Is there anything else you need to discuss with me?"

"Nothing I can think of. I'm at a loss for words over this whole thing. As a matter of fact, I'm still not sure I believe all of it. Wait a minute. I do have one more question."

"Go ahead."

"Assuming all this is real. Why did you contact me?"

"The Captain and your father are the two people I respected the most in my life, and I always wanted to let your father's family know what a tremendous sacrifice he had made, and what an impact it had on another person's life. Not to mention the rippling impact it's had on hundreds of other lives. There's no way to figure, how different things would have been, if the Captain had died that night.

It would've been a shame if no one in your father's family had ever known about the sacrifice he made for others, and the wonderful part is, that his son and grandson learned of it together."

"Ruthie, I want to thank you so much for telling me all this about my father. Although it won't do anything to change the official record, it really makes me feel honored to know I'm his son."

"I am the one who is honored. Well, I have nothing else to tell you, so I guess this will end our communication."

"I'm assuming that some day we'll get to meet face to face."

"We will. Till then I hope the both of you have good lives."

Larry said, "Dad, let's take a walk outside so you can let the star go."

As they stepped out the door Will, opened his hand, and they watched as the star began to lose its bright glow and the color faded. When the light finally went out, the star became snow white, and floated off into the sky till it vanished.

Will and Larry stood looking up into the sky, for a long time.

"Let's go inside and sit down with a cup of coffee while we talk about this."

"Sure. I don't know how much I can fill you in on, though."

"I'm not losing my mind am I? This is what happened that day last spring when you came to the house, isn't it?"

"You're not losing your mind, and yeah, it was similar."

"It was Danny wasn't it. That's why you knew where the car was."

"Yeah."

"How did you come by the box? Where did it come from?"

"I don't have any idea. I just woke up that morning and it was there."

"Did that block of wood you showed us have something to do with this?"

"It did, but I'll have to show you later how that works."

"Ok, you got a star and I got one. I noticed there was another one in there. Who's getting that one?"

"I don't know, because I didn't even know you were getting one."

"How many were in it the day you got it?"

"Five."

"Does that mean two other people have gotten stars?"

"Yes."

"Can you tell me who?"

"I don't know why not."

"Do you know what their situation was?"

"I'm sure I don't know the whole story, but I do know some of it."

"Was Lori was one of them?"

"Yes, but I don't think I should tell you what it was about without her permission."

"Oh, I wasn't asking what it was. You know, Larry, she really likes you."

"I like her, too, Dad. We're good friends. Oh, do you mind if I tell her about today?"

"Of course I don't mind. So, who was the other one?"

"Bob."

"The Bob, that works for us?"

"Yes."

"Man. This is fascinating."

"I know. Maybe we'll all be able to sit down and talk about it someday."

"Oh, I was just wondering, do you think you can handle the business next week?"

"Sure just fill me in on anything special that needs my attention. Are you going to see the Captain?"

"Yes, and I'm going to take your mom with me."

"How are you going to explain the need for that trip to her?"

"Well, hopefully, I can get some help from you."

"What are we going to tell her?"

"Just exactly what happened."

"How do plan to convince her that this took place today?"

"I'll be easier than you think."

"Why?"

"For years she's been telling me, she's felt Danny's presence quite often, and she's firmly convinced that he somehow came to you, and that's what changed your life."

"Obviously, she's right about that part."

"Did you finish the Bobcat?"

"It's all done and ready for Monday."

"Good. Will you go to the house with me?"

"Oh yes, I wouldn't miss this for the world. I'm ready to go when you are. There's just one thing I want you to do first."

"What's that?"

"I'm going to stand back and not touch the box. I want you to put it into my backpack, zip it shut, and you carry it to the house. I'll take the van, and you take the backpack in your car with you."

"Why? What's this all about?"

220

"You'll see, in time."

Will gave him a raised eyebrow look, but did as he requested. Then they left for the house.

***

"I knew it! I knew! I knew it! I just wish I could have been there to see it. Ok, you two, sit down and tell me all about it."

Lunch, a pot of coffee and two hours later, Jeanie was beaming from ear to ear as she said, "I always knew in my heart, there was more than what we could see in our everyday lives. So, where is this beautifully carved box the stars came in?"

"Alright, Dad, show her."

Will placed the backpack on the table, unzipped it and pulled out the…block of wood. Totally stunned he looked at Larry and said, "What the? How did that happen? Did you do that?"

"How could I, Dad? You're the one who put it in the backpack. I never touched it. I don't know why or how, but when it's exposed to someone who has not experienced a star it's a block of wood. I don't have an answer."

"Will, isn't that the same piece of wood Larry showed us the first time he came home last spring?"

"Yes."

For another hour or so they sat and talked about the events surrounding the box and the block of wood.

"Well, folks I'm going to have to go. I owe Lori a dinner out at a restaurant of her choice."

"She really likes you Larry."

"I know Mom, that's what Dad tells me and I like her, too. That's why we're friends."

"It's more than friends Larry. I can see it by the way she looks at you."

"Mom, we're friends."

"Ok. If you say so."

"Dad, give me a call, let me know when you two are flying out. I'll take you to the airport. I love you two."

"We love you, too. Ok, Son, I'll give you a buzz."

***

"Hi, Lori, are you ready?"

"Hi, Larry, Yes I am. How was your day?"

"You aren't gonna believe it."

"Bad or good?"

"It's good. By the way have you decided where you want to eat?"

"You know where I want to go."

"I don't understand you. I'm willing to take you to any restaurant in town, and where do you want to go?"

"Look they've got the best burgers in the world, and besides, I love the owners."

"I knew you'd say that, that's why I told Charley we'd see them later."

"This isn't working the way it's meant to. Men aren't supposed to be able to figure us women out. I'm going to have to change my tactics."

"Hey, I don't have a clue about women; that was just a lucky shot."

"So tell me about your day."

"Let's go, I'll start filling you in on the way."

As he drove to Charley and Barb's he told her about Ruthie and his grandfather, and the Captain. The subject was pushed aside while they ate supper and sat laughing with Barb. As they finished eating, Charley came over and as he cleared the table said, "We're going to be serving dinner for the people in the neighborhood a week after tomorrow, and a couple of our regular volunteers are going to be out of town then, so would you two be interested in helping out?"

At the same time they both emphatically said, "Yes."

"Thanks. We really appreciate it. We'll see you around 11:00 AM next Sunday." Barb said as she was heading for the kitchen.

While finishing off some homemade pie and coffee, Larry finished telling her about the day.

Driving back to Lori's they were both quiet at first then she asked, "How did your mom handle it when you guys told her?"

222

"She was right there. Into it all the way."

"I'm not surprised; she's a very sensitive person. You can tell she's tuned in to everything around her."

Stopping in front Larry asked, "Can I come in for a minute? I need to talk to you about something."

"Of course. You can talk to me anytime you want."

Going inside they sat at the dining room table.

"You look troubled Larry, what is it?"

"Well, I'm not troubled. I've just been thinking a lot recently about where I'm living, and it really doesn't make sense to be running a shop, and meeting with sales people, and business owners on a regular basis, while I'm living on the streets."

"So, are you saying what I think you are?"

"I hope so. I'd like to rent that apartment upstairs, if you don't mind."

"Sure, I told you a long time ago you could."

Suddenly he became kind of shy, saying, "It'll just be temporary until I can get a more permanent place, and I won't get in your way or bother your writing; I promise you."

"Larry, look at me. We're friends, I know you. I know you won't bother me, and you can rent it for as long as you like."

"Thanks."

"What about your former business partner, how will he find you?"

"With everything that's taken place since I talked to my brother, Danny; I believe if it's meant to work out it will. It finally dawned on me that I can't hold myself back for something that might never happen."

"I agree. When do you want to move in?"

"I don't really have a lot of stuff to move, so would tomorrow be ok?"

"Yes."

"How much money do you want for rent?"

"I really hadn't thought about it. It won't be anymore than five hundred dollars a day, though."

"You are such a smart ass."

"You wouldn't want me to be a dumb ass."

"I don't know, maybe I would, then you wouldn't give me all that lip."

"I honestly don't know what to say. Look, after you get your stuff here tomorrow, we'll sit down and talk about it. OK? You know I won't hurt you unless you don't pay me, then I'll have to put you in the hospital."

"Yeah, right, is there any special time you'd prefer me to move in?"

"Here're the keys. You've got your own entrance, so move in when you like."

"Alright, I'll see you sometime tomorrow. And, thanks again."

"You're welcome."

***

The following Friday evening, Lori invited him down for a steak dinner. After the meal Larry thanked her for participating in his celebration.

"What are we celebrating?"

"Five straight days of sleeping inside."

"You really are a case."

"Why do you say that?"

"I've never heard of anyone celebrating sleeping inside."

"That's because you've never spent six years living on the streets."

"You're right and believe me when I tell you that I would never make light of it."

"I know. Once again, thanks."

"You're welcome. Have you told your mom and dad about living here?"

"I really haven't had a chance to yet. They're still out of town and won't be back till Sunday. I'm going to pick them up at the airport late Sunday afternoon."

"It'll be interesting to hear what they have to tell us about their trip. Is it alright if I ride along with you?"

"Sure, you can bet we'll get an ear full when we see them. Well, I'm going to head back upstairs, take a shower, and go to bed. Sometime we're going to have to talk about how much rent you need from me."

"Good night; maybe I'll see you tomorrow, and we can discuss it then."

***

Larry was sound asleep, when sometime in the middle of the night there was a knock on the door that leads to the main house. He slipped his jeans on and opened it.

"Larry, I have to talk to you."

"Lori, if it's about the rent, I'll pay what ever you want. Just don't put me in the hospital."

"I'm not kidding. I can't get this off my mind. We need to talk. Can I come in?"

"Of course."

"Can we go in the living room and sit down?"

"Yeah…I've never seen you so serious, what is it?"

"This living arrangement isn't working. I can't have you living up here any more. I'm in…"

"What have I done? If I've upset you, tell me what it is and I'll make it right."

"It… it isn't you it's me."

"Lori, we're friends. I don't want to lose that friendship. I lo, lo…care, too, much about you."

"I can't have you living here and continue to tell myself we're friends."

"You mean we're not friends anymore?"

"Larry, listen to me. I love you. I want to be more than friends. I want to be your lover, your partner, and your companion. I want to share my life with you, and if you don't feel the same way then I can't go to bed every night knowing I'm sleeping in a room just ten feet below you."

He looked like he'd been smacked upside his head with the biggest surprise of his life.

"Holy cow, I'm stunned."

"Oh my, you don't feel the same way do you?"

"Oh, you have no idea how much I do. The second time you tapped me on the shoulder, and I turned around and looked at you, I wanted to grab you then."

"Then why haven't told me how you feel?"

"Afraid."

"Why would you be afraid?"

After a long sigh, "I don't have a very good track record with women."

"I'm not women, Mr. Lawter; I'm Lori-Ann Mills so you can throw your old track record in the trash."

Taking that as a cue he stood up, grabbed her hand, and as he pulled her up, he wrapped his arms around her, and they kissed.

When he pulled back, he looked into her big brown eyes and said, "I love you Lori-Ann, more than you could ever know. Now, I want to go back to bed, but I'm not going alone."

With a big smile on her face she told him, "Don't worry, you never will go to bed alone again."

Following some tender yet very passionate lovemaking, they finally drifted off to sleep, in each other's arms.

The next morning she woke him up in a way he'd never been awakened before. All he could say was, "Wow!"

She looked at him and said, "I agree."

"Since we stayed at my place last night, does that mean I have to fix breakfast?"

"You better believe it, and I want pancakes, waffles, eggs bacon, ham, hash browns and toast. Oh, and don't forget a whole pot of coffee."

He got up, looked in the fridge and the cupboard and said, "It looks like cereal, and instant coffee, or we can go out."

"Cereal and instant coffee it is, because I'm not putting any more clothes on than I have on now, and I don't think the people in this neighborhood are ready to see me this way. Also, as soon as we're finished I'm dragging you back into this bed."

"You won't be doing any dragging; we'll see who gets there first."

Sitting and sipping their coffees, he looked intently at her and asked, "What made you fall in love with a homeless guy?"

"I don't know. When I first caught up with you, and saw your unruly hair and long shaggy beard, I was kind of turned off, but when I sat down beside you at the bus stop, and looked deeply into your eyes, I knew I was going to love you."

"If we're going to have enough time to get to know each other better we need to get busy, because we have to go to Charley and Barb's tomorrow."

Later, as they were lying on the couch together, he asked, "What are we going to do now? I can't ask you to move in with me, because I don't have enough room in here for all your things."

"Yeah, I know, me and my big mouth, now I'm going to lose all that big rent money I was counting on from you."

"I'm going back to bed, so I guess that's something we'll have to decide after you finish wearing me out."

***

Larry and Lori had a great time working at the tavern with Charley and Barb. They took to it like ducks take to water.

After the meal and cleanup the four of them sat laughing and teasing each other.

"I thought I was going to lose it when Barb threw the plate of food on the floor pointing out the restrooms to one of the guests."

Charley said, "I can tell you this, there is never a dull moment living around her."

"Well, Lori it's time to head for the airport."

"Ok, I'm ready let's get going."

CHAPTER EIGHT

Jeanie and Will were waiting at the loading area by the time Larry pulled up to the curb. After the car was loaded, they climbed into the back seat, and Jeanie said, "Larry, I'm glad you brought your girlfriend."

Shaking his head, he responded with, "Yes, Mom, we are going together."

"I know. I was just wondering how long it was going to take you two to know it."

"Mom, you are really something. You only saw her one time. How could you come to that conclusion in just one visit?"

"You two were easy to figure out; it was obvious by the way you looked at each other."

"I think it's interesting that you knew it before we did."

"Looking over at Jeanie, Lori, said, "You were the only one who didn't know it, Larry."

"I give up how have you put up with this all these years, Dad?"

"Don't worry, Son, you'll find out it's worth it."

"Hurry home Larry I'm dying for a good cup of coffee, and, your dad and I can't wait to tell you two about our trip to meet the Captain. First, I hope you will tell us about your experience with the star, Lori."

"I'll be happy to."

***

By the time they got home, Lori had told them all the details and results of her talk with her deceased friend Judy.

While, Jeanie got the coffee pot, and snacks started; Will, put the clothes and luggage away.

Then the four of them sat around the dining room table sipping coffee, until Lori couldn't stand it any longer.

"So, what happened on your trip to the Captain's?"

"You wouldn't believe what his organization does, not only for veterans arriving home, but they also assist them until

228

they're all settled into where they want their lives to go. They work as go betweens for the vets to the VA."

"And, he set all this up in memory of my grandfather?"

"That's not all; he had assembled a scrapbook full of pictures and mementos of things he and your grandfather did together in the Army, and gave it all to your dad. It was packed up ready for us when we got there, almost like he knew we were coming. He also wrote a book about his experiences with your grandfather. Since he swore on his life he wouldn't tell what your grandfather had done, the book is to be published the day after his passing."

"Is he still doing it?"

"No. His daughter and grandson have been running things so he'd have the time to write the book. He'd been ill for several years. As a matter of fact, his daughter called us on the cell phone when we got to the airport to tell us he had passed on."

"How long were they together before grandfather died?"

"They were stationed together twice before Korea, so they knew each other well."

"Will, you need to tell them what we're going to do."

"Your mom and I are going to start a chapter of Harry's Vets here in town."

"Wow. That's pretty cool Mr. Lawter."

"Lori, please call me Will."

"OK."

"How're you going to handle all that, Dad?"

"Well, for one thing your mom's going to help me with it, and I'm going to retire."

"You're what?"

"You heard me."

"Are you selling your business?"

"My goal is to take six months to phase myself out while I phase you in."

"I don't understand what you mean."

"I'm ready to turn it over to you; that is if you want it."

"I wasn't expecting anything like that. I don't know what to say."

"The response I'm looking for would be, yes."

"Well, yeah, of course I will."

"I have an excellent relationship with my clients, and it took a long time to develop that bond with them, so I never intended to sell it when I retired. I had always hoped to be able to turn it over to you.

When you left six years ago, I was sure that hope was destroyed. Then last spring when you came back I began to hope again. And, when you came to work in the shop I watched how you dealt with those same clients, and I knew you'd be perfect."

"This is personal family business, so why don't I just go home and you guys can arrange all that without me being in the way."

"Lori, I know this seems premature, but, Will, and I both consider you as a part of our family, so we have nothing to discuss that you can't hear."

"Thank you Jeanie."

"Dad, I'd consider it quite an honor to take over, but you've got some pretty big shoes for me to fill. It may take me a while."

"It doesn't matter, because I'll always be available if you need help."

"When do you want to start?"

"Tomorrow morning. Oh, there is one other thing; I hate to ask you to do this, but I think you'll have to."

"And that is?"

"By the time you take over completely you should be sleeping inside."

Grinning, he looked over at Lori and said," I believe we already have that covered, Dad."

"I guess that means we have the first thing checked off the list. I know six months seems like a long time, but it'll go by pretty fast. I hope to open the new office by next April."

"I guess we're going to head for home. I'll see you in the morning and we can start when you're ready. Mom, Dad, I love you guys."

"Home, where is home?"

"Lori has an apartment in her house, and I'm renting it."

"It'll be interesting to see if you ever stay in it."

"Goodnight you two, we're leaving now."

***

The following morning Larry and Will, met in the office to get things started for the turnover.

"How do you feel about Bob replacing me in the shop?"

"The shop has been your domain, so the question is; how do you feel about it?"

"Well, he knows all about the equipment, and he hasn't missed work since he started. I think he can handle it. I'm going to feel him out on it. What are your thoughts on Savanna, and Brooke?"

"They've both been with me several years now. Savanna is the best receptionist I've ever had, and Brooke is a master at taking care of the business paper work. I think they'll do a good job for you."

As the temperatures began dropping and the Fall season was begrudgingly giving in to Winter, the business transition moved along smoothly, and Larry once again sat in the seat of a business manager. It felt better to him than it ever had before. It also occurred to him that a business manager doesn't look right with a backpack strapped on to his shoulders, so he bought a nice bag that looked like a combination gym bag and airplane carry on, so he could take the box wherever he went.

CHAPTER NINE

"You know something we haven't done for a while?"

"What's that?"

"We haven't been to the coffee shop."

"You're right, we haven't. What brought that up?"

"I don't know; it just popped into my head."

"When do you want to go?"

"It's a nice day, and we could go for some coffee and donuts, then, take a stroll around that park over there."

"Sounds good to me; let's do it."

***

"Hello you two, welcome to Mindy's. Wait a minute, you guys look familiar, you've been here before, but it's been awhile, hasn't it?"

"As a matter of it has, I'm Larry and this is Lori."

"Larry and Lori, oh yes, I remember now. I won't forget it again; just make sure it doesn't take that long for you to come back."

"It looks like you've started cleaning, are you getting ready to close?"

"You guys are going to be my last customers today, so take your time. I've got a lot to do before I have to run you off. Besides, my fiancé is going to pick me up and he'll be a little late."

"I don't know what made me think of it, but it occurred to me, we haven't had your wonderful coffee and donuts for a long time."

"No time like the present to remedy that. What would you two like?"

"I'll have a coffee and an éclair."

"What about you Larry?"

"Give me the same please, and if you don't mind, we'll sit over by the window out of your way."

"Sure, here're your éclairs, also take a whole carafe of coffee with you and just relax."

After eating their éclairs, they sat sipping coffee, and Mindy came toward their table.

"Uh, oh, we're in trouble, Lori, she's coming over to run us off."

"I just wondered what you wanted."

"We don't want anything. We're Ok."

"Why'd you call my name?"

"We didn't."

"I heard you. I just wasn't aware that you knew my last name."

"I don't know it, do you Lori?"

"No."

"Look, there's only three of us here, and I'm not calling out, Mindy Lee Adams, so one of you said my name."

Lori and Larry looked at each other, and said, "Uh…oh."

"What do you mean, "Uh…oh?"

"Well, we…"

"Hold it! The voice sounds like it's coming from that black bag on the chair. Don't you hear that?"

"No."

Lori reached over, picked up the bag, and handed it to Larry. He unzipped it, pulled out the box, and set it on the table. Mindy stood wide eyed and exclaimed, "Oh my god."

"What is it?"

"I…I've…seen. I can't believe you don't hear that voice."

They looked at each other in acknowledgement and, Larry, said, "We do now."

"Why don't you open it?"

"The voice is calling your name. I believe you have to."

"This is some kind of joke isn't it? A rubber snake or spider is going to jump out, right?"

"You have our solemn word; it isn't a prank or joke.

"Does it have white cloths in it?"

"What? No. Why would you think that?"

"Never mind."

Sitting down beside Lori, she put her hand on the lid and very slowly lifted it. When it was all the way open she saw a small star inside that was glowing rhythmically and changing colors, while at the same time calling her name. Picking it up, she held it in the palm of her hand, and the voice then said, "Mindy this is your grandmother."

"I don't think so. My grandmothers are both dead."

"People don't die, Mindy. When we pass on, we go to another phase, or level of our lives. Some refer to it as passing on to the other side, and that's where I am speaking to you from."

"Larry, Lori, what the hell's going on here? Who is this?"

"I don't know Mindy. We don't have anything to do with this."

Looking back at her hand she said, "What kind of scam is this? Who are you really?"

"I'm the woman in several of the pictures you've drawn, including the one on the wall behind you."

"I don't believe this. Anyone could come in here and say that, after they saw my drawings."

"I'm not just anyone. Your father is my son."

"Once again, anyone could say that, as long as they don't have to prove it. I don't know who you are, or how you got your voice to come through this little star, but I don't have anything for you to take, so if this is some kind of séance con or scam, it won't work, and you can believe that, because I used to work with one of the best con artists that ever lived."

"I don't know how the star works, but I was informed that I would have the opportunity to pass on some very important information to you."

"You're going to have to do better than that. I'm still not buying it."

"Alright how's this? When you were seven years old, you saved your fathers life by using pressure on a gunshot wound to his abdomen. If you hadn't been with him, he would have bled out and passed before the emergency people got there."

"Alright you've got my attention. How could you know that? If you are who you say you are, you had already passed on several years before that happened."

"On this side we can come back and visit at will, so I was able to see many events of your life as they took place. I've even looked in on your parents from time to time."

"When was the last time you observed them?"

"Just last month."

"I've got you there. You should have checked your history before you started this bull. My parents died ten years ago. It was all over the newspapers."

"Your parents went into the witness protection program ten years ago, and you know that."

Mindy stood there stunned and speechless as the blood drained out of her face, and she felt the cold chills travel the length of her spine, as the goose bumps raised on her arms.

"Mindy, this sounds very personal; I think we need to take a walk."

"No, please, Larry, I'd like for you guys to stay. I have a feeling I may need someone to verify what I'm hearing."

"Ok, we'll stay."

This gave Mindy the chance collect her thoughts. "If you're my grandmother, how old was I when you died?"

"You were three years old."

"How old was I when my other grandmother died?"

"She passed before your parents got married, and you weren't born yet."

"At this point, what's happening with my parents?"

"They desperately want to see you, but they know if they do, all three of your lives would be over, because you are definitely being watched by that crime syndicate, and as long as they believe they're dead you're safe."

"Why are we talking?"

"What do you mean?"

"What is your purpose for being here? Do you have a message for me?"

"Yes. I can tell you where to find the information that will put the ones who run that crime syndicate behind bars for life. The whole system will then collapse, because the ones left to run it will be exposed, and rival organizations will take care of them. After that happens, your parents will be free to come back into the open."

"Something I don't understand."

"What is it?"

"You're telling me these things in front of people I hardly know. Aren't you concerned that they could be in with the ones who are watching me?"

"No. They have each had their own experience with a star in the box. They are not involved in crime. But, they shouldn't hear any of the details, because if anything goes wrong they could be in danger."

"Can I take this star into the kitchen and still talk to you…uh?"

"Yes. We can talk any where you take it. The line of communication will stay open till we resolve the issue at hand. And, you can call me Grandma."

She took the star into the kitchen and closed the swinging door.

"This is all very confusing. I'm still not convinced about it."

"Maybe this will help. When your fiancé was eight years old a tree limb from a large tree fell on him, breaking his arm and giving him a fractured skull. When I saw it happen, I took him into the house where I was living at the time. And, with the help of a white cloth that I pulled out of the same box you took that star out of, I was able to heal wounds that could've threatened his life. By the way that house is the same one he remodeled last year."

"Wow! Ok, I'm convinced. There aren't, too, many people who know that. So, what do you have in mind about this?"

"Since you are being watched, you cannot retrieve the information."

"Who can?"

"It'll have to be someone in a position of power or authority; someone you know you can trust."

"I do know of one person who would take that info and run straight to the Attorney General with it."

"Are you sure this person can be trusted."

"He's a man with a huge ego, but even though he's not beyond bending the rules to do what he feels needs to be done, he refuses to break the law. He is the law."

"Can you contact him discreetly?"

"I have his personal cell number, and I can reach him without anyone else knowing who I am. He told me I could call him anytime I need to."

"How is your memory?"

"Excellent."

"Alright, here it is."

"Ok, Grandma, what's your whole name?"

"I'm Allison Adams."

"Then I'll call you Grandma Alli. OK?"

"Of course it's ok. I'm going to give you the information with the instructions now. If you want to, you can write it down, but you must then commit it to memory and destroy it."

"As soon as you give it to me I'll call my contact."

Mindy listened and wrote down all the info and instructions. Upon finishing, Mindy asked, "Does this mean we're done talking?"

"No. We'll remain in contact till we know that the reason for our communication is resolved."

Reaching into her purse Mindy extracted a small cell phone and dialed a number.

"Hello 'Z'. It's been a long time. It's nice to hear from you again. I hope you're well."

"Yes, I am 'B', and it's good to talk to you again. How are you?"

"Things are going great. What can I do for you?"

"In this case, I have something that might be beneficial to both of us."

"Go ahead."

"Are you familiar with the Seattle Family?"

"Seattle…um, yes I know them quite well. Do you have something in mind?"

"Well, I'm looking at a way to pass on some information to them."

"Ok, I'm capable of doing that. Tell me what you've got."

Mindy proceeded to give him all the info she got from her grandmother, but she did it in a way her grandmother didn't understand. Upon finishing, her contact said, "Are you sure the family will get the best benefit from all this?"

"Without a doubt. Once opened it will reveal everything the family needs."

"Thank you 'Z' it's a pleasure to talk to you again. Of course, you'll know the end result of the family's position."

"Knowing you, 'B', I wouldn't question that for a second. As always, it has been a pleasure on my end as well. You know how to reach me if need be. Take care."

"You, too."

As she turned off the phone and put it back into her purse, her grandmother said, "The names and information you gave that person is not what I told you. What are you doing?"

"My contact is the police chief of a city in the northern part of the country. A few years ago when I was having a lot of problems, he befriended me and helped me get clear of those problems. For a short time we had an intimate relationship, but we've remained good friends since that ended.

He's a highly principled and strong man, and because he won't take crap off of anyone he's made some enemies, so just in case his conversations are being monitored, we talk in a code we've worked out between us."

"So, then, he understood the true meaning of everything you said?"

"Yes. If you don't mind, I'm going to take the star back out to the front where my drawings are. I need to ask you something."

"Sure, go ahead."

"Do you know why I continue to draw you into my pictures?"

"When you were two and a half years old, you contracted a severe case of pneumonia, with a fever of 107. The doctors said you probably wouldn't survive, and if you did you would you'd have permanent brain damage from the fever.

I was determined you were neither going to die, nor would you end up with brain damage. So, I mixed up an old recipe for treating fevers, and gave you a tablespoon of it every hour till your fever broke.

For two whole days, when I sat down I held you to my chest, and when I did have to get up, I carried you everywhere with me. I took you to bed with me. I wouldn't put you down. Finally, your fever started to break on the third morning, and as you woke up you looked at me and smiled, and hugged me. I knew then you were ok."

"Holy mackerel. That was you? And, it was real? All this time I thought it was just a dream."

"It's not a dream; why would you think so."

"I dream that very event periodically, and when I wake up in the morning after having it, I feel warm, and safe, and protected."

"Every time you draw, I'm there beside you, surrounding you with love, so perhaps that's why you draw my likeness into your pictures."

Pointing at the picture on the wall behind the counter, Mindy asked, "Is this what you looked like when you nursed me back to health?"

"Yes."

"It's very interesting, because in my dream I can never see your face. I guess that's why I didn't realize who I was drawing. I'm sorry you died before I got to know you."

"I was very fortunate to be able to spend the first three years of your life with you. You were such a pleasure to be with. I want you to know I'll always be near you to help you if I can."

"Will we ever be in contact again?"

"I don't know, but probably not until you pass to this side."

"Do you know when that will be?"

"This may be hard to understand, but we don't go by time here, just events. I can tell you one thing for sure."

"What's that?"

"When you do come to this side I'll be one of the first to greet you."

"Will I ever get to see my parents?"

"They'll contact you when all this mess clears up."

"Thank you for helping me Grandma."

"You have no idea what a pleasure it has been for me. As much as I'd love stay and talk with you; my real mission has been accomplished, so it's time for you to release the star. I love you, Mindy A."

"I love you, too, Grandma A."

"Mindy, you need to take the star outside and let it go."

"Why, Larry?"

"Just take it out and open your hand…you'll see why."

As she stepped outside a familiar voice said, "What're you doing Min?"

"Oh, hi, Greg. I can't wait to tell you what just happened?"

"What've you got in your hand?"

She opened her hand to show him, "It's a star, and I have to let it go now."

"A star? Where did you get it?"

"Well, it's a long story. Perhaps, the two people inside can help me explain this unbelievable story when we go in. First I have to let this go."

When she held her hand out, they watched as the star began to lose its bright glow and the color faded. When the light finally went out, the star became snow white then floated off into the sky and vanished. They stood for what seemed like an eternity looking up at the sky.

"I'm almost afraid to ask what that was all about, and where it came from."

"Kiss me first and I'll tell you before we go inside."

"You're right I should never lose sight of my priorities."

After they kissed, she told him, "I took it out of a box that looks *exactly* like the one you had with the cloth in it that saved Carla's life."

"What? How...? Does that mean there are two of them?"

"I don't know what it means."

"Where did you get the box?"

"I don't have it. There's a couple inside that brought it in."

"Then let's go in so I can meet them."

As they walked inside, Larry turned toward the door. When he and Greg locked eyes they both just stared at each other. Finally Larry hung his head, and when he did, Greg approached him extending his right hand in a gesture of friendship. At that point Larry stood up, looked Greg in the eye and said, "I know I can't ever expect you to forgive me for what I did to you and our business, but I hope someday you'll be able to not hate me for it."

"I did hate you for a long time, but when I saw you in the camp that day, I could see in your eyes that you had suffered far more for your actions than I had.

Larry put his hand out and shaking Greg's hand said, "Thank you Greg."

Mindy sat there wide eyed in awe. Lori grabbed her hand and said, "I'm so glad this finally happened. Larry's been tortured for such a long time over what he did, and I think he was beginning to believe it was never going to be resolved."

"Larry, during the six plus years since we last talked, I've learned a lot about the real me, so in a way, I feel I should thank you, because if all that hadn't happened I don't know if I would have."

"There's something I don't understand."

"And that is?"

"That day when you came into my camp; how the hell, did you know where to find me?"

"I wasn't there looking for you. That was the camp I lived in for five years. I just went back to see if it was still there and if someone else was able to use it."

"What? You were homeless for five years. Oh my god, I'm so sorry."

"Larry, the experiences I've had in the last year and a half have made those five years worth every minute. For one thing I met this wonderful person next to me while I was homeless. She became the friend I needed when I was at my lowest, and now my lover as well."

"That still doesn't excuse what I did to you."

"We've all done things we have no excuse for, but now it's over, and from this point on I hope we can be friends again. Now I've got a question for you."

"OK."

"Who has the box with the stars in it?"

"I do, why?"

"Can I see it?"

"Well, I'll try to show it to you, but don't be surprised if it isn't a box."

Grinning, Greg said, "Ok. Let's try it anyway."

Larry set the black bag on the table, unzipped it and pulled out the…carved box.

"This has never happened before. Every time I've shown it to somebody it turned into a block of wood."

"Yeah, I know how you feel."

"You do?"

"Oh, yes. Is there anything inside?"

"The stars are all gone, but there is this."

"A business card? What does it say?"

"Thank you for the call. It didn't say that before. What the hell's going on?"

"Look, let's all sit down and get acquainted over some coffee."

"Yeah, that sounds good to me."

Grabbing a pot of hot coffee and filling four cups, Mindy put it all on a tray and walked it over to the table.

"Well, everybody here knows my name is Mindy, but Greg has not met Lori, until now that is. Greg I'd like you to meet Lori."

"Lori it's a pleasure to meet you, and I'm assuming by the way he looks at you, you are the love of Larry's life."

"It's my pleasure to meet you as well. Larry has told me a lot about you. And, yes we do love each other."

While the four of them sat sipping coffee Larry asked, "Greg, how do you know how I feel about the box being a block of wood?"

"At one time I was lucky enough to have that carved box."

"You had it? Where did it come from?"

"I have no idea. I just know it changed my life."

"Yeah, it obviously changed mine, too. How did the stars work for you?"

"It didn't have stars in it when I had it. It had white cloths in it that healed people's wounds."

The four of them were all so busy with their conversations they didn't realize the clean shaven, elderly gentleman in the blue, pin striped suit had walked into the shop.

Walking up to them he announced, "Mr. Lawter I believe it's time for me to retrieve the box."

"You! You're here for the box? Then you're the one who left it in my camp."

"No, Mr. Lawter, you can thank your friend Mr. Fetters for that."

"What? How did that happen?"

"I think you and your friend have plenty of time to work that out later. At this time another person needs the box, so I must be going."

"Why were we the ones to get the box and the items in it?"

"Simple, Mr. Fetters. You both needed them."

"Wow, this is unbelievable."

"I must go now. Miss Adams, Miss Mills, It's been a pleasure to see both of you. By the way, Miss Mills, the uncirculated silver dollar you have, is worth $937,500, but don't take my word for it. Please check with Mr. Fetters' pawn shop friend Stu, he is a numismatist, and he'll verify what I'm telling you.

Good luck to you all till we meet again."

The four of them sat silent and awestruck as the gentleman walked out the door, box in hand.

Dedicated to our best friends Charley & Barb